Road Apples

Karen Kennedy Samoranos

Gallatin Peak Productions

Road Apples
By Karen Kennedy Samoranos
Copyright © Karen Kennedy Samoranos, 2011, 2014

...

...

This book is a work of fiction. While references may be made to actual places or events, the names, characters, incidents, and locations within are from the author's imagination and are not a resemblance to actual living or dead persons, businesses, or events. Any similarity is coincidental.

...

First Edition Published by Musa Publishing,
December 2011

ᴨᴨ

Second Edition Published by Gallatin Peak Productions,
March 2014

...

ISBN: 978-0692398289

Published in the United States of America

Warning

This book contains adult language and scenes. This story is meant only for adults as defined by the laws of the country where you made your purchase. Store your books carefully where they cannot be accessed by younger readers.

Other Books by Karen Kennedy Samoranos

Big Lies in Small Town
Red Rock North
Death By Bitter Waters
The Curious Number
The Secret Life of Richard McCoy

For Felicidad and Domingo

Chapter One

A good friend once told me that the world is a place of unexpected twists and hazards. One moment you're laughing, and the music is playing, and then suddenly, disaster strikes from thin air. Using that principle, I'm always amazed that the first time I heard my baby's heartbeat I was in a hospital examination room, with a rape kit on the tray, and a police officer in attendance.

The very concept of predestination would be endlessly repeated, as great a mystery as the beating heart of the fetus hidden inside the darkness of my own body. My faith would be equally tested in the months to come. I have never believed in love at first sight, or the power of destiny to sway a person's life. Those antiquated human notions seemed more of an excuse for a one-night stand than a solid basis for a lasting relationship.

But the time came when I realized that I had lived most of my short adult life in a stupor, my eyes blind to all the possibilities in front of me. I became a believer one fateful night in the rain, at the appointed hour, and all because of a vintage car, a loyal dog, and a cheating boyfriend.

❖ ❖ ❖ ❖

My adventure began soon after my grandparents, Feliz and Enida Benités, gifted me the title to their 1973 Mercedes when they purchased a newer, flashier C-300. The giving of one's precious commodity is a deeply ingrained Filipino cultural tradition that has endured in my family, reflected in my grandparents' generosity in passing along their classic Mercedes.

Grandpa usually drove the old car, but Grandma was central to making the decision about who would receive the cherished gift. I wasn't without a vehicle to use, as I owned a pickup truck for my construction business, and a house with a garage in which to park it.

Maybe Grandma's pride in my ability to take care of myself was a factor.

I learned early on that my father, Mitchell Benités, is Grandma Enida's favorite son, though she would never make the conscious admission. This fact stands to reason that Mitchell's four daughters would also be her favorite grandchildren without preference to anyone in particular.

The car should have gone to Mallory, my eldest sister, and first in line for this type of inheritance. I intuitively knew that Mallory's succession was in jeopardy when she killed a man, determined by the justice system to have been a legal execution by blunt force. Her attorney, honed by defending cops accused of similar crimes, managed to reduce the District Attorney's suspicions to mere self-defense, and Mallory instantly became a free woman.

Grandma, however, had been quietly disapproving. Her clear-cut assumption is that any death incurred at one's own hands is defined as mortal sin, unless the transgressor repents. I suppose she wouldn't have wanted Mallory, damned and remorseless, driving a car Grandma Enida once carted her own family around in.

There's my second-eldest sister, Miranda, a state trooper, whose only sins would likely be venial. Miranda lives in Lassen County, four hundred miles from the core of family. I can't imagine Grandma Enida, with her shaky hands and questionable driving skills, negotiating a winding highway over the Sierra Nevada Mountains just to haul that car up to Susanville.

Grandma understood that my younger sister, Margot, isn't a vintage Mercedes type. Margot drives a two-seater convertible sports car—a late-model BMW Z4—quite often with the top down. My lipstick-lesbian sibling with her six-inch stilettos and flowery dresses wouldn't be caught dead in that tank-like old Mercedes with its sun-cracked dashboard.

Therefore, it made sense the Mercedes would become mine.

"You like old things," Grandma claimed, when she handed me the title paper.

Sitting inside my bungalow built in 1916, and entertaining my grandparents with fresh coffee, I knew Grandma was right. I remember thinking at the time that my fetish for antiques also included the man I was clandestinely dating, Jake Keene, forty years old to my twenty-five. Jake made a modest income writing novels, another outdated concept.

I'd had a falling out with Jake I was aching to resolve. My peculiar trait is I hate to leave things hanging, probably related to my career choice as a general contractor, which requires a construction job to be followed to completion. When you're a woman working in a field dominated by men, you'd better be precise about everything, including your personal life.

This particular story begins from the point when Grandma passed me the title to the Mercedes, just before Mallory was released of all charges in the murder of a man inside her own carport. I'll factor in my gross misunderstanding with Jake, who was engaged to be married to an attorney by the name of Sophie Whipple all the while we tended our special friendship with stealth sex. I'd been willing to sell my soul to fornicate with a cheater, denying the consequences of my actions.

I wanted a road trip. I needed to get away from the pitfalls of my personal life, and Grandma Enida's gift of the Mercedes was my ticket out of town, in style.

❖ ❖ ❖ ❖

On his way to the airport to catch a flight to Seattle for a promotion of his latest novel, Jake Keene left his dog, Rat, in my care. At first I resented being taken for granted. When I found an extra airline ticket in his coat for his fiancé, Sophie, I understandably went ballistic, and kicked him out of the house.

Later Jake's mother, Charlotte Burgess, in an attempt to bully me into jumping ship from the affair, revealed that Jake had broken off his engagement with Sophie right there at the airport. Rather than taking me for granted, Jake had placed his beloved dog with the only person he felt he could trust. With Rat under my supervision, Sophie would be incapable of compromising the dog while Jake was away. Call it peace of mind, but at least Rat was a gentleman, which is more than I can say of his pet man, Jake.

After Jake's departure, and Charlotte's admission, I decided to get out of the Bay Area. I had a friend in construction who had moved up to Astoria, Oregon, so I planned a week's break to get away from all the peripheral bullshit. If it wasn't Jake and Sophie, and Charlotte Burgess, then it was my sister, Mallory, whose deliberate execution of a perceived enemy raised all sorts of red flags as to the fundamentals of her character.

3

I almost made it out of the Bay Area, when Mallory telephoned me on my cell. Weighed down with my sister's problems, I debated whether I should even pick up the call.

"Madeline, can you meet me for coffee?" Mallory begged, sounding distraught, and I was glad I'd answered.

I was rather hesitant, being that Mallory's state of mind was one of the catalysts for my time-out. Already suffering the wounds of my sister's media fame, I nearly refused, but that would have been incompatible with the definition of Family.

I agreed to meet her at a coffee house near her home, bringing Rat with me.

When I arrived at the meeting place, she was graciously appreciative, but horrified by the dog, an unsightly result of a mix of Shar-Pei and Chinese Crested.

"What the hell is that?" Mallory asked, as though dumbfounded by Rat's blatant ugliness. She kept her distance, and Rat, cavalier to the end, sat back on his haunches and smiled politely.

Seated outside in the spring warmth we broke the ice with small talk. She asked me about the Mercedes, and I mentioned I was on my way to visit my old high school classmate, Kevin Gerard, in Oregon. Kevin was the contractor who had rehabilitated a Victorian I'd been dying to see.

Mallory told me she was no longer being charged with the crime she'd committed with malice aforethought, that calculated murder of her alleged stalker, really a back-room real estate transaction gone sour. Squinting at my sister, partly because of the bright sun, and the remainder my general skepticism in her honesty, I told her I thought it was great.

"Is it because they believed your scenario?" I asked innocently.

Mallory, with a criminal's poker-face, affirmed that her victim's habit of real estate scamming had set the District Attorney's people straight, and absolved my sister of doing nothing more than ably defending herself. She'd secured freedom, after splitting a man's skull wide open with a piece of rebar-reinforced concrete. I had difficulty believing she could sit there calmly with all that blood on her hands.

Mallory then shifted to low gear, and told me she'd broken off her engagement.

I was momentarily stunned. Jesse Ibarra, my sister's now ex-fiancé, was in truth our biological half-brother, spawned twenty-six years ago

4

by our father's extra-marital affair. Dad made his feelings very clear—he didn't consider the young man his son any more than a stranger you pass on the street. Mallory is the scheming type, and had swooped in from left field to pounce upon poor Jesse, playing him as a tool to hurt our father for perceived childhood slights she'd embraced with a vengeance.

I realized at that exact moment how Mallory used people, not only Jesse in order to damage our father, but even me, her mute sounding board. By the limit of our family culture, we are not allowed to criticize an elder, including older siblings, who exert more authority simply by birthright.

Mallory's twisted point of view in relation to our father really hit home. Once Dad showed no interest in contesting her marriage to this so-called half-brother, Mallory quickly lost interest, and dropped poor Jesse like a hot potato.

"You did it to get back at Dad," I blurted. I had nothing to lose in this assessment of my beloved elder sister, whose self-destructive tendencies had nearly proved to be her undoing.

"Yes," she agreed. "But it backfired."

Out there beneath the shade of the coffee house umbrella, I had been about to offer my opinion, uncharacteristic of culture, though inherent to my personality, when my cell phone rang. I was thinking that I could never get out of town fast enough, when I saw the call was from our father. Uncanny, that Dad should telephone at the moment when he was a main topic of conversation.

Dad gravely informed me that our maternal grandmother, Beth McKracken, had suffered a heart attack, and was in a hospital not too far from where Mallory and I sat in the shadow of the café. I told him I was with Mallory, and that we'd be up to meet him and Mom, and then we finished our drinks quickly.

This day was dedicated to reflection and reconciliation. Even as Grandmother Beth lay in the ICU, supposedly on death's door, she managed to say kind words to my mother. Mom, adopted by Grandmother Beth as an infant, had spent a lifetime trying to please a mother figure whose sole purpose in life seemed to be to voice every unmerited complaint. Grandmother's fence mending with Mom melted away the resentment I'd held against my grandmother for so long without realizing its existence.

When I departed the ICU, I saw Dad and Mallory seated on one of those long padded hospital benches. Mallory's head lay on our father's shoulder in the posture we'd all assumed as children, seeking the comfort of unconditional love.

To believe that an embrace could resolve my sister's excesses of temperament seemed much too simple a fix. But I had some measure of emotional security when I finally drove out of the Bay Area, headed north.

Chapter Two

Thirteen long hours of driving were required before I arrived in Astoria. I must have stopped at every rest area on the long Interstate junket. Either I had to make up for the countless cups of coffee meant to keep me awake, or Rat needed to prowl a lawn strip, sniff at invisible doggie markers, and leave his scat after lifting his leg in salute. I had difficulty determining whether Rat was emptying his bladder, or just a wee for the canine message post. At least I had plenty of plastic bags on hand to dispose of his droppings.

The miles passed, along with roadside fast-food attractions, and a constantly changing landscape. I stopped for gas twice, once in Redding, California, and again well across the Oregon border, in Roseburg. I was unnerved to realize that the Mercedes was often the only pair of headlights on the road. Soon the day showed a hint of light, and other vehicles proved the existence of humanity.

Just as I merged onto the Coast Highway south of Seaside, Oregon, the sun rose over the inland hills to the east, and spilled across the land, hitting the heavy surf. Almost instantly, the weariness of travel washed away. Rat, who'd been asleep on the back seat, lifted up his head, and stuck his nose out the window to scent the ocean. I could smell the sea, the tang of endless miles of salt, and the faint rot of driftwood and seaweed.

Another twenty miles, and we were in Astoria, rolling up to the foot of Kevin Gerard's Victorian home. He was standing in the one-car garage with its swing-out doors, when I pulled up in the Mercedes and parked in front of the house. I'd telephoned when I stopped for gas in Redding the day before, and told him when to expect me, so he must have been watching for me since dawn.

He hurried to the car, his arms ready to pull me into his embrace.

"Maddie, damn! It's great to see you."

I hugged him, and then got a good look at his face. The Oregon air must have influenced him, because he'd grown a full beard since he'd moved from California.

"What's this?" I rubbed one hand up his left cheek. Touching him freely felt good in a way, an underlying sexual tension between us we'd never acknowledged—and probably why we were still friends.

"The weather gets kind of cold," he explained, looking down at Rat, who was always polite, especially with strangers, and sat patiently at my side. Kevin crouched down. "Who's this? Is this the Rat?"

Rat wagged his tail furiously.

"I think he likes you."

"I like him, too. C'mon, Rat." He slapped his thigh, and led the way to a redwood gate on the side of the house.

I followed through an alley, and into a delightful garden consisting of raised vegetable beds, a brick terrace and a patch of real grass.

"Rat can have a good time here, while we eat breakfast," Kevin said, climbing the back stairs.

Beneath the kitchen's pressed tin ceiling, Kevin made coffee, toast and scrambled eggs. Rat, done with investigating the yard, snoozed on the back porch in the thin sunlight. Serving out the food, Kevin proceeded to tell me about his projects, involving renovations of older homes.

"You'd love it, Maddie, I'm telling you, these Oregonians are crazy about their homes." He grinned knowingly. "They buy these old houses, pay to get them fixed up, and then flip them. And that's after all the oohs and ahs. But first, they have sex in the house. It's like breaking a champagne bottle, you know?"

Serving myself more coffee to offset the travel blues, I paused.

"Sex instead of champagne?"

"No, I swear it. I caught two couples doing it, right after I basically just completed the renovation. They can't wait, the finished work looks that good."

"Two couples? Uh, together, or separately?" The lack of sleep had made me kind of punchy.

"Two different couples, two different houses, Maddie. Sheesh."

"Is that what you did when you were finished with this house, find someone to break the bottle with?"

"I am an Oregonian now, after all." He glanced at his watch, and stood to clear the dishes. "If you want, you're welcome to come with me, or you can stay here and sleep."

"I'll come with you. I can sleep any time. Besides, I'm dying to see what your renovation work's all about." I began to wash the dishes, while he wiped the table. "What about Rat?"

"Bring him along. There's forty acres at the job site, and another dog to run around with."

The drive wasn't lengthy in terms of distance or time, just a complete change of view. Like Rat, I sat with my eyes on every point of reference, eating it all up. Starting from Kevin's quaint Victorian neighborhood on the slope overlooking the Columbia River, we crossed the Warrenton Bridge, and traveled up Young's River Valley, a region of thickly growing trees and lush green fields. In the filtered sunlight of a partly cloudy Oregon day, I could think nothing but happy thoughts, in spite of Grandmother Beth's ill health, Mallory's predicament, or even my unresolved conflict with Jake Keene.

Kevin pointed at the street sign for the right turn at Peter Johnson Road. That's when our immaturity kicked in, and we found ourselves ribbing like a couple of adolescent boys. This reaction was inescapable when Kevin and I were together, always cruising for locker room vulgarity. True to form, a blameless street sign was perfect bait for our raunchy humor.

"Look at that, Maddie." He snorted at the sign's twofold phallic reference. "I laugh every time I see it."

"I feel sorry for Peter Johnson, whoever he was. I wonder what the other children called him at school."

"Just think how I felt when the property owner gave me the address over the phone."

Done with our juvenile dialog, he parked the truck in front of an odd house with faded cedar shingle siding. We jumped out of the cab, Rat following, cruising around us in circles as he sniffed the air. A pickup truck was parked in the short driveway facing a one-car garage. The faint sound of bleating sheep drifted on the breeze.

My professional experience told me the house had been raised on jacks over a new concrete foundation in the last thirty years to build a daylight basement and garage. I pointed this out to Kevin, who nodded his approval.

"You've got a good eye, Maddie."

He unloaded a portable saw, and handed me a heavy toolbox. After a short hike up a grassy slope and around the buttressed remnants of the original stone foundation, we hauled the gear into the house through the back door, accessed by a key on Kevin's ring. Rat seemed to sense he wasn't allowed in without an invitation, and chose a place in the grass to curl up and wait it out.

The door swung open to a mudroom, finished with a slate floor, tiled wash-down pit, and stained redwood cubbies built against a dun painted wall. A long walnut bench beneath brass hooks complemented the farm atmosphere of the house.

Kevin noted my interest. As a general contractor, I understood the labor required for the aesthetics of a construction job.

"Wait, you ain't seen nothin' yet, Maddie."

Pausing in the kitchen, I could see that Kevin had treated the room like an art piece. He described his renovation work with a serious tone, the use of the original cabinets, stripping off layers of paint, and revealing the oak grain. In the generous morning light streaming through a line of south-facing windows, the cabinet doors were the perfect color of a wheat field ready for harvest.

Up to that moment we hadn't run into the owners. When we climbed the plastic covered stairs to the second floor, I caught a glimpse of a blond-haired woman in a green satin robe exiting the bathroom. She spoke a brief greeting over her shoulder, seemingly not disturbed by our presence, and then she disappeared behind a bedroom door.

We continued up another flight of stairs to the attic. Kevin had evidently been in the middle of drywall work. This often requires more than one pair of arms to hold the wallboard, while the screws are set. I could see he'd secured the gypsum board as high as he could safely reach while sinking the screws in his one-man job.

We set up the saw, and I pointed toward the high ceiling.

"You saved the best part of the job for last, didn't you?"

"I was just waiting for you, Maddie. I know how much you like to hang drywall, and you're a damn squirrel on a scaffold."

"Is that the only reason you wanted me up here, Kev?"

"Dude, Maddie. I missed my favorite drinking buddy."

When a male friend treats you like a man, it's acceptable if that's your expectation of the relationship. Fellowship was the sum of my dynamic with Kevin, despite all my wondering what might have been.

10

We spent a few hours measuring and cutting the eight-by-four-by half-inch wallboard. Before we secured the drywall screws, we pushed in R-30 insulation, and stapled sheets of moisture barrier to hold it in. Next went the drywall, fitted like pieces of a puzzle. By mid-afternoon, and I was surprised how much we had accomplished.

But Kevin could easily read that the long road trip was starting to catch up with me. He offered to take me out for a late lunch.

"What about your tools?" I asked, in reference to the saw and toolbox we'd carried upstairs.

"Leave 'em, I'll be back tomorrow."

We descended to the kitchen, where in better lighting I could see we were dusted in gypsum from the wallboard.

The blond haired woman stood at the sink, gazing out the window at Rat running around in the tall grass with a Border collie. The two dogs' exuberant leaps carried them over a low stonewall separating the small yard at the back of the house from the field beyond.

"Kathy," Kevin spoke, and the woman turned around.

I half-expected her face to match her sleek hair and athletic figure. Kathy's features reflected a woman of at least sixty who tended to work outdoors. Despite her obvious age, her eyes retained the clarity of youthful health.

"Hi, Kevin," Kathy greeted. "Buster is having so much fun with that dog. Is it yours?"

"That's Rat," I informed. "He's with me."

"Kathy," said Kevin, "this is an old friend from high school, Maddie Benités."

We shook hands. Very few women have that sort of grip unless they work with tools or ride motorcycles.

Kathy walked with us to the back of the house, and we called in the dogs. Rat was pooped, but the collie, Buster, accustomed to roaming the forty-acre farm, seemed on his first wind.

"Come on, Rat," I coaxed. Rat followed me to Kevin's truck, asleep almost immediately on the seat between us.

"Kathy seems like a nice person to do work for," I commented, as the farm faded away in the side view mirror.

"I wish all my clients were as great as Kathy."

"What kind of farm does she run?"

"Stock. She keeps alpacas and Icelandic sheep."

"I think I heard sheep when we arrived."

11

"Yeah, she pastures the stock way back behind the big red barn."

"Why alpacas and Icelandic sheep? That's really exotic."

"Kathy's involved with a group of weavers in Astoria, a New Age textile industry based on the hair. Fibers, wool—whatever, shit, a bunch of hippies, if you ask me."

But he was smiling, and I knew he respected Kathy. Deference for a client wasn't a prerequisite in taking a job, though clearly a positive benefit.

"Say, Maddie, guess what. Kathy's name is really Katarina Johnson." He noted my blank expression. "You know, as in Peter Johnson?"

"Whoa!" I understood, nodding furiously.

"Yeah." He laughed. "I almost made the mistake of poking fun at the name, because of the double dick reference, but before I could put my foot in my mouth, Kathy told me she's Peter Johnson's great-great-granddaughter. He was some famous Scandinavian settler in the Young's River Valley."

"Thank you for the information. But I think I have more tact than that. Mentioning the word 'penis' to a stranger I've just been introduced to could be pretty awkward."

"I was really banking on your good manners when I introduced you to Kathy."

He treated me to lunch at a British style pub about three blocks from the Columbia River. The ambience was quaint, with a ship's figurehead of a half naked woman looming over the bar, and the tables made out of used cable spools cleverly sanded and finished. They even allowed Rat to join us as long as the dog remained under the table at my feet.

We ate fish and chips, drank tepid Guinness, and watched the afternoon shadows lengthen between old buildings. I could easily understand why Kevin had gravitated to Astoria. If not the quaint architecture, then the kindness of people like Kathy, and the bartender, Rowan, who brought a bowl of water for Rat to drink.

When we arrived at Kevin's, I fed Rat, and then let him out in the yard. Entering the house, I sensed a kind of soul, the echo of passing time, and a secret history. I was so tired that I think I babbled something to Kevin about the house's psyche. He only smiled at my rambling, and showed me up to my room on the top floor. I remember taking a quick shower to rid myself of sweat and dust, and then fell asleep as soon as my head hit the pillow.

❖ ❖ ❖ ❖

I awoke in the morning, not knowing at first where I was, or the day. The presence of Rat curled on the rug beside the bed brought back reality. I hit the floor running, Rat on my heels.

I was awake before Kevin, so I let Rat out the back door, while I poked around the kitchen. I set up the coffee maker, and prepped breakfast. When Kevin finally made an appearance, I'd already disposed of the dog poop in the yard, washed the dishes, and started cooking breakfast. I'm not much of a chef, never having found a particular enjoyment in the culinary arts, but I can certainly make pancakes and scrambled eggs when I put my mind to it.

"Maddie," he greeted when he saw me at the sink. Kevin has never been a morning person. The trick of the trade is to feign a morning person as one's profession requires.

He found a mug, and helped himself to coffee.

"Man, you're no fun at all," he complained. "You must've slept for twelve hours straight."

"I did?" I plopped a couple of pancakes onto a plate. "Probably the fault of that warm ale. I don't mean to put down the British, but ale kind of reminds me of piss that's been in a bladder too long."

"So…you've had a glass of piss from an over-full bladder? I mean, how else could you make the comparison?"

"Okay, no. But I really think ale should be served chilled."

"If you ask me, it wasn't the ale that got you, Maddie, it was the all-night drive, and five hours hanging drywall."

We sat at the table and ate breakfast, while Rat snoozed by my feet. Kevin asked me to give him the full story of how I'd acquired Rat, so I explained my personal conflicts, and why I had been only too happy to leave the Bay Area. I related the story of Mallory being exonerated of killing a man the cops were convinced had been stalking her. How Jake Keene was engaged to his live-in fiancé, and that we'd had an affair anyway, which ultimately created negative emotions. I included my shame in acting judgmental about my father's decades-old affair, which came to light when the seed of his loins, Jesse Ibarra, sought out Mitchell Benités to get to the truth.

By the time we were done with breakfast and all the coffee, I had exhausted my words, and my heart. Sitting there with Kevin, all I could

13

think about was Jake up in Seattle without me, and evidently without his ex-fiancé, Sophie.

"Jake's mother visited me right after he left for Seattle." I told Kevin about Jake's adoptive mother, Charlotte Burgess, having the nerve to come to my house in Santa Clara, to warn me away from Jake. "She said that Jake should marry his own kind, or else he'll regret it."

"That's such bullshit." He eyed me appreciatively. "You know, I never told you, Maddie, but all these years, I've used you as an example of work ethic. How to be professional, and how to get it done right."

"That's great, Kevin, but—"

"Wait, I'm not saying I thought of you 'that way,' you know? I'll be blunt, Maddie, I've never wanted to sleep with you."

What a terrible truth to admit to a woman who believes she's not much of a looker to most men. He held up his hand when I opened my mouth, though I'm sure there wouldn't have been any words from my corner, just a groan of pain.

"It's not because you're not attractive, because you are."

A hell of a save, Kev, I thought, just staring at him.

"We've been good friends all these years, Maddie. You and I were drinking buddies when I had no dudes as drinking buddies."

"What are you trying to say?" I asked, without seeming hurt or angry.

He held both of my hands. If that wasn't intimate, then I suppose a man could at least hold his sister's hands.

"If you really care about this guy, you should go for it, Maddie. Do you love him?"

"Of course, yes," I said quickly.

At the moment, it seemed the truth, because the words formed so easily. Somehow I'd made the error in equating a sexual attraction for Jake with real love. The problem was I was still willing to continue making that mistake.

"Look. You said he's up in Seattle right now."

"Yeah, at book signings. He's an author, he's up there for a week to promote his latest novel."

"Seattle is three hours away, Maddie. You could drive up for the day, and surprise him."

I frowned down at Kevin's hands, and he withdrew, though I was making the travel calculation, not offering criticism of his clearly platonic affection. Now I was firm on Kevin's intentions, and realized I'd been the only one of us with the issue of sexual tension.

"You know, I really appreciate your hand-holding."

He turned beet red, and muttered some excuse.

"Three hours, huh?" I added.

"A drop in the bucket after driving up here, Maddie."

"I guess I could handle three hours. I don't know where he's doing the promo, or what hotel he's staying in."

"You could use my computer," he offered. "Maybe he's got a web site."

He showed me the basement cubby that served as his office. The update was very modern, not like the bulk of the house, which he'd been meticulous in leaving to period style. The walls were painted a cheerful pale yellow, and a couple of high basement windows let in south facing light. A router blinked its lights from a shelf niche in the cherry wood desk.

Kevin logged onto the computer, and returned to the kitchen, leaving me alone, welcomed privacy after all that mushy holding of hands.

I found Jake's website under his pen name, J.R. Keene, and a calendar of book-signings for the week in the greater Seattle area. If I drove north right at that moment, I could make the evening signing at an independent book retailer in downtown Seattle on Tenth Avenue. I decided to take Rat with me, because I reasoned that Jake would be elated to see his beloved dog. Maybe I'd get to resolve my ill-directed horniness.

I ran back up the steps two at a time. When I reached the kitchen, Kevin was waiting, and passed me a small cooler packed with sandwiches and cold soda.

"You knew." I resisted the impulse to fling my arms around his neck, and kiss him.

"Yeah, dude, Maddie. I know you pretty well."

We hugged goodbye, like a couple of guy friends. I promised to drive back through Astoria on my return trip to California, making a joke about having to return his cooler. He said a few kind words to Rat, and then walked me to my car. He waved as I drove down Franklin Avenue toward the freeway. I was excited for what was in store for me. Had I known, I would have cursed myself for my naïveté.

Chapter Three

I gassed up the Mercedes before I left town, crossing the Astoria-Megler Bridge into Washington State. I pretended a demarcation once I crossed the choppy waters of the Columbia River, an arrival into new territory, but aside from the Washington State border sign, the rest was a simulation in my mind. I was too adult and preoccupied to play that game. I committed to a serious journey, and in retrospect, would soon realize that I shouldn't have been taking myself so seriously.

I drove through beautiful terrain, a part of my mind alert to the road and its hazards, and the rest on Jake Keene. Our last moments together had been grim. I learned he'd only stopped on his way to the airport to ask me to watch his dog while he was in Seattle. I have excellent self-discipline, except for when it comes to sex, so of course we'd had a quickie on the couch. When we were through, I discovered he was carrying airline tickets for both himself and Sophie.

Predictably, I went off the deep end, and threw his clothes into the washing machine. I wasn't too enraged to include his wallet or keys in the wash cycle, knowing he'd need those to make his escape. I created an atmosphere so hostile that he'd had to put his clothes on in the front seat of his car before any of my neighbors spotted a naked man in plain sight, and called the cops.

I'd only found out that he'd broken off his engagement with Sophie when Jake's adoptive mother, Charlotte Burgess, came to my house on Sophie's behalf. This involved leaving her vulture roost at Tanner Valley Vineyards, the family winery in San Martin. I assumed her visit was proof I had evolved into a serious contender in this would-be game of love. According to Charlotte, I was more of an impediment than actual competition, and she took no effort to conceal her harsh opinion of me.

On the way up to Seattle, I kept replaying these uncomfortable events, distracted twice by Rat, who asked me in dog language to stop for his needs. I thanked my wisdom in carrying plastic bags in the trunk of the car, let him exercise on leash at a rest area, and gave him water in a plastic cup. He was happy as long as I paid attention to him, and rolled the windows down for sniff testing while we traveled.

I started to feel sleepy south of Tacoma, so I took an exit and bought a cup of coffee at an independent coffee house. The baristas were friendly, and I'm sure their living depended on keeping one step ahead of their very successful adversaries in the coffee world. I didn't make a point to remember the name of the coffee house, but the coffee was decent, and I made note of its location in case I wanted to drop in again on my way back to Astoria.

This particular café displayed artwork from local artists, some professional, and students from several universities. Oil paintings hung on the walls, and sculptures adorned high shelves. My favorite was the sculpture of a shining eagle made of aluminum. Hanging on a wire near the front windows, the eagle reflected sunlight as it rotated with the air currents. I remarked to the female barista who served me at the counter that I admired the eagle, impressed with the detail in its layers of metal feathers.

"So do I!" she gushed, giggling like a bimbo.

I couldn't figure out why this young woman would go out of her way to give strangers the impression she's an imbecile.

I pocketed my wallet, and grabbed the coffee. "Who made it?"

"Jason," the scatterbrained barista spoke to her male co-worker, who was making the more expensive mixed coffees. "Is that Wyatt's piece?" she asked, pointing up at the eagle.

"Uh, yup," Jason confirmed.

"It's Wyatt's," she told me, as though I'd somehow missed their verbal exchange. Leaning forward, she spoke candidly. "He's like, kind of old, you know? But, like, he's kind of hot, too." She giggled again.

Jason rolled his eyes, and mumbled an expletive.

I think it's an ego bruise to a young man when a woman his age declares an attraction to a man she's already termed "old." I was snickering when I departed with my coffee.

I would have rolled into Seattle by four p.m., in plenty of time for Jake's five o'clock book signing, but I got a flat tire just south of Kent. There I was, on the side of the freeway with a broken jack, frustrated as hell, and cursing myself for not inspecting the jack before the trip. I at least had the prudence to check the tire pressure on the spare, but that did me no good if I couldn't lift the wheel off the ground. I finally called my tow service. I should have done that to begin with, but I have a lot of confidence in my ability to handle a simple tire change.

Within thirty minutes, the service sent a tow truck, and the driver changed out to the spare. I was back on the road, knowing I had to get the damaged tire repaired in the event of another unscheduled flat.

I found a guy in an automotive outlet in Renton who was willing to fix the tire while I waited, and sell me a replacement jack. They removed a nail from between the tread, repaired the hole, and I was on the highway by six p.m.

I was running out of time, but I miscalculated in thinking an hour was plenty of leeway to work it out, as downtown Seattle is a nightmare of one-way streets and surface traffic at rush hour on a Wednesday night. I didn't know how in the world I was going to make this book signing before it was finished at seven. By the time I actually located the bookstore on Tenth, and then a convenient parking garage, the time was almost seven thirty.

With Rat on a leash, we jogged to the bookstore. I tied the dog to a bicycle rack in front, and hurried in, hoping Jake had lingered over a crowd of admiring fans. There were the eight-by-ten ads with his headshot, but Jake was nowhere to be seen.

An employee was just cleaning up the last traces of the book signing—a folding table, chair, and a stack of Jake's latest novel.

"Excuse me. Ma'am?" I inquired tentatively.

She turned and gawked at me, and I realized that I had just addressed a teenaged girl as an elder.

"Sorry," I apologized. "You definitely don't qualify as a 'ma'am.'"

She laughed, and waved her hand, already having forgiven me.

"What can I help you with?" she asked.

"J.R. Keene." I pointed at the table.

"I'm so sorry. You just missed him. He finished the signing a little after seven."

I groaned, slapping my forehead in theatrical exaggeration, which seemed to alarm her.

"I came from California," I explained, hoping to erase the impression I was completely nuts. "Jake is a friend of mine."

Apparently name-dropping "California" and "Jake" simultaneously seemed to do the trick, because she patted my shoulder kindly.

"You could check with the hotel," she suggested. "They might be able to get a message to him."

I snapped my fingers. "You know, that's a great idea. I'll just go over to the Marriott right now."

"He said something about staying at The Edgewater Hotel," she volunteered.

"That's right." I chuckled. "He usually stays at a Marriott, but now I remember, he did mention The Edgewater. Gee, thanks."

I made a mental note to tell Jake he shouldn't reveal to giddy teenaged girls where he was staying in the event a stalker was following his itinerary. But at that moment, I was grateful the giddy teenaged girl was a blabbermouth.

I had no idea how to locate The Edgewater, so I consulted with a meter maid who was printing out a parking ticket for some inconsiderate jerk who'd double-parked a Hummer. After a moment of dubious suspicion, and my assurance that I wasn't the owner of the Hummer, he gave me the directions.

I retrieved the Mercedes from the parking garage, and we were off for The Edgewater, Rat excited by the sights and smells of Seattle. He wagged his tail constantly, caught up in my high spirits, even when steel gray clouds looming over the tall buildings of downtown began to drip rain.

At first, there were a few drops, a cautious prelude, and then the heavens broke, setting loose a deluge not unlike a Hollywood movie set. This torrent seemed the true face of Seattle, though no one seemed concerned. People conducted their business either with or without umbrellas, not bothered in the least about getting rained on.

I finally found The Edgewater. After I parked—this time leaving Rat locked in with the windows cracked—I hurried to the lobby to find Jake.

The hotel was plush and expensive looking. I was thinking I'd love a night in a bed in this beautiful hotel, naked in the arms of Jake Keene. I was rewarded with that carnal train of thought, by the sight of Jake, stepping off an elevator.

Strangely, when I saw him, I was trying to figure out how to get in touch with him. I had his cell number, but I wanted to make a romantic gesture, not announce my presence in Seattle with such a mundane device. I knew the terminology used in high-end hotels, "concierge," though I saw Jake before I could locate the front counter.

I was just about to call out to him, when I realized he wasn't alone. He was holding the hand of a very attractive and feminine woman. She wasn't dressed in jeans and Converse sneakers. Unlike my tendency to boyish attire, she was stylish, the epitome of a *Vogue* ad. To further the depths of my stupidity, I was making the rationalization that Sophie surely would be furious if she were standing here in my shoes.

Jake kind of twirled the woman, as though on a stage and dancing to the piped-in music. Both had flushed faces, and the woman's hair was disheveled, to me an obvious indicator that Jake had probably already gotten laid up in his hotel room. Pulling her close, he kissed her. I'm not talking about a peck. That kiss was sexually charged, with opened lips, and a hell of a lot of tongue.

After an instantaneous jolt of revulsion, my first thought was that I didn't ever want to touch that man again.

He glanced up at the precise moment I was staring...no, riveted—you see the bloody car wreck, but you can't break away—and our eyes met. Jake Keene has a dark, exotic look about him, though I swear he turned white as a sheet out of the horror of getting busted.

All I did was turn tail and run. I heard him call out my name, but I kept going, determined to escape. I jammed it out of the lobby, into the rain and back to the car, trying to drown the high tone of his panicked voice with the sound of my tennis shoes on the streaming pavement.

The rain was falling so hard that when I accelerated onto the freeway, I had difficulty discerning the lines on the road. I had intended to return to Astoria that night, but I didn't think I'd make it. The wipers were flinging lickety-split, defrost was on full-blast, and I couldn't drive any faster than fifty. I was an emotional mess, and as I drove, I cried and cried, while Rat, always patient, whined softly for me to feed him, and allow him his toilet.

I regrouped, and located a gas station south of the Kent turnoff. Rolling beneath an overhang out of the rain, I fed and watered poor Rat. He sensed I was distressed, and kept pushing against me with his shoulder as though trying to comfort me. Eventually he did his toilet thing, which I cleaned up, and then we were back on the Interstate.

Though all those bitter tears had been good for my self-respect, the time was past nine p.m., and I was really, really tired. Maybe the endless road trip to Astoria, combined with the tediousness of hanging drywall, Jake's disingenuous behavior, and despair that was quickly turning into disgust—but I knew I needed to stop. Maybe a motel would be the answer. Notice that I use the term "motel", not "hotel", the difference between the m and the h being roughly a hundred dollars a night.

Fortunately, I remembered the coffee house in Tacoma, and the bright eagle hanging from the ceiling, created by an older man the air-headed barista, Cindy, had declared "hot." I needed hot, at least in a cup of coffee, so I made the decision to take the next exit.

The rain was still bashing the pavement when I pulled into the parking lot of the coffee house. I was grateful the place was open for business, and appeared to be packed with people on this rainy night. Just as I was climbing out of the car, two shadows slick with rain pounced on me and tried to pry me out of the Mercedes.

"Give me the fucking keys, bitch," one of them demanded, while the other fumbled around inside the car for a purse, a female contraption I never carry. Maybe they expected an easy mark in a woman, but I surprised them by kicking and screaming, and even landed a few solid punches, accustomed to being in the thick of the occasional bar brawl.

But amazingly Rat saved us, turning from a gentle companion into a vicious defender. I'd never heard a dog snarling in tongues. He fought dirty, biting down on an attacker's arm or leg, and yanking backward with his entire body, then releasing only to choose another extremity to sink his teeth into, repeating the nasty process.

The two muggers, terrified at Rat's speed and aggression, tried to hide in the car as a last resort, but Rat was swift, and countered every attempt at escape. There was blood on the ground, though not mine, and surely not Rat's. All the while Rat inflicted damage, I was landing punches, kicking with my feet, and yelling my head off.

In spite of the rain, the commotion of Rat's snarling rage and my maniacal screaming seemed to catch the attention of the people in the coffee house. The thug who'd demanded the keys to the Mercedes used the distraction of numbers, and fled down the rain-washed street. I'm sure he'd been brutally punctured by Rat's canines and was bleeding, little dots that probably melted away beneath the force of the rain.

The other thief who'd been scrabbling around for my non-existent purse was lying on his back upon the pavement, terrified of the growling forty-pound dog arched over him, teeth anchored in the man's forearm.

The first coffee house patron to arrive was over six feet tall, weighed at least two hundred pounds, and would have seemed terrifying popping up suddenly in a dark rainy parking lot. He just stood there, considering Rat and the thief, while the crowd surged behind him. Rat might have kept ripping away, but the man spoke to the dog in a low voice, urging retreat. Rat dropped the perp's bleeding arm, and returned to my side, grumbling resentfully.

The tall man grabbed the perp by the bloody sweatshirt. Hauling my attacker to his feet, the man half-dragged him into the café to hold him for the police, who arrived soon after to take the report.

One of the baristas was kind enough to place me at a table far across the room. Rat sat on his haunches with his back pressed against my legs, growling whenever he got a whiff of the perp. Though the leash was slack, I was glad I had clipped it to Rat's collar ring.

The perp had been revealed by then, and some of the coffee house customers knew him by first name. There was a general feeling of disbelief that the young man could have attacked me so ruthlessly in the parking lot. The fact of the assault gained him very little sympathy for his numerous dog bites, and Rat's display of good behavior inside the coffee house added to the dog's credibility.

With the perp's identification, the police had his name, an address, and a possible route to his accomplice. The onboard police computer also brought up a list of priors—several for felonious assault—so I knew I was fortunate that neither Rat nor I were physically harmed.

I was exhausted by the emotional drain and lack of food. I hadn't eaten since Kevin's sandwiches, which had fueled my mad dash to Seattle. While I cooperated with the police, my hands were shaking. I was relieved that Rat allowed one of the officers to touch him, even going as far as to examine Rat's mouth. The officer inquired about Rat's last rabies shot, and I was grateful Jake had the forethought to hang Rat's vaccination tag with his license. This prevented the police from quarantining the dog for any extended period of time. Rat's cooperative and friendly attitude toward the police officers eased our situation. In the end, they gave me an incident report, and told me we were free to go.

I had been keeping my eye on the man who had helped Rat and me. Even after the cops arrested and removed the perp, the man sat quietly by himself at a table, long legs stretched out before him, one foot hooked over the other, and hands tucked into the pockets of a black wool pea coat. He never once looked at me, but his demeanor suggested the patience of a man who had spent a lifetime waiting, and so had perfected it.

His dark hair, stringy from standing out in the rain, reached halfway down his back. Small gold hoops glittered in the lobes of his ears. I'm not at all attracted to long hair or pierced ears on men. My personal bias tells me that long hair is often an excuse for a lack of proper hygiene, and pierced ears occasionally flag excessive drug use and hidden tattoos. But this man seemed meticulous about his hair, and radiated vitality unlike most chronic potheads I've met.

Determined to offer gratitude for his assistance, I picked up Rat's leash, and walked across the room, Rat following obediently. Standing near the man, I wasn't sure how to break into his cloaked silence, so I only said, "Sir?"

He immediately looked up at me with these incredibly beautiful eyes. I could tell he was sad, though I didn't understand why until later that night. He owned a depth of kindness you don't often see in strangers, a warmth that offset his melancholy. Once he smiled wistfully, I was encouraged to continue.

"Sir," I repeated, "I just wanted to let you know I'm grateful for what you did for us."

"I didn't do anything, your dog did it all." His voice was warm and deep. "And you seem to have no problem kicking a little ass, too." He slowly rose to his feet, as though concerned about frightening me. He was very tall, and loomed over me, though his demeanor wasn't threatening, just an aura of caring and safety.

"Are you hungry?" he asked.

"Yeah, actually, I'm real hungry."

Rat, who stood next to me at leash, decided to be forward, and nosed the man's hand gently to gain his attention.

"Good boy, you're a good dog." The man leaned down, and patted Rat's head affectionately. "What's your dog's name?"

"Rat." I didn't bother clarifying the technicality of Jake Keene's ownership.

"He sure looks like a wet rat from being out in the rain."

"He always looks like that."

"Hmm." He considered Rat's odd appearance carefully. "You're lucky he was with you, strange-looking dog or not. I think your friend here saved you."

"I know. I owe him big time." I held out my hand. "I'm Madeline Benités."

I don't know why I didn't tell him I was "Maddie." At first I wanted a formality to my name. When I rehashed the memory, I believe my introduction reflected the need to frame my femininity, often concealed beneath blue jeans and pullovers.

"Hi, Madeline." He shook my hand gravely. "I'm Wyatt McLain."

"Wyatt?" I was strangely elated at the mention of his name. I pointed to the sculpture floating effortlessly above the caffeine-junkies. "Are you the Wyatt who made the eagle?"

"Yeah, I'm that Wyatt. How did you know? I've never seen you around here." He regarded me with growing amusement. "You're not one of those ditzy college kids, are you?"

"Not at all. I'm not from around here. I'm a general contractor, and I've got my own business in California. I was in Oregon visiting a friend, and then decided at the last minute to drive up to Seattle." I explained my arrival at the café earlier, and how Cindy had given me Wyatt's first name when I asked about the eagle. I held back Cindy's description of Wyatt, but he only guffawed. His outburst of uncontrolled laughter was startling, and trailed away as quickly as it surfaced.

"Yeah, here, let me?" He briefly rested a hand on my shoulder, before drawing away. "She called me 'kind of old, but kind of hot,' right?"

"That's right." As I nodded, my cheeks were red from embarrassment…or maybe the passing touch of his hand made my face burn.

"Don't let it bother you," he assured. "Cindy's got air and kindness in that skull of hers." He rubbed his chin. "Look, you said you're hungry."

"I'm starving."

"Would you let me take you somewhere to eat?"

"Well…" No matter how kind he seemed, he was a stranger.

"How long has it been since you ate?"

"I haven't eaten since…since before I got a flat tire, maybe five hours ago."

"Then, what are we waiting for?"

What indeed?

Without wasting another moment, we walked to the Mercedes. The rain had diminished somewhat, and fell only lightly. I opened the door, pulling the seat forward so Rat could climb in, and noted that Wyatt was not at all self-conscious when he helped himself to the front passenger seat, and belted in. He even located the lever, and moved the seat back to accommodate his long legs.

24

"Nice car! It's what, a seventy-two?"

"A seventy-three, but, uh, excuse me. Wyatt? I…kind of figured I'd follow *your* car."

"Sorry, Madeline, I have a car, but not here. It's parked a couple of blocks away in front of my place. I walked to the coffee house. It's not too far. I know where the closest all-night diner is. We could just eat, and be done with it. Or eat and talk, if that's okay with you."

He smiled, which expressed that sweetness, and removed the edge of his melancholy.

I eyed him suspiciously, taking my time so he could see I wasn't a pushover. I didn't know this man, and yet, I had to trust Rat, my canine chaperone, who seemed to have a sixth sense about human nature. I remembered that Rat had treated the scent of Jake's mother, Charlotte Burgess, with a high degree of hostility, and had attacked the two thugs without hesitation. The fact that Rat was now sniffing the shoulder of Wyatt's black pea coat, and wagging his tail eagerly, told me that I had more to trust than to doubt about this man.

Rat will take care of Wyatt if he gets out of line.

"Besides, your dog will bite me to death if I so much as think bad thoughts," he added, as though reading my mind.

Shaking my head, I started the car, and off we went. He pointed the direction to a diner near the Interstate, where we were seated in a corner booth. Rat had to stay in the car, though I parked the Mercedes in full view of the plate glass windows. I was relieved it seemed to have finally stopped raining.

We both ordered comfort food from the waitress—pancakes, hash browns, sausage and eggs. There's something about breakfast fare I find calming. Unfortunately the diner coffee tasted like hot water with a tint of brown. But I didn't mind. I was famished, and the anticipation of food was a reprieve to that desperate feeling I'd achieved after my encounter with Jake in Seattle.

While we waited for the food to arrive, I excused myself to the bathroom. When I returned to the table, Wyatt had gone missing, presumably to the restroom. I used the free time to call Kevin on my cell and briefly explain what had happened, promising to get a motel for the night, and drive back to Astoria the following morning. I had just signed off, when Wyatt returned to the booth.

"Your boyfriend?" he asked, as though entertained by my swift exit from the phone conversation.

"No, just a friend, the one in Oregon. I didn't want him to worry about me." I almost slid the phone back into my jacket pocket, when it beeped, and caller ID prefaced Jake Keene's cell number. I decided I wouldn't answer any communications from Jake until I had time to cool down.

"That was my boyfriend," I informed. "Well, he's not officially my boyfriend, just somebody I was seeing." I told Wyatt a little of what had transpired that day in Seattle.

"Wow! And you're this rational?" He shook his head. "Man, if I caught a woman I was seeing romantically having tongue fights with some other guy, I'd be hurt."

I had thought he'd say "angry," the natural response to a cheater, but "hurt" was as violent a word he used. The description of his "tongue fights" made me laugh in spite of my resentment toward Jake, and Wyatt grinned at me, pleased I'd reacted favorably to his wisecrack.

"I couldn't stay," I said, of my disgust with Jake. "He'd already been intimate with her."

"How could you tell?"

"Well, she was dressed-up for a night on the town, but she wasn't wearing any lipstick, and her hair was a mess. And they both looked sweaty."

"You're an amazing judge of character, Madeline, and wise, too."

That's when I admitted that Rat wasn't my dog, and actually belonged to the sometime boyfriend.

"I've been dog sitting. Jake was away on a business trip, and didn't have anyone else to watch Rat for him."

"Well, it's a good thing Rat was with you," he reasoned, "or else tonight's outcome might have been different."

He asked about Rat's lineage, and I related Jake Keene's story of Rat having a Shar-Pei dam, and a Chinese Crested sire. Both breeds are valued and never intentionally crossbred, but somehow the two prized breeding dogs managed to sidestep their owners' supervision, and mate anyway. The result was Rat—the most hideous from a litter of three ugly puppies.

"He *is* ugly," Wyatt agreed, "though he's so nice, it makes you forget to look too closely."

He wanted to know what part of California I was from. I described the Bay Area, and its collection of cultures, religions and ethnicities.

"Are you a collection of ethnicities?" he wondered. "Because I can't seem to categorize you to any one race." He was looking me up and down without bothering to hide his interest. "You're definitely an eye-catcher."

"You wouldn't believe it if I told you. Let's just say I'm a little bit of everything. How about you?"

He revealed he was Quinault Indian, and lived in Tacoma, but would return often to the reservation in Taholah to visit his Aunt Doreen.

"She's my mom's sister," he explained. "She raised me when my parents died. She's the only family I have left, except for my little sister, Katie. Wait. She *hates* being called 'Katie,' so I have to get this right the first time. Kate lives in California, so I don't see her all too often."

"I have a sister who lives far away, too." I knew how it felt to see Miranda only rarely.

"Does your sister live in Washington State? 'Cause it would be kind of funny to have *my* sister live in California, and *your* sister live up here in Washington."

"No, Miranda lives in Susanville, it's a little town in northern California."

He threw himself back against the seat as though I'd struck him.

"No!" He inhaled sharply. "No shit!" he added, for effect.

"Excuse me?"

Now he was leaning over the table. "No. Shit," he spoke slowly, in case I didn't hear him the first time. "My sister lives in Susanville too."

"You're full of it," I dared, taking a bite from my hash browns.

"No, *really*." His eyes became very intense, not frightening, but attractive, despite the pain that lurked behind his grin. Now I knew why Cindy considered Wyatt "hot."

"Yes, you are," I challenged. "You're probably making that up."

"Look, Madeline, I wouldn't lie to anyone, and especially to you. My sister, her name's Katie—ah, Kate Sumner, and she lives on a ranch near Susanville. Well, it's closer to Westwood. Up near Goodrich Creek."

Now I knew he was telling the truth, because you have to know the Susanville area in order to name those towns, and that pretty creek.

"So, Wyatt. Let's just…pretend I believe you."

"It's true," he insisted, as though there were no other possibility. "What about your sister?"

"Okay, get this, her married name is Miranda Snead, she lives on North Gay Street in Susanville, and she works as a trooper for the California Highway Patrol."

"Hah, Snead." He laughed again, an abrupt roar that came and went so quickly. He didn't even bite at the "Gay Street" reference.

"Yeah, I know, Snead took some getting used to. Doesn't flow off the tongue like Benités."

The food and conversation were making me sleepy. The hour was late, close to midnight, and I knew I was going to shut down soon. I asked if he knew of any cheap but decent motels in the Tacoma area.

He told me a motel was nonsense, that I was more than welcome to stay the night at his place. I think his exact words were "You can bunk at my loft."

I surprised myself, and agreed without hesitation. Wyatt was what I can only describe as warm-hearted. Though clearly a man of great physical strength, he radiated compassion, and his eyes reflected vibrancy, even with the hidden pain. There didn't seem to be an evil bone in his body.

At least I gave him an out.

"You don't even know me," I contended. "As far as we're concerned, I could hit you over the head, and then rob you when you're out cold."

Which only made him laugh again.

"Right, Madeline. Hah!"

Once more, we got into the Mercedes, with Rat sniffing at Wyatt's hair. He gave me the route to his loft, close to the University of Washington. The streets were wet and shining, empty of traffic, and it had started to sprinkle again.

Outside of his address, he paused a moment to show me his car, rapping his knuckles on the hood of a dark blue Ford Crown Victoria, as though to prove he hadn't been lying about that.

"Why do you drive such a big car?" I asked, as Rat and I followed him into the loft space with its high ceiling. "Doesn't it have a V-8 engine?"

"It is a gas guzzler, but do I look like I'd be comfortable in a subcompact?"

"Well, no, of course not."

"And besides, when you're Indian, and you drive around in a Crown Vic, the police up here assume you're one of them, and they tend to leave you alone."

I noted a wood stove in the common area on the main floor. To ward off the chill of the rainy night, Wyatt loaded the box with fresh wood.

While he stoked up the fire, I studied a large oil painting hanging above the stone backstop. The study depicted sage plains flowing into the distance, where little snow-capped mountains sat like pearls beneath an enormous blue sky arched over by thunderheads. The caption beneath read, "Surprise Valley, Modoc County." The painting seemed almost real, as though a window to another world. I felt I could climb inside and walk across the golden plains to the distant mountains.

"This is extraordinary, Wyatt. Where did you get this?"

"That's my sister's. She's an artist." He pointed out the tiny signature, "K. McLain," in the lower left corner. "The need to create runs in the family."

"What about that?" I motioned to a tenor ukulele lying across the top of a sofa-back table. "Do you play?"

He picked it up sheepishly, the koa grain of the instrument shining richly in the firelight.

"I fake it pretty well."

"My father is a professional musician. He's got a nice ukulele too."

"I'm no professional when it comes to music. But I'll give it a try." He plinked out a few notes, and then began to strum. I recognized "Pearly Shells."

"That's one of my dad's favorite songs."

I told him about my parents singing "Pearly Shells" at my sister Margot's sweet-sixteen birthday party, much to her pained embarrassment.

"Hawaiian shirts and all?" Wyatt asked, carefully setting the ukulele onto the tabletop.

"Yeah, the whole outfit. Their performance was so corny. Margot's only recently been able to talk about it without breaking into a sweat."

Digging around in a cabinet, he pulled out a carton of wine, and offered me a glass, explaining that I'd hit upon luck, as he rarely kept alcohol in his Tacoma diggings. After unsealing the cardboard box, he produced a bottle of red wine. Uncorking the wine, he poured two long stemmed glasses, and handed one to me.

"You caught me with my pants down, Madeline."

Snorting at his description, I accepted the wine. "That's a handy metaphor, about the pants. It kind of forms a picture, you know?"

"I like it, too." He laughed softly. "I wouldn't have the wine, if it wasn't for my sister's man. He was a vintner from way back."

Turning the bottle, he revealed the label of the Reserve Red, from Clay Creek Winery in Lockeford, California. This was another shocker, one of my favorite wineries, boutique and obscure. I'd even given Jake a bottle of Cabernet Sauvignon for his fortieth birthday from that very winery. Wyatt didn't simply have a case of this wine. He was directly affiliated with the winery through his sister, and that was about as far-fetched as our sisters living near Susanville, or a commonality in the song, "Pearly Shells."

Wyatt observed my face as I explained the connection between us—first our sisters, then the song, and now the wine. I could feel tiny hairs stand up on the back of my neck, out of a thrill of odd coincidences than any sensation of fear.

"Do you believe in kismet?" he asked seriously, and I'm sorry, but the word took me by surprise, and I laughed outright. He was an understanding man, and grasping my foolishness, changed his tack.

"Or in fate?" he suggested.

I watched Rat pad around, and make himself a bed on the carpet close to the stove, the glass windows displaying the flame. Rat's demeanor reflected ease in Wyatt's proximity I was willing to accept.

But I shrugged, dismissing the myth of destiny. I like to believe I always have the power to choose the course of my life.

"I'm not sure about destiny. I know life has its obstacles, and sometimes you've got to watch out where you step."

"Not things that get in the way, Madeline, not missteps, or dog scat. I'm talking about things that are meant to be."

"Are you saying somehow fate decided I was meant to get robbed at the coffee house?"

"Well…maybe not robbed, but I think you were at least meant to stop in there again."

He held his glass before the flames, and pondered on the wine sloshing back and forth like an ocean current.

"I don't gamble, so I'm not too keen on odds, or coincidence, Wyatt."

"What're the chances, then, that our sisters would live in the same county, near some dot on a map? That you would prefer wine from my brother-in-law's winery, or that I would play a few notes of a song that holds a special meaning for you? That I would be at that particular café on this particular night—or the fact I almost didn't walk there, because of the rain?"

"So, in your reasoning, fate is the preponderance to us meeting by chance."

"I haven't been to the café for almost a month, Madeline. I've been in Taholah, staying on the rez with a friend of mine, a tribal lawyer, who's also a wood carver, as part of a group working together to make a canoe."

He described a streamlined boat hewn from a single log of old growth red cedar, carved for the canoe races held during the celebration of Chief Taholah Days, the annual commemoration of the 1855 Treaty with the United States government.

"Yes, undoubtedly, what *are* the odds?" he repeated, eyes searching mine in the firelight.

"How old are you, Wyatt?" I asked, in my cynical habit. "If you don't mind the question."

I needed to know, because his age could fall anywhere between thirty and forty. He had smooth skin with a suggestion of sun squint, and curves from smiling, but his eyes were clear and youthful, like Kathy Johnson's had been.

"I'm fifty-two," he said without ego. "I'll be fifty-three next time around." He laughed at his own straight talk, a man willing to face his age, and take a chance admitting it. "I'm quite aware, Madeline, that you can do the math."

I knew he could read the shock in my face, as I'd grossly underestimated his age. When he told me he was over fifty, I had a bombshell moment.

"Wyatt, I'm twenty-five. I'm young enough to be your daughter."

"Right, I know. You just don't feel like a daughter to me." He stretched his legs. "I think you should know that I never involve myself with women from your generation, not because of the age difference, as much as the cultural difference. But with you there's no time lag."

"Time lag?" My puzzlement made him grin.

31

"You know, idiocy, vapor-heads. Like that Cindy at the coffee house? You and I can have a real conversation, and I don't find myself in need of a translator, or having to dumb down to be understood."

He was tall and muscular, a man who expressed his fitness carving boats out of cedar trees, and building metal sculptures like that huge eagle talon that stood on a table just to the left of the wood stove. He saw me studying the talon, and put aside his wine.

"That particular piece," he told me, "saved my life."

He related the story of a home-invasion robbery, how he'd caught three young men in the midst of stealing copper from his loft. He would have let them go, but one of them stabbed him repeatedly, so he clubbed the man once across the back of the head to prevent the knife from penetrating through his chest to his heart. Before the police and the paramedics arrived, the perp bled out on the concrete floor.

Wyatt's account revealed why he carried the underlying grief in his eyes.

"I killed a man. I hit that poor guy hard enough to crack his skull wide open. I killed somebody's son."

"But he would have killed you," I pointed out. "What else could you do? And then we wouldn't be sitting here like this."

"Yes, that's true. You're right." Though I could still see the remorse in his eyes.

We talked further, mostly about art and music. He professed a love for seventies rock, and I told him about my preference for jazz standards. He conceded that his demeanor toward me in the diner would have gotten him into trouble at the rez.

"It's considered a social indiscretion to openly look a person up and down, especially a woman. I didn't mean any disrespect, it's just…you're probably familiar with Western culture, and then I feel very comfortable with you, Madeline."

"I understand, it's the same with my dad's family. You're not supposed to stare or point at people. But you're correct, I'm acculturated, so I'm not at all offended."

"I'm glad. I wouldn't want to scare you off, or give you the wrong impression about me."

And then, he offered his bed to me. I didn't mull over the moment or weigh alternatives. I accepted his proposal readily. I know it was forward of me when I climbed the stairs with him, our hands linked together, an unmistakable energy between us, more than the simple craving of two lonely people.

In the half-light of his bedroom, he removed his sweater and undershirt, casting exaggerated shadows across the wall. He showed me the scars from the knife wounds that described the details of that terrible attack. The scars started at the height of his left shoulder, and spread down the pectoral muscle, red ribbons of healed tissue that mimicked the undulations of wind in the clouds.

I think he was startled when I ran my fingertips gently along the upraised lines with their dots from sutures marring his bronze flesh. I suppose those scars would be horrific to some, but to me, they were strangely beautiful, a badge of survival in a man who lamented the brutality that had gone into killing his attacker.

I started to kiss his scars one by one, first his chest and his shoulder, and then I made my way up to his lips. He was a great kisser, and that led to making out, and then some fooling around, while we slipped out of our clothes an article at a time. There was shared wonderment between us, a keen awareness of the moment when the body swears by the sincerity of the heart.

When we finally moved to more serious intention, and slowly started to make love, ours was an elegant dance, where every movement has a nuance and a meaning. I was half his weight, and half his age, but I could feel the sensibility of luck and destiny, stars that aligned to bring us together, two uncommon strangers with oddly common ties.

Afterward, we fell asleep in the mutual peace of loving arms. Sometime around dawn, we awoke, and realized our profound good fortune to still be together, and so we made love again. I can only describe intimacy with Wyatt as fiercely powerful, and softly poetic. Being with him reminded me of the ocean, endless to the horizon, how the sea appeared in the light of the dawn when I first approached the Oregon coast on my way to Astoria.

Even when Tacoma was long out of sight, I could feel his incredible pull. I am a woman who makes a habit of facing facts, but the dreamlike nature of my first night with Wyatt created emotions I tiptoed around, wary of the implications, and afraid of deluding myself into making another mistake in judgment when it came to love.

Before I departed, we sat down in the kitchen for early morning coffee, drunk on the afterglow of our memorable night. I couldn't forget his eyes, the sensation of his fingers on my cheek, and the soft whisper of his voice when he spoke, as though reluctant to break the spell.

Hand in hand, Wyatt walked me through his studio, a practical space cluttered with wood carvings, clay proofs, and finished works: glittering hummingbirds in flight, flocks of bronze shorebirds, and a shining falcon, suspended from the ceiling by a wire, gliding above all the catalogued pieces on sickle wings.

He pulled a labeled box from a drawer deep in his workbench. The memento he released from its cardboard prison was the fired clay proof of a flatfish, scales and eyes realistic in the studio light.

"For you," he insisted, pressing it into my hands.

I ran my fingertips over the piece, in awe of its intricate beauty, and then recalled feeling the ridges of his scars.

"What kind of flatfish is it?"

"Alaskan halibut. The final piece is on display at the Seattle Aquarium. It's over seven feet long. I made it out of copper, so it's green where it oxidized, but shiny where children get to touch it." He smiled. "The way you're touching it right now."

I slid the halibut into the pocket of my jacket, fingers curled around its shape.

"I'll cherish this. Thank you."

He put his arms around me, and hugged me close. "No, thank *you*, Madeline."

We walked outside with Rat, holding hands like besotted lovers. Down by the street, while we waited for Rat to do his thing, he revealed to me that his father had named him "Wyatt Earp," after the historic lawman from Tombstone, Arizona, made famous by the conflict at the OK Corral.

"Why do you think he named you Wyatt Earp?" I asked, loading Rat into the car.

"My father was a humorist, I suppose. I'm probably a lot like he was, always looking for the joke. I figure people can't argue if they're laughing together."

But something troubled him, even as he leaned down to the window to say farewell.

"Would you believe me if I told you that I'm not a killer, Madeline?"

Knowing how it had felt to defend myself, I placed my faith in Wyatt.

"I believe you," I promised, touching his face.

I would have kept my hand on his cheek forever, looking into his eyes, except I had to put the car in gear. I could see him standing there when I drove away, framed in the rear-view mirror, his long hair streaming in the wind. Leaving Wyatt in Tacoma far more difficult than leaving Jake in Seattle, because I had this strange conviction that I belonged. Our meeting on a rainy night was more than simple coincidence.

Chapter Four

I arrived in Astoria in time to have lunch with Kevin at the Franklin Avenue house. We spent the afternoon hanging the last of the drywall at Kathy's farm.

When we were finished, we sat out back of the house, and watched Rat play with Buster, leaping the wall, and wrestling in the grass. Kevin picked a long blade, and stuck it between his teeth, while I suggested by virtue of the dogs he might be introducing something to his mouth that he wouldn't normally eat. That was the fastest I've ever seen a man spit.

I didn't say much to Kev at lunch about the tribulations of my Seattle adventure, especially about Wyatt, as though in fear of ruining an intensely beautiful memory. Kevin knew me well enough to know that I was holding back the whole story.

But in the afternoon light of Young's River Valley, I had need for candor, and found the words. They seemed to fit together as I described in detail the drive up from Astoria to Seattle, and the numerous impediments to my timely arrival. Stopping at the coffee house, the flat tire, and the subsequent fix, how I felt when I finally found Jake, and he was ardently kissing another woman. How my pain was killed by my anger, and how my anger died when I realized that I had ceased to care what Jake did.

"Maybe all those events got in your way to keep you from getting to Seattle on time," Kevin concluded. He was suggesting the same path of destiny that Wyatt had spoken of.

"I didn't think of it that way. It was all so frustrating, but now it seems logical."

"Maybe you were supposed to catch Jake by surprise. If you got to the book signing, you never would've busted him at the hotel."

"That's true." I remembered Wyatt's word, "fate," for which there is no concept as logic.

"I'm really sorry that happened to you, Maddie."

36

I picked a ladybug off a grass blade, and let it walk up my hand, before it flipped its wings from a spotted orange shell, and buzzed away. I was in that zone, buffered by the singular effect of the night with Wyatt, that a creature as seemingly pedestrian as a ladybug was sublime in the residue of my euphoria.

"I thought about it, all of it, Kevin, and I'm glad I went to Seattle."

"You're *glad* you busted Jake?"

"I'm glad, because I got a chance to see who Jake really is. Well, and then I met somebody."

I awkwardly related what had transpired after I left Seattle in a downpour. When I was finished, Kevin was staring out at the distant barn. When he finally spoke, he had a trace of sarcasm in his voice.

"I'm not your brother, Maddie. I can only put myself into that state of mind. But if I were your brother, the first thing I'd ask is, what the *hell* were you thinking?"

I shook my head. "I don't know. It seemed…right."

"You just got jumped by a couple of car-jackers, and then you go home with a total stranger? *And* have sex with him? And that seems right to you?"

"You make it sound sleazy, and it wasn't."

"I just hope this guy feels the same way, Maddie, 'cause us guys, we tend to think less of women who let us act out our sleaze."

I sorted through the memory, trying to put my emotions into words. I decided to use the comparison factor, with Jake Keene as example.

"I never introduced Jake to my parents," I explained. "Margot knew I liked the guy, but she never knew I was sleeping with him. Nobody knew how much time I was spending with him. I felt like a secret agent or something."

"You have to ask yourself then, 'what if?'"

"You mean, what if I'd told my dad about Jake?" I sighed. "I wasn't in that place yet. I don't think I even told you what I was doing with Jake, until it all started to fall apart."

"You never told me he was already engaged to someone else when you started sleeping with him, not until just before you came up here to visit me. As a man, I have to admit we tend to take advantage of these situations. As your brother, I would have advised you to move on, before it became a situation."

"I know, and you'd be right. I should've moved on a long time ago."

"So, let's go back to last night. Why did you sleep with a total stranger?"

"That's just it." I struggled to find the words. "He *wasn't* a total stranger."

I explained about our sisters, the song, and the winery, about being at the same place at the same time, when neither of us had crossed paths in our entire lives.

"And Rat liked him, too." As though Rat's opinion constituted Wyatt having passed the greatest litmus test known to humankind. Though I was grasping at straws, it meant everything to me that I believed.

Kevin looked off at the barn again, the centerpiece that apparently prevented him from berating me. Even with my one sided sexual undercurrent, I had sensed long ago that Kevin and I were never good for anything but friendship, and I appreciated the brother concept. When he spoke again, I had thought he was going to scold me further, but he'd returned to a point of reason, which for Kevin, involves a shade of intrigue.

"This sister," he mused, "would you be willing to meet with her?"

"Do you mean Wyatt's sister?"

"No, Maddie, the sister of the fucking governor of Kentucky. Who the hell do you think I was talking about?" He was back to reproach.

"Wyatt said her name's Kate, and that she lives in Susanville, or near Westwood. Maybe Miranda can help me find her."

"Would you take that chance, Maddie?" He finally smiled, and I started to feel better since revealing this profound, brief love affair, my errant pause on the road of life. "Damn, you took a chance with this man, a God damn leap. Now are you willing to take a chance talking to his sister?"

"I mean." I shrugged, "I guess it couldn't hurt."

"Think about it, a sister might speak more honestly about her brother, especially to another woman." He pointed his chin at me. "Like you did about Mallory being a nutcase, now that's what I call honesty."

"What should I say about you, Kev? You know. If a woman ever asks?"

Kevin snorted. "That'll be the day." He scrambled to his feet, and offered me a hand. "Let's go eat, and we'll do some sleuthing on the computer, my secret agent girl."

38

We returned to Astoria, and he took me out to a seafood restaurant near the Riverwalk, where we could watch boats cruise by on the Columbia, and joggers and dog walkers negotiating the edge of the land. Astoria owned certain shades of the Bay Area, except that the city rising on the river shore was far more picturesque. I understood Kevin's attraction to Astoria, and even felt a hint of that longing that must have been powerful enough to rip a man's roots out of California.

Back at the house, we sat side by side in front of his computer, while I pondered on what to enter. Kevin decided we should first find Wyatt in Washington State, before looking for his sister. I typed in "Wyatt McLain Tacoma," and was immediately redirected to "Wyatt Earp McLain," and a link to his web site.

The screen filled quite suddenly with images of fantastic metal sculptures, from delicately tiny birds, to a wolf eel, and a giant copper sea turtle. There were accolades from the City of Tacoma, a reprint of an arts feature from *The Seattle Times*, and a list of his upcoming gallery events, scheduled twelve months out.

In a photo, Wyatt stood shirtless beside a gorgeous cedar canoe with several other men equally in a state of undress, Wyatt the tallest by at least a head. The caption read, "Quinault Cedar Canoe Carvers, Taholah, June 2005," and was headed with a seal of the Quinault Indian Nation.

Kevin whistled, and prodded the image of a broad-chested Wyatt with a fingertip. "Wow, now I know why you sucked into it, Maddie. The dude's built."

"Yeah, he looks just like that."

"Still? This picture was taken six years ago."

"Maybe that was before the burglary, because he looks the same, except for the scars."

"What scars?"

I told him about the home invasion robbery, and how Wyatt was stabbed.

"He clubbed the man to stop him from using the knife, but the guy bled to death before the paramedics could get there."

"Your lover's a murderer?"

"Well…so is Mallory," I reasoned. I seemed to surround myself with people who'd done away with other people, though I knew there was a distinction between Mallory and Wyatt, and the engine that drove their ultimate acts.

"Which is why I wouldn't touch your sister with a ten-foot pole, no matter how fucking hot she is."

"But he didn't seem like a violent man."

Wyatt's use of the eagle talon in the midst of being stuck by a knife-wielding thief seemed more reflexive than retribution. I recalled the tenderness of his arms, and knew without any doubt that Wyatt wasn't a cold-hearted killer.

"Let's get this shit cooking," Kevin muttered, tapping away on the computer, searching through the pages of Wyatt's web site. The site was filled with photographs, mostly of sculptures, and a few that included Wyatt with local dignitaries, both in the Puget Sound area, and elders from the Quinault tribe.

"Look at this."

Kevin clicked on a photo of Wyatt standing with his arm around a tiny woman. Studying the photo, I could see that the two shared certain facial characteristics. The caption verified my suspicions, when it read, "Wyatt & Kate."

"I think that woman is his sister. Seeing this might make it easier to find her once I get to Susanville."

"So you're really going to go through with it, huh?"

"I'd really like to talk to this Kate."

Kevin did a new search using "Kate McLain Susanville California," and came up with links to both "Katherine McLain" and "Katherine Sumner."

"Either she's twins, or just a busy woman," he joked.

The site using the woman's maiden name referred to photos of oil and acrylic paintings, while the Sumner site depicted American Paint Horses. The horse site made mention of the Spotted Horse Ranch, but the address listed a P.O. Box in Susanville, instead of a physical address.

Kate's site hosted a photo of Kate and Wyatt, and people who had a Native look about them. I said as much, and Kevin scoffed at me.

"Hey, aren't you part-Indian Miss Hoity Toity?"

"I am, and I wasn't being a snob," I assured. "I was just making an observation."

Kevin rubbed his eyes. "I need a shower. What do you say we go find a place to eat, and get a drink? I'm still hungry from all that work."

I agreed. On separate floors of the Victorian, we took our showers to wash off drywall dust, and the sweat it clung to. With Rat safely stowed in the back yard, we were ready to hit the nightlife of Astoria.

Which amounted to a neighborhood bar & grill complete with country hits on a restored jukebox, and a pinball machine.

"This is a lively place," I told Kevin sarcastically.

We sat in the front window of the narrow rectangle known as Boo-Teak, which owned a nautical theme, from fishing tackle strung across the top of the bar, to the teak seating, adorned with striped chair pads. An old brass ship's lantern in the center of our table served as a candleholder.

While we shared a platter of fries and calamari, Kevin commented on the passing foot traffic. He hovered over a draft beer, but I stuck to coffee, too tired for alcohol, no matter how weak the content.

With all of my mental pauses about Wyatt, a point occurred to me.

"Who was it you hit the champagne bottle with?" I asked, which caused him to pause the giant glass mug raised halfway to his lips.

He carefully set down the mug. "What are you talking about?"

"Sex for champagne," I reminded. "When you finished your house, you said you did the christening thing. You told me that you're an Oregonian."

He spread his hands on the table, seemingly on the brink of tears.

That's when I remembered when Kevin lived in San José he'd had a roommate, Jeanine, a lawyer, who paid Kevin rent to offset the pricey home mortgage. Jeanine had worked in the District Attorney's office, and it was a standing joke between Kev and me that she paid him for his sexual talents. When she became engaged to another man, she stopped sleeping with Kevin. A few months later, she moved out, and then Kevin sold his San José home to relocate to Astoria permanently.

"Maddie, it's been just me," he said softly. "I didn't hit the champagne bottle with anyone."

"I'm so sorry, Kev. You haven't dated since you moved up here?"

"Not yet." He toyed with the mug. "Maybe I'm not ready."

"Is it because of Jeanine?"

He nodded.

"You were in love with her, weren't you?"

I had to ask. I felt bad for Kevin that the reason he chose to move to Astoria had less to do with an old Victorian house that needed his care than a choosy woman who wanted more out of life, and from her partner.

"I sure was. I loved her a lot."

"Who did she end up marrying?"

"Another lawyer in the DA's office." He smiled wanly. "She wanted a guy who worked with his brains, not his hands."

"And you fell in love with the house as consolation."

"No, I fell in love with the house because she needed me."

"How does a house tell you it needs you?"

"By looking like hell, Maddie, you know that. You should've seen her when we first met. She was so sad."

"I only saw the finished pictures, or the mostly finished ones. I never saw what it looked like when you found it."

He tossed back his beer, threw some bills on the table, and grabbed my hand.

"Come on. I'll show you."

We hiked up the few blocks to Franklin Avenue. After high school, Kevin attended USC on a football scholarship, but injured his left knee during freshman year, and had to leave school. The knee still bothered him, and gave him an awkward limp, though I had to really work to keep up as we climbed the grade.

Beneath the recessed lighting in the basement office, Kevin pulled out three photo albums that recorded the renovation from start to finish. Laying these out on the worktable, I saw the face of a house that hinted at a gracious past, but had been battered by the years. Painted gray, the floors tacked over with worn carpeting, stained wallpaper and institutional tile squares completed the grimace of a Victorian crying out for rescue.

Kevin bought it on the cheap, similar to my Santa Clara bungalow, a classic piece of garbage, until I ripped out the carpeting and stripped the floors. Room by room, Kevin revitalized the Astoria house, lightening the load of decades of abuse and shabby wear. He brought out the burning color of fir floors, and stripped paint off the pressed tin in the kitchen ceiling. The walnut planks that lay beneath sections of linoleum and plywood in the kitchen were refinished to the color of dark chocolate. The result stood over our heads, a house that reflected the pain of a man determined to make a new life from the dreck of a broken heart.

"It was ghastly," I commented. "You did something special with it."

"Yeah, well, she was hard work." He didn't bother to hide his utter passion for the house. "I'm too into her to sell her now."

"That's crap, Kevin. You could get a couple hundred grand more than what you bought it for."

"No, Maddie." His voice broke. "I mean that I'm too attached to her. I couldn't bear to sell her to some stranger. And you won't believe how many times I've been asked."

Later, we sat in the kitchen, and ate tacos Kevin made on the Wedgwood gas stove, the conclusion to a day of food, as though we were both determined to fill up our hungry spaces. There's a Wedgwood stove just Kevin's in my Santa Clara house, a vintage original, cleaned and restored. Standing next to his stove, I ran my hand along the curves in appreciation, and then thought about following Wyatt's scars with wondering fingertips.

Kevin noticed my gesture, and laughed crudely.

"You're just like me, Maddie, a hopeless fucking degenerate for old houses."

"You're such an asshole." I knew he wasn't. "Just for that comment, I'm going to drive down to Susanville tomorrow."

"Really?" He raised his brows. "You have the balls to see this thing through?"

"I don't know what you mean by seeing this thing through—"

"Because of your gigantic balls?" he cut in quickly.

"But I *am* going to talk to his sister."

"You gonna see Miranda while you're there?"

"She'd be pissed at me if I came to Susanville without at least trying."

"Yeah, I never told you this, but Miranda's pretty hot, too. Only, I'm scared of cops, so it'd never work."

"And never mind that she's already married. Do you think that might've been a deal-breaker once you got past her being in law enforcement?"

"Maybe. Or, maybe not."

The stars would have come out over the Columbia River if not for the fog gently creeping. At least there were plenty of lights from the Downtown Historic District, as we sat on the porch wrapped in our jackets. The glow of Astoria beckoned, but I knew it wasn't my town.

"Anyway, I do have to drive back home," I reminded, leaning against Kevin for warmth. The air was cold, and I could smell the ocean on the breeze.

"Don't be coy. You just don't want to help me mud all that drywall tomorrow." He stood. "Looks like I'll have to rent a sprayer and just lay it on."

"That's so much like a man, you're not happy unless you've got a big hose in your hand."

We retreated indoors, and played a few rounds of cards, while Rat stretched out beneath the table. Tired, we parted for the night, and that was the last I saw of Kevin until morning.

Chapter Five

I departed early, around seven a.m. I didn't want to let myself off the hook, as Susanville was a ten-hour drive across the mountains that separated the Oregon coast from eastern California's high desert plateau.

Kevin packed me food and drink in the small cooler. I started to object, but he pressed it on me.

"This way, you'll have to come back to Astoria."

Before I left town, I filled the Mercedes' tank with premium, or else the engine knocks. While I gassed up, I went through the car to rid myself of garbage, like gum wrappers, the sleeve to a fast-food hamburger, and a slightly crushed paper coffee cup.

I stared down at the cup, unable to toss it in the trash. The crushed paper cup had come from the coffee house in Tacoma, and the contents had kept me awake through the flat tire, and up to my sorry destination in Seattle. The café had been a place without a name, and I'd never even looked at the marquee. I was staring down at a cup that read quite plainly, "Road Apples," with a row of red and green apples to either side of the logo.

Road Apples was an amusing name for a coffee house, and often used as slang for horse manure. I shrugged, and tried to loosen my hold on the cup, but for some reason I couldn't let it go. The cup was days old, and whatever liquid remaining had dried completely. The plastic cap fell to the ground, and that went straight into the trash, but I had developed a sentimental attachment to the cup. I folded it in half lengthwise, and tucked it into the glove box with the registration and a weathered map of California my grandfather had used in an era before smart phones and GPS.

Rat was a good companion on these long drives. He never felt carsick, took great interest in the scenery and scents that came through the opened windows, and always let me know in advance when he needed me to pull over. The day and the miles carried us from the lush

45

coastal hills, through pine-covered mountains, and out to high desert, where sage hills rolled toward the distant horizon. I thought of Kate's painting in Wyatt's loft, and smiled at the intimate memories invoked.

Once I reached Klamath Falls, and cut across to Lakeview, Oregon, I knew I was getting close. I threaded through Modoc County, and crossed the Madeline Plains into Lassen County, a region that seemed to be holding its breath in anticipation. I recall the distances grown over with mule's ear, a wild *asteraceae*, splashing the flats and bulges of land with bright yellow, and filling the wind with a spicy odor.

When I reached Susanville, I was ready to find a motel, and hit the pillow. But I had to at least try to reach out to my sister, Miranda. Visiting another gas station on Main Street, I topped off a tank I'd already filled in Alturas, and then drove up the hill to my sister's house, a Craftsman on North Gay Street.

The time was almost five-thirty, and Miranda wasn't home, gone to swing shift and a beat of the Interstate, but her husband, Gilbert Snead, was there. Finished with his day's work as a deputy with the Lassen County Sheriff's department, he was sitting on the front porch in civvies and drinking a beer when I pulled up.

At first, he didn't recognize me, with the dog and strange car, but once he figured out who I was, he jumped to his feet. For some reason, he was calling back over his shoulder, and then another man came out of the house to join Gilbert on the porch—Gilbert's younger brother, Duke.

Gilbert is a man's man, a regular guy, and when I'm not stuck in my cynical groove, I find many qualities to admire in my elder sister's husband. Miranda is happy, and that speaks volumes about Gilbert.

Duke is Gilbert's polar opposite in all matters, including apparel. In the heat of early summer, Duke was dressed in khaki shorts, a wife beater, and a denim vest with a large Confederate flag patch sewn onto a front pocket. I was appalled at the redneck motif, which reflected a serious lack of sensitivity for both the members of the local Indian Confederation, and Duke's US citizenship. I imagined Duke wearing this outfit, and driving around Susanville in his rusted Ford truck, complete with "Hannity Up!" scrawled across the tailgate.

During my last interaction with Duke, he'd offered me a particularly unpleasant marriage proposal. His overplayed rural attitude, coupled with a habit of dressing like a media caricature of a poor uneducated white man had the effect of a bucket of ice water. But—he is Miranda's brother-in-law, so I'd used diplomacy in turning him down, and promptly fled town. That occurred months ago. I hadn't been to Susanville since, and wouldn't have come today, except for the strange urge to find Wyatt's sister, Kate.

Both men were ignorant of my silent criticism, and waved to me as I approached.

"Well, looky who's here," Duke spoke first, in the worst of white trash drawl. I'd determined long ago his accent was acquired, an integral part of Duke's wacky backwoods ensemble.

"Boy howdy," I returned without cracking a smile. "How's it goin', fellas?"

I shook hands, and introduced Rat, while enduring the expected laughter at Rat's general ugliness. There should be a warning in the literature about breeding a Chinese Crested with a Shar-Pei, though in the case of Rat's conception, owner incompetence was to blame.

"No one would make a dog like this on purpose," went my standard excuse for Rat's appearance.

Gilbert invited me in for a soda, and once at the table, I related the story of being nearly car-jacked in Tacoma. I didn't include why I was coming from Seattle, or my unbelievable tryst with Wyatt, but I did reinforce Rat's bravery.

"That's some great shit!" Duke declared. In spite of one-track admiration for his own dog, Rascal, Duke seemed genuinely impressed with Rat's aggression in saving my weak female ass. Smooth sailing, until Gilbert asked me how I obtained possession of the dog in the first place.

"He belongs to an ex," I said, with a tone and facial expression that guaranteed I wasn't going to elaborate, so the matter was wisely dropped.

"What brings you to Susanville?" Gilbert asked.

"Yeah, besides that righteous car," Duke added. Apparently he'd seen the car from the kitchen window, before called out to the porch by his brother.

"I'm looking for somebody." I patted Rat's head to bolster my courage. "I'm trying to find a Kate McLain, or Kate Sumner."

Gilbert laughed. "That's easy. I thought you were going to give me a name I couldn't help you with."

"Do you know her?"

"Well, not exactly. We don't socialize, if that's what you're asking, but I know *of* her."

He proceeded to tell me about how, over twenty years ago, Wyatt's sister killed a man in self-defense. The man had broken into Kate's house, and threatened the life of her then toddler daughter, Sara White Owl.

"Around here, law enforcement goes by the rule, 'Never monkey around with Kate McLain.' It's become a universal cliché."

I was rendered speechless, and believe me, I'm outspoken, so it requires a hell of a force to shut me up.

"Don't forget to tell Maddie that Mrs. Sumner also shot what's his name, Robert Simms, about three years ago," Duke reminded his brother. "Man, what a hell of a way to go, popped in the head with a forty-four Mag. Whoo-hoo, what a mess."

"Duke," Gilbert warned his brother, when he noted my slack jaw and glazing eyes.

But Duke was on a roll.

"And that was only a year after her daughter Kristina smashed that dude's head in, remember? The kid who was gonna shoot it up at Susanville High? Shit, I never knew you could kick a guy to death. I'm gonna get *me* some steel-toed boots."

I recall thinking, *Lord; this compulsion runs in the family?*

"Wait, *wait!*" I waved my hands to hush them up. "Kate Sumner killed *two* people?" I wanted to at least keep the subject matter on Wyatt's sister.

"That's right." Gilbert nodded, unemotional in the wake of Duke's jumbled outburst. "She was exonerated both times. They were determined to be acts of self-defense." He eyed me curiously. "Why are you looking for Kate Sumner?"

I had to think of a lie, and fast. "I like…horses." I'm not very good at lying. And then I rubbed my nose, the sure sign of a falsehood.

"Well, they've got plenty of those," Duke said, not intuit like his brother Gilbert. But I guess being in tune as a law enforcement officer lets one see much more than a simpleton such as Duke.

Gilbert gave me a look that said, *I won't ask, but I know you're up to something.* Then he let it go, with a steady gaze that passed between us without ever hitting Duke's conscious radar.

"Where do you think I can find her?" I asked Gilbert bluntly.

He pointed to the telephone, sitting on top of the local directory. "The phone book," he advised.

Trying to hide my eagerness, I pulled the book out carefully, and flipped through the pages to find "Sumner." I almost laughed at the simplicity, until I realized there was no address.

"There's no address!"

"Of course there's no address," Gilbert said smugly. "It's a ranch, it's off the highway, and they probably don't even get mail delivery."

"You ever been out that way, Gil?" Duke asked his brother.

"Once or twice. My beat's normally south County. I'll tell you what, Maddie, you could go to Parker Gallery, and ask Gladiola."

"Where's Parker Gallery?"

"South side of Main, between Gay and Greeno."

"That's where I'm going."

I put the phone book away, and, clucking my tongue for Rat, said goodbye.

"What do you want me to tell Miranda?" Gilbert asked, at the door. "In case she wants to see you."

"Tell her to call my cell. I might be in town for a day or two."

I returned to the car with the feeling that two pairs of eyes were boring into the back of my head. In loaded Rat, and we were off to Parker Gallery.

❖ ❖ ❖ ❖

Parker Gallery is inside of one of those old false-front buildings on the south side of Main. I easily found a parking spot in the street shaded by the block, and left Rat locked inside the car with the windows cracked. That way he would have no problem keeping track of me.

All around Susanville, local artists have painted murals depicting historical events, or important people such as the settler, Isaac Roop, and his daughter, Susan, after whom the town was named.

On Parker Gallery's uphill wall was a mural entitled, "Lassen County Competition," with delicately painted footnotes suggesting that one of Lassen County's founders, Anton Parker, was a lecherous womanizer, mimicking the excessive plural hoarding of the Fundamentalist Latter Day Saints in the sheer numbers of female partners, many of whom were Native American. In the corner of the mural was the inscription, "Kate McLain–1989," so I knew who'd created the mural. Seeing Kate's name only deepened the urgency to locate her.

Inside the Gallery, the walls and shelves were crowded with paintings of varying styles and medium, great clunky ceramics created

49

without the benefit of a potter's wheel, and handmade jewelry. There was even a hulking metal sculpture of a giant lizard standing in the corner, and my heart leapt, until I realized the style wasn't even remotely Wyatt's.

A heavyset woman stood behind a long glass counter, having a conversation with another woman, whose back faced me. The second woman was petite, shoulders and back covered by a long fall of incredible dark brown hair that shimmered with a natural red tint in the light through the plate glass windows.

They both turned their attention toward me when I entered. My first thought was to apologize for the interruption, and then to inquire about where I might be able to find Wyatt McLain's, sister, Kate Sumner.

But I realized that Wyatt's sister was the woman with the unbelievable hair. And I heard Wyatt's voice speak in my head, in that awestruck tone.

Yes, undoubtedly, what are the odds?

"Kate!" I said loudly, with a nervous quiver in my voice. "Kate," I repeated, like a stuck needle of that old phonograph my Grandpa Feliz had gifted me when he realized how much I appreciated antiques. My nervousness was amplified, how I imagined I'd behave in the presence of, say, a rock star, or someone famously affiliated.

"Do I know you?" she asked, immediately on the offensive.

"No, we've never met, that is, your brother told me your name, but he said you didn't like being called 'Katie,' and I came here to find you. That's my car outside," and I motioned with a thumb to the Mercedes, and Rat lolling his snout out the window crack. "Because, you see, it's like this." I held out my hands as though for mercy. "I really need to talk to you."

Both women gave me their version of the skeptical glare. All I could do was shake my head helplessly.

"I don't know about this one, Kate, she might be a spy," said the woman behind the counter, who I learned was Gladiola Parker, the gallery owner, and a long-winded descendant of the lascivious Anton Parker. She seemed to enjoy being upfront about her ancestor's lechery, if only for the shock factor she could gain from the reaction of strangers.

Fortunately, Kate wasn't in the mood to play mind games. She approached me and grasped both of my hands, and to my thrill, she spoke her brother's name.

"What about Wyatt? Is he all right?"

"Oh, he's fine, just fine," I assured. "He's just…listen, could we…I guess, have a talk? Coffee maybe? I'll buy you a coffee."

Kate studied my eyes for a moment. I'm sure she was wondering, here's this stammering stranger, claiming to know Wyatt, and apparently having come quite a distance in a dusty, bug spattered car, complete with an ugly dog, and requesting an unscheduled conversation.

"I'd be happy to talk with you," she accepted, which amazed me. I certainly wouldn't talk with me, in the state I was in, and with the approach I'd made.

"Are you insane?" Gladiola asked frankly.

"Of course I'm not insane," I replied.

"I wasn't talking to you, Missy," Gladiola bristled.

"It's okay," Kate reassured her concerned friend. She pointed out the window at Rat. "Is that your dog?"

"Yes. Well, not exactly. The dog's a friend of mine." I shook my head. "It's a long story."

"I have plenty of time for a long story," Kate told me, without even looking at her watch.

Gladiola came around the counter, and after brusquely introducing herself, she sat us down at an oak bar table by the window, and then went into the back to make a pot of coffee.

"No way I'm going to miss this," she announced.

While we waited for the coffee, I told Kate about my ordeal from the beginning, when I left the Bay Area, shortly after Grandmother Beth was hospitalized for a heart attack. I mentioned that my sister had killed a man, though she hadn't been prosecuted. I spoke about Mallory, not to make some sort of connection with Kate for what she'd done twice under duress, but because Mallory's experience factored into me leaving town.

Gladiola, having served out the coffee, snorted derisively.

"Go on, don't mind her," Kate urged.

I picked it up in Astoria, working with Kevin hanging drywall at Kathy's farmhouse, and the bright idea to visit my secret boyfriend in Seattle.

"I wanted to surprise him," I explained, in defense of finding him locking lips with that attractive woman in the lobby of The Edgewater.

"*I'll* say," grunted Gladiola, who never once hesitated to add her commentary to my story. "I'm betting he was plenty surprised. Young

51

lady, you should never sneak up on a man. You know you're going to catch them all cheating eventually."

"Gladiola," Kate cut in, giving me space to continue.

"I was upset, so I left pretty fast, and it was raining buckets coming down from Seattle. I was tired, and decided I'd find a motel, and then I ended up back in Tacoma." The terror of being surprised by the two thugs in the parking lot of the coffee house was accentuated by the complete transformation in Rat.

Gladiola thoughtfully studied the dog through the window. "He weighs, what, forty pounds maybe?"

"Thereabout," I confirmed. "And then, Wyatt came outside to help me."

Here, I stopped. I couldn't continue with my story, as though the words were plugged up in my throat. To think *Wyatt,* or to hear Kate say his name didn't affect my equilibrium, but to speak his name choked me with emotion.

Kate grasped my hand. I'm not a touchy-feely person, though I didn't at all mind Kate's method of connecting in a conversation.

"You care very much for my brother, don't you?" Her voice was kind and gentle, much like Wyatt's, and I could only nod, while tears welled in my eyes.

I wiped them away impatiently. "I do. I *really* do."

"What happened next?" Gladiola prompted, but Kate cut in.

"I *know* what happened next."

"What? *What* happened?" Gladiola was either completely clueless, or trying to string me along to get all the prime dirt.

Kate stood, and picked up her purse. "Come on, Maddie, did you say?"

"Yes." I'd told Kate my name was "Maddie," because I felt that "Madeline" belonged on Wyatt's lips alone.

"I think your friend, the dog, could use a walk. We could take him to the park. There's one not too far from here, and then we can talk some more."

We left Gladiola behind. According to the placard in the window, she had obligated herself to keep her gallery open for business one more hour. I also doubted that Kate would have allowed Gladiola to tag along now that my tears indicated a momentous declaration in the offing. When we walked away with Rat, Gladiola was standing in the window, face pressed against the glass, like a child staring longingly at a retreating ice cream truck.

Meanwhile, Kate and I headed toward Uptown with Rat, north of Main, to Memorial Park, where we sat in the bleachers, and let Rat run up and down the wooden steps like a jock in training. I brought along a bag of grapes from Kevin's cooler, and we shared these while we talked.

Kate went right to the point, without wasting time on trivialities.

"How old are you, Maddie?"

"Twenty-five." I felt miserably young, and somehow undeserving of how I felt about Wyatt. He was older and sophisticated, and had lived an entire lifetime before I'd even been born.

"Twenty-five," she mused. "I remember being twenty-five. It doesn't seem all that long ago." Her statement undermined my insecurity in the age difference, and I was grateful for her wisdom.

"What were you like at twenty-five?" I imagined her very much as she was right then.

"Oh, I was passionate, just like you." Though she didn't frame the focus of her passion, it didn't matter, because she'd acknowledged a characteristic we both shared.

My time with Wyatt could have been a dream, and I said as much.

"I know I should leave it as it is. It was…beautiful, indescribable, and a great memory. I don't know if I can ever go back."

"My brother has this way about him, a magic," she agreed. "He has a quality that's infectious."

"He's not…Wyatt's not married, is he?"

I couldn't imagine an attractive and vital man like Wyatt McLain out in the cold with no love to keep the home fires warm. Though I hadn't seen any indication that a woman shared his loft residence, the thought of myself as a possible instrument of adultery, however blameless—or blameworthy I'd be—made me cringe.

But Kate settled that issue quickly.

"No, he's never been married. He has no children, and I'm positive he doesn't have a regular girlfriend, or else he wouldn't have slept with you."

"I didn't say anything about sleeping with Wyatt. How did you know that he slept with me?"

She smiled that same sweet smile that I'd seen on Wyatt's face.

"When you said his name, and then all the tears, I knew, Maddie, plus your sentiments about that night. You're utterly transparent about

53

your feelings for my brother. And no woman could be so deeply affected without some physical connection to a man." She flicked a grape stem across the bleacher seats. "Did Wyatt tell you that he's almost fifty-three?"

"Yes, he was completely honest about his age when I asked him."

"And his age didn't scare you off?"

"Wyatt's age really didn't seem relevant to who he is or how I felt about him. I had wondered, but at the time, I thought he was maybe thirty or forty, not fifty-two." I took a deep breath. "I know I'm only twenty-five, but I run my own business, I'm level-headed...well, for the most part, except for that stupid choice of mine to go surprise a man in Seattle. Though I'm really glad that I did."

"I'm not at all worried about your chronological age. In this life, it doesn't mean a whole lot in real love, except for that lawful difference between right and wrong."

She gazed down at the shadows the trees cast on the ball field, considering. And then she told me about how one of her own daughters had fallen in love with a thirty-one-year-old man at the age of sixteen.

"It was real love," she nodded. "You know it when you see it." She studied my face for a moment. "I believe I see some of that same quality in you, Maddie."

"I'm not looking to fall in love. I don't need the trouble. I have enough issues."

I realized it was already too late, that Wyatt had me absolutely, though even on the bleachers talking with Kate, I was silently pouring on denial in a fruitless attempt to protect my heart.

"Whether you want it or not, sometimes love catches you when you least expect it. You can't control the cards forever."

"I had no intention of going home with Wyatt, or even spending the night with him. And I never would have stopped in Tacoma a second time, if it wasn't for the eagle."

"What eagle?"

"Wyatt lent a sculpture to the coffee house, a place called Road Apples, and they'd hung it from the ceiling. I asked an employee who crafted it, and she mentioned Wyatt's name."

"And that's why you went back?"

"Yes and no. I can't explain the draw in a way that makes rational sense, so I won't even try. I just needed to go there. But there's more." I told her about my sister, Miranda, who lives in Susanville, about Wyatt playing "Pearly Shells" on his ukulele, and that bottle of Clay Creek wine.

"My husband, Paul, he grew up at Clay Creek," she revealed.

"I know, Wyatt said he'd been a vintner."

Rat, done with his endless up and down exercise, sat beside me, and rested his head on my thigh. I stroked him gently, and affectionately murmured his name.

"Rat likes my brother, too," Kate observed, before I could mention the fact.

"Yes, he does."

"I'm sure that means everything to you. It's a special gift when an animal likes a person, it implies a trust."

"And that's why I trusted Wyatt right away. Rat has good intuition about people."

"Wyatt has no reason to deceive you," she agreed. "That isn't part of my brother's character." She paused a moment, as though considering. "May I ask you a personal question?"

"I don't mind at all. This is already a personal conversation."

"Did you see the scars?"

Kate seemed concerned about asking the question, but I was relieved the subject had been touched on.

"I did. Wyatt wasn't shy about showing them to me."

"Then I'll conclude that you weren't frightened away."

"I was honored that he'd trust me enough to reveal them to me. I thought they were..." I tried to recall the moment Wyatt removed his shirt. "To me, Wyatt's scars were the consequence of taking life with deep regret. As though he'll always remember the other's life with respect."

"That's true."

I frowned. "You've been more than generous, Kate, giving me your time, and hearing me out. I know I should have just kept driving, and yet here I am. I never would have come to talk with you, if it weren't for that one night."

"What about that night, Maddie?"

"I'm stuck on that night. Wyatt reminds me of the sea, the way it was when I drove out to the coast on my way to Astoria."

"What was that like?"

"The sun was coming up over the land, and the breakers were pink. I felt like I could dive right in, and nothing bad would happen to me."

"Wyatt's like that, I suppose. You probably don't know this, but we never even met until I'd already grown up."

"I didn't know."

"But when we finally did meet, I felt as though I'd known him forever."

"That's right, that's how I felt too. There's something very familiar and inviting about Wyatt."

"Wyatt's a dynamic man, I'm sure he makes a lot of people feel that way, like they've known him forever."

I tried to comprehend what she was getting at, that her brother, though an honest man, loved the world and the women around him.

But her next words disputed any worry I might have had about being just another woman in a chain of sexual liaisons for Wyatt.

"Don't get me wrong, Maddie, Wyatt's not a womanizer. I don't believe for a moment that he duped you into a one-night stand, or that he deliberately falsified his intentions just to get you into bed. No matter what he's been through, he's an idealist, and you were probably as real to my brother as he was to you. I sense something very genuine about you, Maddie, and I would even bet that he's stuck on that night, just like you are."

"He said to me, 'What are the odds?' He even used the word 'kismet,' and I laughed. Not at the idea, but because it was such an old-fashioned word. I've never heard anyone use kismet in a conversation. With Wyatt, it seemed to fit."

"He gave it up to fate?"

"Yes, he said that. He described it as fate. And it all seemed so very real to me, Kate."

"It *was* real, Maddie. You know, because otherwise, you and I would not be sitting here, talking. But I have my doubts."

"About me?"

"No, my dear, about my brother. And not because he's in any way insincere, but because he's the kind of man who knows what he wants, and when he makes up his mind, that's pretty much it."

"Why does that make you doubt Wyatt?"

"Let's just say that sometimes Wyatt is a force to be reckoned with."

We talked for a few minutes more, and then she walked me back to my car, the art gallery now closed, and no Gladiola to press for the gory details of our conversation. I felt that as soon as Rat and I got inside the

56

car and headed down the hill, that would be the end of it, and I would never come back to Susanville, not even for Miranda. When I hugged Kate goodbye, I almost started to cry. I liked her so very much, not only because she reminded me of Wyatt in face and mannerism, but in her compassion. A person with the ability to form objective thought and see both sides is a rarity.

I watched fade Kate in the rear-view mirror, in the way that I'd watched Wyatt. Her arms were wrapped around her shoulders, as though she were cold in the high desert heat, while her long hair waved out behind her like a banner.

Chapter Six

I drove as far as Reno, where I paid for a room at a cheap motel that was pet friendly, though they charged me a fee to keep Rat in for the night. I lay on the bed with the curtains closed, listening to the beeps of my cell phone announcing that Jake Keene was still trying to contact me. I hadn't yet answered, nor listened to any of his voice mails. I really appreciate a cell phone that allows you to tailor a ringtone to the incoming caller.

But I made a point to answer the phone when Miranda called close to two a.m.

"Maddie, are you okay?" she asked, first thing.

I looked at the time on the illuminated face of my watch.

"Yeah," I breathed. I could hear Rat's tail whacking the floor at the sound of my voice, and I trailed my hand down to pat him.

"Gilbert said you might be staying in town. Are you still in Susanville?"

"No, I'm in Reno."

"Listen, Maddie, if something's wrong, maybe I can help you. Are you in trouble?"

"What makes you think I'm in trouble?"

"You were looking for Kate Sumner." As though by association, I was now a first-class murderess.

"Miranda, it's not what you think. Here's why I was looking for Kate." I told her everything. Honesty was easy, really, and though our sisterhood does not always gear smoothly, we do love each other unconditionally. I knew that while she probably couldn't offer up much in the way of actual assistance, I would at least find comfort in conversation.

"You've had quite a week," she observed.

"Yeah, well, it's not over yet, I still have to drive home tomorrow." I considered the time. "Today. I have to drive home today."

58

"Then you haven't heard yet, have you?"

"No-o-o-o," I said warily.

"Grandma was just diagnosed with colon cancer."

Dummy me, I heard "Grandma," and instantly thought about Mom's mother, as Grandmother Beth had a heart attack before I left for Astoria.

"No, it was a heart attack." I was trying to correct what I assumed was her gross misinformation.

"Maddie, I'm not talking about Grandmother Beth, I'm talking about Dad's mother, Grandma Enida."

A moment of silence, while, staring up at the ceiling, I tried to grasp the concept of colon cancer. Fortunately, Reno is never completely dark, so I could see the smudge of shadows, and cavities of texture.

"What does it mean?" I asked her softly. "What happens now?"

"Dad said the doctor will do the surgery in a few days, when Grandma's digestive system is cleared out."

"How did they find the cancer?"

"Grandma passed out in the house."

She proceeded to explain that when Grandpa Feliz called for the ambulance, and they brought Grandma to the hospital, they took her blood count, and diagnosed her with severe anemia. Grandma had apparently been bleeding for months during bowel movements, and never told anyone.

The blame lay, not in my grandmother's inherent stubbornness, but in stoicism that many of the Filipino elders embrace, a by-product of World War II, and the global Depression. There's a common belief among the elders that you take what God gives, remain silently appreciative for the good, and openly grateful for the bad, just to avoid tempting providence.

After we ended our conversation, some time was required to go back to sleep. Rat took advantage of my racing mind, and asked to be taken out for a pee. I walked him along a strip of ragged grass, while he sniffed and peed, and then sniffed and peed some more. One of the motel's male inmates seemed to be having a slightly raucous party, complete with a hooker, who joined the man in front of their room, where they smoked post-coital cigarettes and watched me tend to Rat. I was wary about their interest, but Rat never even blinked.

❖ ❖ ❖ ❖

In the morning, I checked out, and drove back to the Bay Area, returning to the real world. Being home felt good, embraced by a house reflecting my deep appreciation for antiques that flourish when they're treated with love. The house smelled of staleness, so the first thing I did was open up all the windows, and let the breeze blow through.

The second thing I did was place the clay proof of the halibut Wyatt had given me in a place of honor—the fireplace mantel in my bedroom. The fish lay sideways, watching me with bulging eyes, propped against the wall between a pickling jar filled with hawk feathers, and a tiny American flag on a wooden stand.

The next task involved clearing out the numerous messages Jake Keene had deposited on my cell phone voice mail. Just to be cautious, I erased them without even bothering to listen. I suppose had I come home without the revelation of my night with Wyatt McLain, I would have suffered Jake's long-winded monologues, but in my present state of mind, I found life simpler in deleting them.

I spent a half-hour reading through countless e-mails that had backed up during my absence. Some were worth reading, and others meant only to discard, such as the junk messages that told me I could "grow a long and hard one," or if I purchased their herbal remedy, I'd "become a love hurricanes center." I had never given Jake my e-mail address, so there weren't any wordy letters to trash.

There was plenty of snail mail stacked up in the huge plastic bucket that stood beneath the mail slot in my garage: nothing too difficult, no hoops to jump through, nor great hurdles to overcome. As Wyatt had claimed when I mentioned obstacles, he was more focused on the world as it was meant to be, in mystical alignment.

I dumped the bucket of mail upside down on the worktable in the smaller of the house's two bedrooms, which I used as a home office. Just like Kevin's basement cubby, my office was a practical space with no nonsense arrangement, and without frills. Besides the birch table, I had an uncluttered desk, a combination printer/scanner/copier, and a desktop computer. The laptop in its case was seldom used except when I needed it on a job.

I let Rat have the run of the back yard, and was just starting to make a dent in the pile of mail, when Rat galloped around to the gate, and started barking forcefully. I jumped up, remembering he'd done this once before, the time Jake's mother, Charlotte Burgess, climbed down from her high-horse at the Tanner Valley Vineyards, and tried to work her manipulative charm on me.

The doorbell ringing soon followed rat's ferocious barking. Annoyed at being interrupted in the midst of sorting through the mail, I was completely prepared to eject Charlotte from my front porch. When I opened the door, there stood Jake Keene, suitcase by his side, and his blue Mitsubishi Eclipse parked at the curb.

I know he probably expected me to scream and shout, and make a terrible scene, but all I did was open the door a little bit wider, and beckon to him with a inward gesture of my hand. I headed toward the kitchen, noting he'd left the suitcase behind, perhaps contingent upon my reaction. If he wanted to follow, that choice was his, but I was positive I wouldn't allow that suitcase past the threshold. I also knew I wanted no part of Jake. Before, as Jake's lover, the concept of Sophie had been nothing more substantial than a rumor. To actually see Jake in the process of swapping spit with another woman disgusted me. I could forgive, but I'd be damned if I'd ever forget.

I could hear his footsteps following behind me, which meant he was playing the odds. I concluded he gambled fairly often, though only on relationships.

"Maddie." He spoke my name, while I pulled out a chair for him at the table, and proceeded to make a pot of coffee.

Wisely, he sat down in the proffered chair, and kept his mouth shut, while I found a package of lemon sugar cookies, and slid them onto a platter. The coffee was soon done, though the waiting, at least for him, was awkward. I spent the hang time slowly rinsing dishes that had collected dust after spending a week on the dish drain rack. When the coffee maker finished its task, I deliberately served Jake's brew into a cup depicting a raging dragon wrapped around the mug like a snake.

"Maddie," he repeated.

I finally glanced at him sharply, surprised that he looked like hell. I had expected, if not a well-rested man, then at least one generally relaxed from constant sex in a luxury accommodation, and with a smile of debauchery on the corners of his mouth. Now that I could study him closely, he seemed ill, or possibly troubled.

"How was Seattle?" I asked, taking a cookie, and casually nipping off an edge with a canine. "Did you have a good time?"

"You know how Seattle was." He hung his head, a dramatic gesture for a man who seldom worried about how others might judge his thoughtless behavior. "I saw you in the hotel."

"Really? Why, that's absolutely incredible. You won't believe this, but, hey, I saw you, too. Isn't that an amazing coincidence?"

"Come on, Maddie. She didn't mean anything to me."

I blinked at him, incredulous. I suppose that many men use this line, in the hopes that the woman they've just been caught with by their wife, girlfriend or significant other, has the self-respect of a rock. Conversely, the wife, girlfriend or significant other must also have an intelligence rating very similar to the aforementioned rock to believe this spiel. These men very seldom understand that it's far worse if the focus of the affair they've just been caught committing means nothing. They're suggesting the other woman may just as well have been the palm of his hand, and in the end, would have served as the smarter choice.

"That's laughable." I shook my head. "She was a beautiful woman, Jake, well-dressed, and well put together. Are you telling me that you could have been tonguing a banana slug for all it mattered to you?"

"You know that's not what I meant."

"No, really, what did you mean, Jake?"

"I mean—I don't have any feelings for her."

"Jake." I hushed him with one hand held up in front of me. Mine wasn't a *talk to the hand* gesture, but a way to get him to shut up, because he was digging a fairly large hole with that mouth of his.

"Look," I continued, "I know our relationship has its limits. I know you didn't dump Sophie to be with me, and marriage isn't your deal, as long as you're still out there on the prowl with a dick in your pants. I'm betting you meet a lot of babes at those book signings, and I can accept that, Jake. That's the kind of person I am. I can take honesty. I can take the truth. What I can't take is this load of bullshit you're trying to shovel. That just proves you don't know me, that you never knew me."

I'd made a brave speech, though admittedly beneath all the lavishness of my words, I was angry. I reflected it was a good angry, though I wondered if I'd be so well adjusted had I not that secret inside of me, the memory of the glorious night spent with Wyatt.

I knew I didn't want anything from Jake that involved getting naked or professing our love. I was relieved I'd busted him in Seattle, because witnessing him joining tongues with his anonymous lover was an impetus for me stopping in Tacoma, and meeting Wyatt.

"Maddie, I just came to say I'm sorry," he told me, once he figured out that I was finished with my strangely calm tirade.

"You're forgiven," I said quickly. *That* was easy!

"And to pick up Rat."

I froze. He could mumble heart rending apologies until Hell froze over, and I'd accept each and every one, if only to get this business over with. But to take Rat?

"You're going to take Rat?"

"Yeah, Maddie. Sophie's moved out, so I don't have to worry about anything happening to him."

"Well," I stalled, foolishly thinking a miracle would occur, and Rat would magically get to stay with me. I knew the dog belonged with his legal owner. I sighed painfully, and rose to my feet. "I'll go get him."

All I had to do was open the back door, and Rat darted in through the laundry room. He'd already caught scent of Jake, and practically jumped all over his pet man, thrilled to see the master once again. I felt guilty for even wishing Rat's change of heart, and just handed the leash to Jake.

He stood up, and snapped the leash on Rat's collar, regarding me thoughtfully. Noting that my teeth weren't bared and my claws were sheathed, he approached me, and hugged me, kissing me briefly on the cheek. In the end, he must have known me pretty well, as any normal woman would have decked him for his infidelity. Which made me wonder what kind of legal maneuvering Sophie might have up her sleeve for this rotten tomato of man who couldn't manage to keep his penis exclusive of other women.

"Thank you, Maddie. You don't know how much this means to me."

She didn't mean anything to me.

His hollow rhetoric echoed in my head. I wondered how often he'd spoken these same words to Sophie in reference to me.

I stared at the wall, listening to the clicks of Rat's nails along the wood floor, as he walked with Jake to the front door. Jake opened the door to a rush of air, and they were gone. When that door closed, the ending felt like forever. I could accept never seeing Jake again, but I hated parting with Rat. I thought about how the dog stood by me in the pouring rain, fighting for the same cause. We had shared an experience that included Wyatt, and knowing Rat was gone didn't seem fair.

I sat alone in my living room for a long time, hearing the noises around me—airplanes from San José Airport, a rumbling freight train on the Agnew line, and cars passing along Bassett Street. I felt very much alone without Rat, but I also knew that I'd kept my dignity, which seemed vastly more important than contesting who had more right to Rat's favor.

Eventually, I returned to the pile of mail in the office. Somewhere near the bottom—which was once the top, probably the last mail delivered on this day, right before I returned from Reno—I found the letter.

It was mailed in a sky-blue envelope, with the logo on the return address, "W.E.M. Corp., LLC." I thought, *what the hell?*

And then, when I realized it hailed from a P.O. Box in Tacoma, Washington, it hit me like a ray of sunshine; this was a letter from Wyatt. I couldn't rip it open fast enough, my fingers clumsy in their haste to yank out the contents.

Dear Madeline,

I know I'm being forward in sending you this letter, but I have every intention of being forward. It seems to me we got our foot-shuffling out of the way. All that awkwardness of the first date will never be our problem again. Lying naked with you was a revelation. I'm no registered genius, but I could swear we have a physical compatibility. I already know we have no impediments to great conversation.

I'll admit, it was difficult watching you drive away. In the event that you think of me as a dirty old man, or a hopeless pervert, let's just get right down to the facts. I concede—I am dirty and hopeless, an old man, and a pervert.

You're probably asking yourself, how did I find you? I have access to this tool, called the Web, and you wouldn't believe how easy it is to find someone you want to find, whether or not they actually want you to find them. Sounds complicated, doesn't it? But it's not complicated. You were right there in the telephone listing, address and all, though I decided a letter was less threatening than an actual telephone call.

Alas, this is my first and last letter to you, Madeline. I heavily stepped over the line last night, and I'm doing it now, stalker-style. But I promise I won't write you ever again, if you don't respond to this letter. You can choose to say yes or no. It's up to you, my friend.

I'm still thinking of you,

Wyatt

With the letter in hand, I went to my bedroom, lay down on the bed, and gazed at the halibut on the fireplace mantel. What an incredible turn of luck, receiving a handwritten letter from Wyatt. I could only wonder whether Kate telephoned him after our meeting in Susanville, though by the postmark and the date on his letterhead, he'd written and mailed the letter the very day I left Tacoma. For it to arrive here in Santa Clara exactly three days after meant that he must have run straightaway to a post office to get the letter to the counter before noon.

Knowing there was no time like the present, I hurried to my desk, sat down with pen in hand, and wrote Wyatt a letter. My attempt was passé, and I could easily have found the e-mail link on his web site, or even picked up a telephone. But he'd taken the time to write on paper with a pen, transcribing his emotions, laying bare the essence that could tip the scale of success or disaster, and I felt I owed him. Actually, this gesture was more than gratitude. I was excited to hold a piece of evidence that revealed he'd taken such care to reach out to me.

Dear Wyatt,

Thank you for being forward, and taking a chance by writing to me. Just before I found your letter, I was feeling blue, because Rat had to leave. As for us—I haven't been able to stop thinking about you. It's uplifting to know you've been thinking about me, too.

After I left Tacoma, I went back to Astoria to say goodbye to my friend, Kevin. I then drove to Susanville to find Kate. Your sister is your best representative. I like her a lot, because she reminds me of you.

I never would have slept with you, Wyatt, if I didn't believe. I can't explain my feelings, or the sense of having already known you somewhere in the distant past. I don't want to call what happened to us fate, because I subscribe to free will. But I do know that something momentous happened to me in being with you. I'm trying to find the answer. Kate asked me, too. I told her that when I was driving to the Oregon coast, and saw the ocean in the sunrise, I connected you to that moment. There is the sea, and the tide, and I hit the perfect wave.

Please keep in touch, Wyatt. It feels right to hear from you.
Thinking of you too,
Madeline

I folded the letter, slid the paper into an envelope with his name and address, and made sure the stamp was secure. I drove to the post office, which was less than a mile from my house, and thrust the sealed envelope into the slot.

Afterward, I felt a sense of letdown. What I really wanted to do was go home, and telephone Wyatt, though there was something to this letter writing. Old-fashioned snail mail suggested romance, a concept that rarely visits me, and which I am never seeking out.

Chapter Seven

I had a couple of construction jobs to handle the following week, which kept my time occupied. The first was a complete bathroom renovation in Cupertino, right down to the structural floor and studs. I'd done this owner's master bath six months ago, so I knew her expectations.

The next job involved building a wheelchair ramp up to the back door of a house in San José for an elderly man who was recovering from major surgery, and couldn't climb stairs. I had to hire a couple of day laborers for this job, Juan Jiminéz, and his cousin, Humberto. Because I had worked with Juan so many times in the past, our partnership was second nature. The ramp was built in a day and a half, much to the delight of the elder's adult children. The county building inspector was even personally impressed with the finished product.

I could go along on autopilot with procedure, while performing re-enactments of lovemaking with Wyatt in my head. Therefore, I seemed to always be walking around slightly distracted, and horny too.

There was a day or two before my next scheduled job, a kitchen renovation in Modesto. To the layman, it might seem odd my construction contracts carried me all over the map, up to a seventy-five mile radius, but I'm self-employed. I'd secured many construction jobs by word of mouth, which explained why I had to rove to pay my bills.

During that brief down time, I went to visit Grandma Enida in the hospital.

Grandma had been operated on twenty-four hours prior. After discovering a huge tumor nearly blocking her colon, the surgeon had been able to remove not only the tumor, but resect the remaining organ so that Grandma avoided the inconvenience of a colostomy bag.

When I arrived, my father's younger brother, Mark, was in the room, joking around with Grandma, who looked a little bleak, and was hooked up to tubes and wires. She was on several medications, including a morphine derivative for post-surgical discomfort, but she recognized me even though Uncle Mark declared Grandma slightly delusional.

"She's on drugs, Maddie," he told me, accepting the kiss on the cheek I wasn't allowed to tender to Grandma, in order to avoid the potential for infection. "Right, Mommy?" he goaded his mother. "You're on drugs, Mommy, the doctor's got you all doped up."

"Shee!" This was Grandma's version of a cuss word. If her mind was delirious, then at least her mouth still worked.

I stayed about twenty minutes—long enough to feel satisfied that Grandma's recovery would go smoothly. Tired though she was from the surgery and the numerous drugs, Grandma tried to extract the promise from me to drive her to her favored Indian casino.

"When I go home, Madeline, you take me to Cache Creek. Your Grandpa no longer drives at night. She's too old now."

I savored Grandma Enida's lackadaisical use of English pronouns, as the Ilocano-Filipino dialect owns no word for "he" and "she". When I was a lot younger, I told myself the Ilocano people were unbiased through the power of language. However, there is a word to describe a homosexual, *bakla*, so I concluded the tolerance of the Ilocano people is only halfway to acceptance.

Uncle Mark walked with me to the parking lot. He said he'd been at Grandma's bedside for nearly two hours, and had to return to his day job at a tech company in Santa Clara.

"Good thing they like me there, or else they'd fire my ass," he joked, eyeing me curiously. "Something up with you, Maddie?"

"Why do you ask, Uncle?"

"I don't know. You seem, hmm…self-satisfied. Anything you need to talk about?"

"Maybe, Uncle. That depends how much time you have."

He rubbed the scant whiskers on his face grown together in the shape of a goatee. "I'm already in deep shit," he remarked, which meant he had plenty of time to hear the whole story.

He followed me on his Harley Fat Boy motorcycle to the closest chain coffee house, close to the hospital. Over a couple of large coffees, the excuse to linger at a table, I related to him what happened to me after I left town. I even admitted to the one-night stand with Wyatt, though I didn't name any names.

"Tell me, Maddie, was it payback, or a separate issue?"

He was referring to me having taken a man to bed immediately after catching my casual boyfriend with another woman. But this was an easy answer for me.

"Completely separate, Uncle."

He studied my face. "You're supposed to be pissed," he concluded. "And yet you've got this glow." He paused. "Are you by any chance pregnant?"

"What? No way, Uncle."

The idea was absurd, and to me, totally implausible. Though I'd had sex with Jake just before he had to fly to Seattle, we'd used a condom. And Wyatt had used condoms during both of our interludes.

"You have this glow," Uncle Mark repeated. "I don't know about that, I've always been one-hundred percent, right on the money, about women and pregnancy. Wait, except for this one chick I went to high school with. I ran into her about ten years after graduation, and asked when she was expecting. She sort of look pissed off when she told me she wasn't pregnant. Oh well, maybe she had a beer belly."

"I'm not pregnant," I reiterated firmly. "It's impossible."

"Well." He shrugged. "There *is* the Virgin Mary." Though we both knew I was no virgin.

After we parted—Uncle Mark back to work, and me straight home—I was preoccupied with not only that replay of Wyatt in my head, but now this questioning from Uncle Mark whether I was pregnant. I was irritated and worried at the same time. Rolling down my street, I adamantly told myself pregnancy was out of the question, though if it were true, I'd have a problem trying to figure out whose condom somehow failed. Even a pinhole will let in a little light.

When I pulled into the driveway, I spied Rat lying on my front porch in the shade, and was instantly put on the alert for Jake. Thankfully his blue Eclipse was nowhere in sight, nor was Jake lounging on the edge of the redwood planter boxes. I was baffled, though at least it was wonderful to see Rat again.

He seemed very excited to see me, whining and dancing around in circles. When he was through celebrating our reunion, we sat for a few minutes while I hugged him close, his tail endlessly whacking the porch boards. After I brought him into the house, I dug out his water and food dishes, and set him up in the laundry room, having dog chow left over from our trip to Oregon. He was famished, and not only downed the kibble in record time, even for a dog, but he lapped up all the water in the bowl.

I let him out in the back yard, and then telephoned Jake. He didn't answer at the house, but he did pick up his cell. I told him in a civilized manner that his dog was at my house, and he could retrieve the animal anytime, preferably sooner than later.

"Thank you, Maddie."

His voice sounded odd. When I hung up I figured I'd ask Jake why he decided to dump Rat, when he'd had been so cautious about the possibility of Sophie disposing of the dog while Jake was away in Seattle.

Jake arrived not too long after my call, in less than an hour, with leash in hand. He appeared upset at me, though he seemed to be trying to stifle the emotion. He was almost successful, until I asked him why he'd left Rat on my porch, and then his annoyance immediately dissipated.

"I didn't leave Rat on your porch."

"Then how did he get here?"

"I don't know. The last time I saw him was two days ago when I let him out to use the crapper."

"You haven't seen Rat for two days?" *What the hell is wrong with you,* I thought. "And…and you didn't worry about him? At all?"

Jake shrugged. We both stared down at the ragtag Rat, who looked up with sweet brown eyes, loving and innocent of scheming.

Jake caught his breath suddenly. "Do you mean to tell me that Rat *walked* to your house, Maddie?"

"But that…that only happens in movies."

"Sometimes I read about this." He patted Rat's head. "A cat or a dog, missing for months, turns up on its owner's doorstep."

"But…I'm not his owner. And anyway, that would mean he traveled here from Ben Lomond in two days. He'd have to work his way through the Santa Cruz Mountains, cross highways, and negotiate city streets. In two days."

He frowned. "Are you sure you didn't come out to Ben Lomond, and pick him up in your car?"

"What are you suggesting?"

"Nothing." But nevertheless he persisted. "Are you sure you didn't come get him, Maddie?"

"What are you accusing me of, Jake?"

"I think maybe you kidnapped my dog."

70

"Why in the hell would I kidnap Rat, and *then* tell you he's here?"

"To get me back. Hey, I mean, it's possible, right? Women do these things to work men over."

I decided this is what a hot flash from menopause must feel like, a ball of fire within the body's core that spreads to the extremities, and draws an instant sweat. I couldn't believe the audacity of Jake to point a finger at me for something I'd never do. And to suggest that I was conniving by virtue of being a female, clinched my contempt for him.

"You can go now." My voice was deadly calm.

"Now, Maddie." He tried to change his tone, and his allegation, but I wanted no more of this conversation. In fact, I wanted his sorry ass out of my house, and was almost willing to eject him physically, had I not my good sense tightly reined-in.

I suppose he could see some quality in my features that spoke a warning, because he left quickly with Rat. I even heard him scratch rubber with the Eclipse.

Sighing from frustration, I ducked out to the garage absentmindedly to clear the mail bucket, and found an envelope with a check from Kevin, prefacing the drywall work I'd performed while on vacation. I was touched by the professional gesture, and made a mental note to write him a thank you card.

When I saw the sky-blue envelope with Wyatt's logo, my heart swelled. Like Kevin's check, Wyatt's letter helped alleviate my anger, but only just, and I actually had to clear my mind before I opened it. Honesty is very important, both in myself and in others, and to be accused unjustly was aggravating.

Dear Madeline,

Well, well! You talked to my sister! It's a good thing she likes me, or else I'd be up Shit Creek without the proverbial paddle. There's nothing so pivotal as having a woman talk to your sister. If any man asked me why integrity is so important, I would advise to always be respectful to women, as they are the stronger sex. This is an Indian cultural rule all men must learn and abide by.

I'm so happy you decided to write back to me. I've been distracted with thoughts of you. Don't misunderstand. This is a good distraction, but a distraction nonetheless. I'm not confused about the physical element, and the natural tendency for a man to think with his dick. However, I think it's fair to warn you that I am a hopeless romantic.

It's been sunny in Tacoma. I've been left with only half a brain, but enough intellect to be able to get myself together for a show I've got scheduled in Portland next week. I'll pull through, thinking of you, dear Madeline.

Wyatt

I was amazed that he should be just as concerned with integrity as I had always been. This attitude is a side effect of being the daughter of Mitchell Benités. Thinking about my father, I had a sudden urge to go talk to him. I mustered a tremendous surge of self-control to swallow the impulse, though I nearly choked.

Wyatt mentioned he had a show in Portland, and I mused on the possibilities. I imagined taking a few days off, driving up to Portland, and laying around in his motel room. Here the fantasy grew, anchored in the memories of his body, his scent and taste, the way he felt when our skin brushed, the color of those scars against his flesh. Sexual fantasy is one thing, but this was more of a relationship daydream. I could only picture the raw sex, if fornicating was connected to an emotional love affair.

Impatient with my sexual idiocy, I sat at my desk for five minutes, working through the veil of arousal so I could once again focus on commonsense. I think I did the utmost to unravel the mystery in my letter.

Dear Wyatt,

It's interesting that integrity is important to you, as it was foremost when I was growing up. My father is Filipino-American, and though he was raised in the U.S., he retained very strong cultural family values. I don't know if it would interest you, but my mother is Caucasian, and 1/4 Sioux, adopted at birth by a white family, so her acculturation is complete. This makes me a mutt even more than Rat the dog.

I couldn't resist going to see your sister, Kate. When I left Susanville, I was nearly as sad as when I drove away from Tacoma. For the last week, I've worked two construction jobs, and half of my mind has been filled with nostalgia about my brief time with you. Call it fate—call it compatibility.

I'm twenty-five, Wyatt, and like you, I've never been married. No husband, no children. I am what many would call a loner, dedicated to my career, but obviously not bitter or bitchy (at least I hope not!). My little sister is a lesbian, so you can see my liberal leaning. And my father's culture seems to create strong women, so I find what you describe as an "Indian cultural rule" easy to accept.

I also find it very intriguing that circumstances put us together for one brief moment in time, and we could celebrate our similarity. But I'd like to know—how are we different? Are these differences, if they exist, too weighty to ever mean that fate was right?

Waiting for your thoughts,
Madeline

Once again, I addressed an envelope, sealed it, and firmly pressed on a stamp. I remembered Kevin's check, so I searched through my desk until I found a nice flowery thank you card, and hurriedly wrote down my gratitude for the monetary compensation, and a promise to return that borrowed ice chest.

Both envelopes in hand, I drove up the road to the post office. After dropping them in the slot, my thoughts were on Wyatt, though I knew Kevin would understand. I imagined Wyatt tearing the envelope open with his hand; or perhaps he might use a letter opener. I own one of these, a bamboo blade in a sheath crafted to appear like a sword, which smoothly slits open envelopes. Miranda gave it to me for my twenty-first birthday. Both of Wyatt's letters, however, had avoided the letter opener, and were torn open violently, with my feverishly trembling fingers.

I brooded on the mail slot, and then on my conversation with Jake. Here, I felt concern for Rat, afraid that he might turn up again on my porch, or perhaps injure himself trying. I thought to call up Jake, and offer to build Rat a kennel. I then knew my wisest move would be to not say anything. One of my pet peeves is being misunderstood, and I wanted no wrong ideas between Jake and me.

Sighing, I loaded into the car, and headed home, one hand resting on Wyatt's letter, which I'd brought with me as a proxy passenger.

Chapter Eight

I spent a week in Modesto working on a kitchen renovation in an older home in the center of town. Not familiar with the day laborers in this area, I instead hired up my cousin, Jerry, a licensed general contractor in the Central Valley.

One thing about working with family is that you have evolved from the same gene pool with related parents, so you seem to know what to do without asking. Also, construction work is sort of like being a surgeon—the more you do, the more you know. I can rip out a row of kitchen cabinets, and though the wall looks like hell, I'm confident that when I install fresh drywall and hang the new cabinets, no one will ever see scars.

Jerry lives in a late-model subdivision in Lathrop, adjacent to the San Joaquin River. The location is excellent for a man like Jerry who lives his life for family, to work construction, and fish for striped bass. The house he bought is enormous, five bedrooms, three-and-a-half baths, and nearly four thousand square feet. I asked him about his homeowner's insurance, and he admitted that living on a flood plain and covering so much space beneath the roof guarantees his premium remains high. Fortunately the house was paid for in cash at the end of this vicious recession, and three of his wife's relatives hit hard by the economy rent rooms to offset the inflated price of insurance.

I stayed in a spare room on the first floor, right next to the kitchen. Unlike Miranda's home which has a full bar in the basement guest bedroom, Jerry's household practices teetotalism, not out of any religious stuffiness (like me, Jerry's a Catholic, with a singular appreciation for a good wine), but because two of his in-laws are under the age of twenty-one. Jerry's wife, Gigi, is a great cook, and there was plenty to eat, just no liquor. That didn't bother me at all. I enjoyed the hospitality, paid Jerry a living wage, and was too tired at night anyway to find a liquor store. Most of the time I was asleep as soon as my head hit the pillow.

By Friday, the job was done, and Gigi's bon-voyage gift was a three-day supply of Filipino victuals. I drove opposite the direction of the evening commute traffic, and arrived home with my belly rumbling for the delights sealed in snap-lid boxes on the passenger seat of my truck.

Once again, I was surprised to find Rat on my porch, only this time, he seemed a bit worse for wear. His collar was missing, he appeared much thinner at the flanks, and was limping a little, as though his pads were sore. He scented the food through all that plastic, and nearly jumped on me to get to it.

Bringing Rat into the house, I set him up in the laundry room, where he went through two bowls of food and water respectively. Finally, he lay down with a sigh, and a break to allow his belly settle, so he wouldn't vomit.

I watched the dog closely, while I called up Jake, trying both his home and his cell. He didn't answer, so I left messages on the two voice mails. I let Rat out in the yard, and he did his toilet thing, too exhausted to waste time with urine marking. The dog seemed relieved to come back into the house, and throw himself down for a nap beneath the table in my office.

Two hours later, sifting through paperwork with Rat still deep in slumber by my feet, I heard the doorbell ring, and a pounding on the door. Rat didn't move a muscle, as he was so overcome by his travels, so I left him alone to turn on the porch light, and warily peek through the spy-hole to see whom it was I'd somehow pissed off.

The aggressive visitor was Jake Keene.

I opened the door to his livid face and clenched jaw.

"What the fuck, Maddie," were his first words.

No, "Thank you, Maddie, for saving my dog," or "Gee, I'm as stunned as you are." He instead acted like a complete asshole.

"Do you want me to deck you?" I asked calmly. "Because I will, if you don't shut the hell up."

"Where is he? Where's Rat?"

"In my office." I pointed, and Jake took off.

Jake's voice barely registered in poor Rat's brain. The dog nearly had to be shaken awake, but Jake dragged him out from beneath the worktable anyway.

"You should take him to a vet," I advised. "He was really exhausted this time, and he was limping too. I think he has bruises or abrasions on his pads."

"I'm going to go to court, and get a restraining order," he threatened. He hadn't even heard me.

"What? What's your problem?"

"Maddie, quit fucking stealing my dog!"

Now Rat was awake, but he seemed confused, looking back and forth between the two of us, like a blameless child caught in the middle of a parental argument.

"I didn't steal your dog!" Had my voice ramped up a bit in volume?

"Then how the hell did he get here, huh?"

"I don't know, Jake, I've been in Modesto *all* week!"

"You're fucking lying to me, Maddie!"

Oh, *that* did it, because of the integrity thing. I grabbed up the pile of my neatly stacked receipts, and I literally threw them in his face. They hit him on the forehead in a single clump, and burst apart, showering the floor at his feet.

"You're an asshole, Jake!" I hotly declared. "I've been working with my cousin Jerry all damn week! You fucking jerk!"

He picked up the pieces of paper one at a time, taking the time to check the dates and even the times of my purchases. For my vindication, included in the formerly neat stack was a gas receipt that proved I'd departed Modesto on that very day, close to five p.m.

His face changed, when he realized that Rat had voluntarily come all the way from Ben Lomond for a second time.

"Maddie, I—"

"Fuck you, Jake!" I snarled, opening the front door.

"I'm sorry, Maddie," he tried again. "I didn't mean it."

"Yeah? Apparently there's a *lot* of shit you didn't mean!"

"Really, Maddie, please, I'm sorry."

"I want you to leave!" I demanded, in case he was that stupid. Just to impress my desire, I stuck out my arm, and pointed violently at his car.

This time he picked up Rat, and carried the dog to the Eclipse. I turned off the porch light, not wishing to suggest an invitation.

I almost had a drink after that, but, recognizing that medicating was not what I should be doing with liquor, I decided instead to take a shower to cool down. Somewhere between shampoo and conditioner, I thought I heard the doorbell ring. This irked me, as I imagined Jake trying to make up for being a thoughtless bastard. If he were back on my porch again I'd let him wait it out. I kept showering, and even deliberately took my time.

Finally done, and shutting off the flow, I distinctly heard the doorbell ringing, and, without even drying off, I wrapped myself in my terry robe, and huffed to the door. Looking through the spy-hole, I knew that it wasn't Jake, because the person standing on my front step was way too tall. Still, I was having trouble making out a face, until I switched on the porch light, and instantly recognized Wyatt McLain.

I pulled that door open so fast, not giving a damn whether my hair was streaming, or that the robe stuck to every protrusion of my female form.

"Well!" He smiled charmingly, and the irritation I felt for Jake dissipated right away. No, it melted, just like my heart.

"Wyatt!" I was so excited, I felt breathless.

"I was wondering if maybe you weren't home, and then I heard the shower running." He pointed toward the side of the house. "I, uh, investigated."

"You actually went to my bathroom window, and checked it out?"

He pushed the hair out of his face. "I wanted to be sure you were home."

"Did you see anything?"

"Maybe."

"Because I always open the window a crack to vent the steam. I mean, there's a fan, but I always open the window out of habit."

"It's not like I didn't *try* to see something, but your bathroom window's too high up, even for me."

"I'm glad my neighbors didn't think you were a peeping Tom, and call the cops."

"I don't make a habit of acting like a peeping Tom." He frowned. "Did I forget to tell you that I'm a dirty old man? I thought it was in that first letter I sent to you."

I swept him inside, feeling a little shy being caught wet and undressed. But he didn't seem to mind my dampness, and the residual water dripping from my hair. He carried no luggage, nor did I ask about that red compact sedan at the curb.

"What are you doing here?" I asked joyfully, my arms laced around his neck.

"Why? Do you want me to go?"

"No, silly, I'm excited." I pressed my body close to prove it.

Holding me with one hand, he dug a crinkly paper out of his pocket with the other. The well-worn paper was the letter I'd sent before I went off to Modesto to work on the kitchen remodel with Jerry.

"It says here your little sister is a lesbian," he pretended to read. "I thought maybe I could help change her mind. Get a little two-for-one."

I knew he was teasing me, so I only kissed him. This lip-lock had to be accomplished by standing on my tiptoes to reach his mouth, because he was so tall.

"I'm not a lesbian," I informed. "You don't have as much work cut out for you."

He was kissing my neck, and getting wet in the face for his efforts.

"I hear you like power tools, Madeline," he whispered, when he came up for air between kisses. "Your turn-ons include table saws, jackhammers...nail guns...and...and...industrial strength...adhesive."

I dropped my robe, to Wyatt's hushed praise. Eventually his clothes went the way of my damp robe, and we ended up on the couch right there in the front room, ready to do the deed, but lingering with the kisses. Rubbing my naked body against gorgeous muscled curves was an excellent form of foreplay. At some point, he fumbled for his pants, and pulled a condom from a pocket before the real action began, but I didn't mind the sidebar. You can do a lot of sexy things while putting on a condom if the mood is right—and believe me the mood was flowing.

Making love with Wyatt was amazing and explosive after my pent-up horniness, like acting out a fantasy that's been smoldering for days and days. Finally the flames ignite, and you pretend you're no longer responsible for your actions in the heat of the moment, though to prevent disaster, caution is now ever more critical.

Afterward, we went to my bedroom, and lay in the bed side by side. He touched me tenderly, and I traced his scars with my fingertips in awe of him. Wyatt said he'd figured out our only difference, he being male and me being female, and then he apologized for his advanced age, and claimed to have an extended refractory period. When I began to run my tongue slowly along the pleasing contour of his naked body, I could see he recovered fairly quickly, and was ready again in no time, though he had to retrieve his jeans from the living room to access a fresh condom.

Finally, when we were finished with the severe sexual tension our letters and thoughts had nurtured, we sat in the kitchen, and ate Gigi's leftovers washed down with hot cocoa, and just talked. I asked him about his art show in Portland, and that's when he admitted he'd been inspired by my last letter to come and see me.

"I flew to Portland for the show," he explained, "and then I traded in the other half of my plane ticket for a one way to San José. Homeland Security and the TSA, they don't like one way flights, and some ignoramus gave me a hard time, until I flashed my tribal card."

"Why the tribal card?"

"A tribal card is proof I'm more of an American than they think I am."

"How did you find my house?"

"I rented a car with GPS." He was beaming with pride in his ingenuity. "I usually have trouble with those newfangled devices, but this time I had incentive to learn how to use it."

"What incentive are you talking about?"

"The incentive to get laid, Madeline. I'm hooked on you, like booze or drugs. I've been walking around with a hard on, and that has a knack of getting in the way of higher brain function. I had to do something with the thing, and I couldn't think of anyone else to share it with but you."

"I think it's sweet you'd come all this way for sex."

He reached across the tabletop, and grasped my hand.

"You've got it wrong, Madeline, it's not just sex. I haven't been able to stop thinking about you since we met." His eyes changed. "I'm stuck on that night, apparently."

I knew Kate had told him what I'd said when I'd met with her in Susanville.

"How did you manage to fit into that little rental car, anyway?"

"What choice did I have? I just wanted to be with you."

We returned to bed, and made love again. I've imagined the theoretical mechanics of size difference, though being with Wyatt, and experiencing his tender care allowed me to forget we were so physically mismatched.

"Whew," he said, grinning, after I'd reached pleasure, and he obliged with a wildly passionate ending.

"You're so good," I agreed, touching his cheek.

While we lay there in recovery, I told Wyatt about my work, and related my latest tribulation with Jake Keene. I added the fact that Rat had twice traveled quite a distance to find me.

"Today was the second time?" he marveled. "Rat must really care for you." He paused. "What about Rat's master?"

"Jake doesn't love me, and I don't love Jake," I said matter-of-factly. "Otherwise, I wouldn't be lying here with you right now. I would've made up with Jake, and that would've been that."

"Do you mean if you'd made up with him, this bed would be really full right now?"

"No."

"I don't think a double bed does justice for two people, let alone three."

Wyatt deliberately ignored my previous comment with a passing joke, as though unfathomable he would be superseded by Jake, a foul presence sharing the warmth of my bed in Wyatt's place.

"What I'm *saying*, Wyatt, is that if the possibility existed when I left Seattle that making up with Jake was in the cards, I never would've gone to the restaurant with you, nor would I have gone home with you, and I certainly wouldn't have slept with you. I would've shaken your hand and thanked you, and gone on my way. There would have been no night to get stuck on for either of us."

"I'm relieved you didn't make up, Madeline." I could feel the motion of him nodding in understanding.

"Look, I need to tell you something, Wyatt. About a week before you and I met, I had sex with Jake. It happened before he left for Seattle." When I was greeted with silence, I added, "I used a condom."

I felt a need to tell Wyatt the truth. I wanted no secrets between us. My worst fears were of Jake possibly attempting to undermine the happiness I'd found with Wyatt, and I didn't want any lies or withholding to complicate our newfound romance.

"Well, you're certainly not dead yet," he observed. There was benevolence to his statement, instead of accusation, and I knew he appreciated my honesty. "It's not like I've been celibate my entire life," he added.

"I just needed you to know, so there wouldn't be any surprises."

"Do you still want Jake?"

"No. I lost all my desire for Jake when I finally saw who he really was."

He reached out, and rested a hand on one of my breasts, not in a possessive gesture, but a lingering sexual caress. This is how we fell asleep, and how I awoke in the morning, to his seeking hand.

❖ ❖ ❖ ❖

During breakfast, I asked him when he was intending to leave.

"Why? Do you have a construction job?" His was a mature question, not the insecurity of *Are you trying to get rid of me?*

"I don't have a job starting for another three days," I promised.

"Good," he affirmed. "I get to be with you."

After breakfast, we took a walk, and I toured him around my Agnew neighborhood, with its collection of mismatched older homes. I told him about how my father would take us four girls down to the railroad tracks, and lay pennies along the rail, so a passing train could flatten them.

"I still have a bunch of flat pennies," I said, revealing the sentimental side of my nature.

"You grew up near here?"

"*And* my parents still live in the same house, only a mile or so up the road. Would you like to meet them?" I asked, without second-guessing him.

"Of course I would. I probably have a lot to talk about with your dad, like the Vietnam War and Woodstock."

I knew what he was up to. He was attempting to magnify the reality of his age, and the fact that he was of my father's generation. But I didn't flinch.

"Well, my dad *is* in his fifties," I pointed out. "Though it's not possible for you to both remember Woodstock too clearly, since you were, what, barely ten years old, Wyatt? And the Vietnam conflict was over just before my father qualified for the draft, so I guess that means you were pretty safe too."

We walked up the main drag toward my parents' home, forsaking the use of a car on such a beautiful morning. We were hand in hand like a couple of teenaged lovers, Wyatt's six-foot height considerably blocking the sun.

"Did your folks ever get to meet Jake?" he asked, just as we were turning the corner, their driveway in sight, the bulk of the house hidden by a few large mulberry trees that crowded the street. I could see their cars parked out front, an indicator they were home.

"Never. Nobody even knew I was seeing him."

"Wow, I feel special, then."

I glanced up at him, meeting his gaze, and smiled. "You *are* special."

81

On approach, we could view the entire house. There was my father, mowing the lawn in preparation for his pending Saturday music students. Mom was standing in the garage sorting laundry.

We were still holding hands, when they both turned to look. I'll never forget Dad's response, the sudden halt of the power mower, and his spontaneous grin. When I introduced Wyatt, he wiped off the grin, and tried to look scary, but he obviously liked Wyatt too much to continue with the farce.

They invited us inside, and while we sat like guests in the living room, Mom made coffee. There was at least an hour to kill until Dad's first music student arrived, and we passed the time with conversation. I was so pleased that neither of my parents made a fuss about Wyatt's apparent age, or even asked why I was with a man who seemed to be old enough to have sired me.

I knew my father trusted me as an adult. My liaison with Jake Keene had been hidden, and my behavior secretive. I'd probably sensed my liaison with Jake wouldn't last. Wyatt was different. I wanted to shout out our association, and share his kindness with my family, especially with my parents, whose respect was paramount.

And then Dad dropped the bomb.

"Christ, Wyatt, you're a hell of a lot better than that last guy Maddie was seeing."

I scrambled to think of who that might have been.

"I think she was embarrassed to be seen with him, because she never even brought him over," Dad went on. "Though she did take care of his dog."

That's when I knew I could never put one over on my father. Either he knew me well, or he was just lucky, and had seen me with Jake Keene sometime during what I had always assumed to be covert hanky-panky.

"Mr. Benités, let me ask you something," said Wyatt gently, ignoring the obvious—such as referring to his contemporary as "Mr."

"Anything."

"Do you like me because your daughter's out in the open about it, or because I'm just a real nice guy?"

"Both!" Dad crowed. "I can tell you make my daughter happy, and that's all that matters to me."

"Well, I can appreciate that," Wyatt agreed.

"It doesn't even matter to me that you're a little older than Maddie by a couple of years."

Dad smirked knowingly—although I'm convinced he was as off target as I had initially been in regard to Wyatt's true age. Quite a bit later, he commented that Wyatt looked great "for being forty," so I know Dad was as suckered by Wyatt's youthful vigor as I had been.

Dad's first guitar student soon arrived, and we said goodbye, but didn't depart right away, which prompted Mom to ask us to come for dinner on Sunday.

"So you can meet two of Maddie's sisters," she proposed.

I looked at Wyatt, who only nodded and smiled, and then I said we'd be there at six.

Having gotten that over with, we walked back to my house, still holding hands, which meant that my parents had passed Wyatt's test too.

"Why do they call you Maddie?" he asked.

"That's my nickname."

"Do you want me to call you Maddie?"

"If I'd wanted that, I would've told you my name was Maddie when we met."

"You told Kate your name was Maddie."

"That's different, I'm not attracted to her, and I don't need the added thrill of hearing my name on her lips."

"You could be named Bill, and I'd still think you're a woman. It's your tits, I think," he concluded.

When we arrived at the house, I asked him where he wanted to go, and he said to me, "Take me somewhere the tourists don't normally go."

I drove him up to San Francisco in the Mercedes, but first we unloaded his only luggage, a gym bag, from the trunk of that rental car, a red Nissan Sentra. Stowing the bag in the house, we dropped the Sentra off at the rental agency.

"You don't need a rental car when you have me," I pointed out.

"At least your car has lots of leg room." He seemed relieved to be able to stretch out, once the passenger seat was pushed back all the way.

Though the City is a prime tourist attraction, I didn't bring him to the usual spots that visitors would seek. They usual practice is to join ferry tours of Alcatraz, drive down Lombard Street, walk to the height of Coit Tower, or peruse Fisherman's Wharf, with its cheap souvenir trinkets and over-priced eateries.

Instead, because I knew he'd grown up near the ocean in Washington State, I drove out to the coast, south of the Golden Gate Bridge. Avoiding the crowds in Golden Gate Park, I found a parking slot on the bluff overlooking the ruins of the former Sutro Baths. We hiked down to the cove containing pools of seawater, and stone buttresses that once formed the foundation for the beautiful facility. There is an easy trail down the face of the bluff built by the Park Service, but we negotiated the south face, descending the steep ledges through high weeds.

I soon noted something was amiss with me, a subtle feeling that I needed to protect Wyatt. My intellect told me this was absurd, but some maternal spark inside forced me to hover. I imagined six towering feet of man taking a fall off the slope, and I was appalled at the very thought.

Down by the pools, I started to worry that we might be mugging victims, and I had to suppress that, because it was an unreasonable fear. I felt that we were vulnerable, and I decided that I was projecting Wyatt's own experience of being robbed in his loft, or the attempted car jacking in Tacoma, upon our Saturday ramble.

After Sutro Baths, we walked along a footpath at the edge of the Great Highway, past the touristy Cliff House, and down to Ocean Beach. Out on the wind blasted landscape, we watched little shore birds run up and down the sand, deftly prying out marine worms and sand crabs with their agile bills.

I had a vague feeling of danger here, due to the legendary undertow, notorious for pulling unsuspecting greenhorns out to sea and drowning them. I knew Wyatt was no novice to the vagaries of the sea, but I kept myself as a guard of the crashing surf. This meant that occasionally a wave would shoot up the beach and inundate my feet, soaking my shoes and the cuffs of my jeans.

Wyatt had no idea of the twisted depths of my thought process. He only laughed at my lack of vision, and chased me up to where the sand was dry and deep, and I couldn't easily get away. He pulled me down, and we wrestled, until a middle-aged couple, alarmed at our commotion, waded through the sand to rescue me. I could see the scene from their point of view—here's a man over six feet tall, and a muscular two-hundred pounds, bronze skinned and long haired ruffian harassing a woman half his size. When they realized I wasn't being assaulted, that my cries of seeming pain were actually wild shrieks of laughter, the man scolded us severely. Sobered, we promised to behave.

84

While we sat on the beach, Wyatt pointed out the birds by name. I recalled doing this with Jake when I'd first met him on the municipal pier in Pacifica, and how impressed I'd been when he knew their Latin names. Jake had seemed so learned and cultured, and had served as part of my attraction for him. I imagine this is the mechanism behind female college students becoming enamored with their world-wise male professors. Jake probably was apt to use this ruse often to get women into his bed, such as that flashy babe in Seattle.

This time was different, because Wyatt used general terms, like "raven" and "gull" and "sandpiper." He didn't mention the sub-distinction of the many species, and he didn't quote those lengthy scientific specifications. I really didn't care that he didn't use the scientific names, meaningless triviality for how the birds related to our purpose of discussion.

But I could see that he was fascinated with birds, that he understood their unique body forms just by the fact of the eagle sculpture hanging in Road Apples. His connectivity to the natural world gave me an insight into his mind, and a respect that Jake never earned. Maybe the pretentious side of Jake was a projected element he put on like a costume for the benefit of his audience, while Wyatt was crystal clear, and wholly open.

Right there on the cold sand of Ocean Beach, I wanted to tell Wyatt that I had fallen in love with him. That's when I secretly admitted my feelings to myself. I'm convinced love probably occurred the moment he'd said "kismet" to me that first night at his loft in Tacoma, as he was the only person I've known who had ever used the word. My emotions on our first night together had been mixed up with an acute physical attraction for Wyatt that was steadily building into a more complex allure. Now at the beach, I owned a conscious acknowledgment.

I decided to hold back, as women are not supposed to say these words to the man first. I may have been raised as a strong female, but I knew the subtlety of social expectation.

He gathered me close with one arm, tucking me into his side.

"I really like you, Madeline," he declared. "I like you a lot."

Okay, so his declaration wasn't "love." For the moment I was satisfied with being liked by him "a lot." You can love someone, though liking is a separate issue entirely. For instance, I love my sister Mallory, but liking her is something I really have to work at, due to her tendency to twist facts, and use them to plow relationships under when they don't

85

suit her current needs. So, Wyatt liking me felt like an honor, and a special gift.

I made a stupid move. I gazed into his beautiful eyes, and lost my good sense.

"I love you, Wyatt," I foolishly declared.

Oh God, I'd said it! I leaped to my feet at the stunned expression in his eyes.

"Dammit!" I cursed. "I didn't mean to tell you that."

He stood, and brushed off the sand, and put his arms around me, so he could embrace me and still look into my eyes while we talked.

"Are you saying you mean it, but you didn't want me to know yet?"

I nodded, feeling close to tears. "Yes," in a voice not quite my own, "I mean it. But I wasn't ready to say it to you."

"Unless I'd said it first?"

"Yes. You know, so you wouldn't feel like you owed me."

I felt bad that I'd jumped the gun, and somehow made him obligated. I started to cry, worried he might think of me as insincere to my true feelings, and that I had to wait for his declaration in order to clear mine. We sat down again, and he put his arm around me, and kissed away the tears. Though he didn't tell me he loved me, he reassured me in a way that made telling him acceptable.

"I must confess something to you, Madeline," he said, once I decided that crying was a waste of our precious time.

"What's that?"

"I've never told anybody ever in my life that I loved them."

"Oh. Why?"

"I think because it's not part of my vocabulary."

"Why is that?"

He told me his story.

"My father, who was a white man, died when I was four. He was a test pilot for the Air Force, and he was killed in a jet crash in 1962. We were living in California, near Sacramento, and my mother was pregnant at the time. I remember that she cried a lot afterward. She was very sad, but she was loving toward me too. After my father was killed, we had to live off base, in Stockton, I think. My mother worked menial jobs, because nobody would hire a pregnant, obviously minority woman. When she went into labor, she was admitted into the County hospital, and then may have been told that the infant was stillborn."

"Is that really what happened?"

"No, Madeline. In fact, that baby was my sister Kate, stolen from the hospital by a white nurse who did that sort of thing out of twisted social obligation. The nurse believed that Indian babies shouldn't be raised in poverty, or as heathens. My mother's medical records were changed to reflect a stillbirth, but oddly enough, an actual birth certificate was issued for Kate as a live birth. To add to the offense, back then, hospitals often administered scopolamine to women in labor, which made them forget the details. Anyway, this nurse didn't understand that she created a type of poverty for Kate by stealing her away, because Kate never got to know our culture until she was already a woman herself."

"Your mother must have been devastated."

"My mother was probably so filled with grief, I don't think she ever would have recovered, even with me to take care of. First her husband is killed, and then her child dies. My mother was killed on the way home from the hospital in an auto accident. I was immediately placed in foster care. I was extremely lucky to have been claimed from Social Services by the Quinault Indian Nation. My mother was full blood, and a tribal member. I was probably too old to have anyone want to hide me away, like they did with Kate."

"Do you remember it happening?"

"Yes, I was only four, but I remember most of it, and only from the point of view of a four-year-old boy. My mother's sister, Aunt Doreen, she adopted me and raised me on the rez."

"Why didn't your mother return to the reservation after your father died?"

"I don't know, I can only assume that she was out of money, and did what she thought was right. Being a pregnant widow with a young child certainly can put a crimp in your plans. And I believe, though I can't prove it, that she was probably evicted from the Air Force base soon after my father's death. The military wanted to rid themselves of a woman who was a citizen of two nations, the U.S. and the QIN. "

"Like you?"

"Yes, like me. But here's the kicker, Madeline, it's not as though I don't know what love is. It's in me and part of me. I always knew that Aunt Doreen loved me. I remember being loved by my father and mother, and I had a sense of belonging, of familiarity. Oftentimes, I was blindly loyal to my own detriment. But I have never in my life been able to tell any one person that I love them. Even Kate, when I finally met her, I never told her. I still haven't told her."

"Did Kate ever tell you she loves you?"

"Sure, yes. But there was never a requirement to tell me. If she never said it, I'd know it, because that's how it is."

"You don't have to tell me, Wyatt. You don't even have to feel it."

"Well, that's a different thing, now, isn't it, Madeline?" He tweaked my nose. "How do you know I don't feel it?"

I shrugged. "I only know you're here, and that means everything to me."

He laughed softly. "A lot of men would be happy to take a flight for some great pussy, Madeline. To them, it'd be no big deal. And you are a pure delight. But, do you know what? I *really* hate to fly."

I concluded that he loved me. The world was really that simple. I was overcome with the revelation that life and love are both convoluted and understated.

We talked endlessly, and I learned more about him, and told him about my life. In the return trip to Santa Clara, I brought Wyatt to my favorite noodle house. While we ate, I took subtle note of his likes and dislikes, pleased to find out afterward that he had also been in close observation of me for the very same reason.

When we arrived back at the house, he took me by the hand, guided me to the bedroom, and made love to me with a deep tenderness I have never experienced. His eyes in the gloom said more to me than his words ever could.

When he finally slept, I stayed awake, just watching him. Maybe it's strange, that I thought about the years of Wyatt's childhood, growing up under the care of his aunt, surrounded by a rain forest and a windswept shore, where the sea appears to roll away to forever. I conjured fantastical, giant fir trees draped in moss, and the echo of ravens croaking unseen high in a canopy that seldom let in the sun, because it was so often cloaked in rain.

Something inside of me connected to Wyatt. I felt the bond just before I drifted off to sleep—a spark, or a dream, where you can walk in your memories without being harmed.

Chapter Nine

On Sunday morning, over warm oatmeal and a pot of coffee, he asked me to bring him to my church.

"Why do you want to see my church?"

"I want to know everything there is to know about you, Madeline."

"That's presumptuous. How do you even know I go to a church? I may not even be affiliated with any type of organized religion."

"I saw the Jesus statue at your parents' house, up on the top of their entertainment center," he claimed. "You're a Catholic."

"The fact of my parents keeping a Jesus statue doesn't make me a Catholic. They could be art collectors, or Protestants."

"Protestants don't keep figurines of Jesus. They equate statues to filthy idolatry. I conclude that you must be a Catholic for your parents to house a Jesus statue."

"My parents may have taught us Voodoo. Or *Santeria.*"

"That's absurd, that's movie fluff. Come to think of it, I saw a likeness of the Virgin too, at Mom and Dad's. No Protestant puts any store in the Mother. That's why their women are stepped on by their men."

His reasoning was mind-boggling. There are plenty of Catholics who honor the Blessed Mother, and strive diligently to repress women, but at least his was just my kind of thinking.

"Maybe it's only my parents who are Catholic."

I was actually having quite a bit of fun being blandly difficult. He also seemed to enjoy the dance, a witty repartee that thrilled me deeply.

"Once a Catholic, always a Catholic," he quoted a flexible truism, where the noun can be substituted with words like "slut" or "deviant."

I finally relented, and showed him the crucifix my parents had gifted me on my Sacrament of Confirmation. I rarely wear it because of the danger of jewelry around power tools, and keep it safe in a cedar jewelry box high on a shelf in my closet.

"Why don't you have a statue, Madeline?" he asked, deliberately offering me a perplexed expression.

"You just wait," I slyly threatened.

I drove him to the nearest Catholic parish situated by a busy freeway in Santa Clara, where a gleaming metal statue of the Blessed Mother rears over thirty feet toward the sky.

"Good Lord," he declared, standing at the statue's one giant foot that peeked out from under the gown, and where the faithful had left buckets of flowers and tossed coins for luck. "This is serious fetishization."

I was both impressed with Wyatt's intelligence, and relieved that no one in our vicinity was likely to understand what he had just implied. One of the facets he'd told me was he'd acquired an MA from Central Washington University in Ellensburg. He was, in fact, an educated person, vastly more so than myself, who'd attended the street school of construction to obtain my skills, savvy and State license.

"What you've earned, dear Madeline, is known as a PHD," he claimed the day before, over steaming bowls of noodle soup. "A 'Pool Hall Degree.'"

I'd found that humorous, and a common theme among Dad's jazz musician friends, especially those who hadn't gone to college, but whose formidable talent, knowledge of music theory and performance experience supported what academia never could impart.

We entered the church, and attended the mass, though afterward, I had to explain to Wyatt that this wasn't my favored house of worship.

"It's old school, pre-Vatican II. Women are excluded from any liturgical involvement whatsoever at this parish, and only the priest serves communion."

"Then why did we come here? Should I be thinking that all Catholic churches prescribe to misogyny?"

"I just knew you'd appreciate the figurine."

Into the Mercedes we went, though I had no idea where I would take him today. A fat guy on a Harley Sportster roared past, and I was suddenly inspired.

I drove up to Skyline, where we could glimpse the fog-laden sea from the top of the ridge, though I didn't descend to the ocean. Instead, I turned south, winding through Madrone and oak woods that clothed the ridges, beneath the shadow of fir and laurel, until we reached the little restaurant at the junction of Woodside Road, where bikers hang out in the adjacent parking lots, showing off their axes.

Wyatt was amused at the fact there were very few cars, but a massive gathering of motorcyclists, who seemed more prone to lounge around in the shade, and bullshit with each other than to eat at the diner. This meant that we were able to find a nice booth in Alice's where we could watch the road, and listen to the roar of pipes.

"You don't know this, but I have a big motorcycle," I told him, over burgers and coffee. "It's a street cruiser, 1600 cc's."

"That's so damn hot." His eyes grew wider. "You'll have to show it to me."

"I keep it covered in my garage. I've been too busy to take it out riding."

"You're a brave woman to ride a motorcycle."

"No, I'm chicken-shit, and that's why I keep making excuses not to ride. There are too many potholes, and too many crazy drivers on the road."

"Will you at least model it for me sometime? Naked?"

"I promise I'll try. If we're naked, we might not make it to the garage."

"*That's* something to look forward to."

When we finished eating, I drove us south, toward Saratoga, where we wound down through the high-priced town with its multi-million-dollar bungalows.

"I'm betting you like that house," he said, pointing to a beautiful Tudor home, painted sea blue, and built around 1928.

"Of course, though I prefer Craftsmen style, pre-1920."

"I'm sure you wouldn't turn up your nose at that blue house."

"You're right. It's lovely, but it would take several million dollars to buy a house like that, in a town like Saratoga."

He was briefly astounded at that concept. "Real estate's like that in Seattle," he conceded, "though not so much so in Oregon."

"That's what Kevin told me. He said he bought his battered Victorian in Astoria for a song, and now it's worth much more. He won't sell it. He's too much in love with it."

"Are you attached to your house very much?"

"Well, I guess so, yeah, meaning I doubt I'd ever sell. I put a lot of work into it. The house used to belong to the grandfather of a high school classmate, and let me tell you, the house had really great bones, but it was a piece of shit when I bought it. The old man died inside the bedroom, the family didn't want it, and no one would even give them an offer with that type of disclosure."

"You're not afraid of ghosts?"

"I kind of got used to the ghost of Grandpa Gus."

"Have you ever, in your life, thought of moving away from the Bay Area, and living elsewhere?"

I glanced at him, knowing he was up to something, though I didn't want to assume what was the most obvious. He'd mentioned Oregon with a purpose, which made me think he wasn't going to ask me to have anything to do with Tacoma. I was intrigued, though I curbed my excitement.

"When I traveled to Astoria, and saw Kevin's place, relocating crossed my mind. But most of my family lives here in the South Bay."

"Except for one of your sisters. She made the move, right?"

"Right. It's because my parents have vacation property in Susanville, though Miranda's the only one who actually wanted to live up there full-time. After college, she got a job with the Highway Patrol, and stayed in our parents' home, until she bought a Craftsman in town. I performed a lot of the updating."

"I know you're wondering what I'm getting at."

"Yes, I am."

We were nearly home, as the route was a straight shot from Saratoga to Santa Clara on back roads.

"I like Portland," he said. I could sense he was studying my profile. "Oregon's somewhat different from Washington State. Portland is not as pricey, quainter and very homey. On the cab drive to the motel, I saw tracts of old houses."

"Lots of places have tracts of old houses." I pulled into the driveway, and shut off the engine. "Have you seen photos of Detroit recently?"

We entered the house. I knew he was still in the middle of this matter, and wanted to finish, so I made coffee, and we sat in the living room, staring at the dark screen of the television.

"The art gallery was in downtown Portland," he continued his angle. "Even with all those tall buildings, Portland is modest, kind of folksy, different from Seattle, or Tacoma. Portland still has rain, but there's more color to the surroundings. You know, in people, and the buildings. The first thing I thought of when I walked the streets was that if I were white, I mean, *completely* white—not so much the Quinault part of me, the part of me raised on the rez—I'd be happy living and working in Portland."

"Is that how you feel about Tacoma?"

"Tacoma is convenient, I'll grant it that, and more of an industrial shipping town, blue collar and rough, though comfortable. The only reason I've stayed on is Tacoma's close to my favored metal supplier. But I managed to locate another supplier with good pricing in Beaverton, which is not too far from Portland."

"I drove through Portland. It's on a series of rivers, right?"

"Partly on the Willamette, and partly on the Columbia. It's a city of rivers, and maybe that's why I like it, that and the rain. The people there seem very intellectual, extremely interested in art, enhanced by the wineries in the Willamette Valley, which are close enough to an urban center. There's really great public transportation. You could get on light rail, and just about go anywhere from the hub. Portland's got the bustle without the hustle."

"What about the reservation? Portland's got to be further away, compared to Tacoma."

"Tacoma's less than three hours from Taholah, and Portland is only one hour more. I could get used to that, especially if I had some really great company for the trip."

"Please tell me what you're trying to tell me, Wyatt," I begged softly, no longer able to bridle my eagerness. "None of this beating around the bush."

"I found a house, a great old house," he revealed. "The best of all, it's on South East Salmon Street, which is like a sign to a man from the Canoe People, who literally grew up in flowing water. And I have the cash for the down. The house needs some work, but I don't know anyone in Oregon."

"You could ask Kevin Gerard," I proposed. "He specializes in renovating vintage homes."

"But he's in Astoria. I want someone who'd do the work, and who lives in Portland. Somebody who understands the substance of a vintage home."

"I don't know any contractors in Portland. Maybe Kevin could recommend somebody for you. He must have made some professional contacts by now."

"I want you, Madeline." He finally got to the point, as I knew he would. "I want you to fix it up. I want you to live in it with me."

I let the moment wash over me, feeling and inhaling it. I expected to choke, to drown, to suffocate, but this was Wyatt's magic, and I soaked it in.

"Oh." I couldn't manage to speak further.

"I know it's…weird," he translated. "All I could think of when I saw it was how much you'd like it. The way I like you."

His affirmation popped the lid off my reticence.

"Wyatt, if we had sex right now, right this very moment, I'd break open." I attempted to explain the sudden fragility in my emotional state. "You've stunned me. I'm stunned."

"Right now?" He seemed intrigued by the concept of me being a cracked shell.

"Yes, right now."

He reached out to grasp my hand. "I don't want to lose you, Madeline. I know what having a passion for something feels like, and I figured you'd really enjoy working on this house. I thought that maybe if I got the house, you'd go along with the idea. That's all it is, an idea, but I seem to be hanging onto it, ever since I traded my plane ticket for San José."

"Do you need an answer? Because I could answer you, if you want me to."

"Answer when you're ready to answer."

"Because I'd be very likely to agree with your idea."

He seemed surprised. "Really?"

"The way I feel about you, right now, right this very moment, actually, since I first saw you in Road Apples, there's a high probability I'd go to Portland to live with you."

"Without knowing everything there is to know about me."

"Yes, without clear knowledge, I already know you, Wyatt."

"I'm happy about that, Madeline. Because when I saw that house, I came to the realization that I can't picture my life without you in it."

I supposed that was as close as he'd get to "I love you," telling me he couldn't live without me.

"I'll think about it some more, Wyatt, if you don't mind."

"I know you will."

The time was getting on toward six o'clock, and we'd promised my mother we'd come for dinner. We showered separately to avoid that

94

inclination for the gymnastics of sex in a shower stall that I doubted both of us could easily fit into together. He showered first, and then me after, and when I came out, he was drying his long hair with a towel. He had the most marvelous hair, long and straight, so dark that you could barely see the few threads of gray that ran through it.

I went to him, and leaned into him, and we just hugged. The embrace was self-supporting, and when we parted, I knew I didn't want to be without him either. I've never felt this way about any man, Jake included.

I drove us in the Mercedes to my parents' house, which smelled of my mother's wonderful cooking. Wyatt met two of my sisters, Mallory and Margot, and Margot's female partner, Julie. As always, I could see the love between Julie and Margot. But I was concerned about Mallory, whose single state would probably be her lot, having killed a man with the excuse that it was done out of self-preservation. That had been Wyatt's defense as well, justifiable homicide.

I knew better. I could see the differences between Mallory and Wyatt—he having killed with great remorse and lingering sadness, and Mallory, to be rid of financial ruin disguised as self-defense.

I could see they all loved Wyatt. He was sincere and intelligent, and had this way of putting out a snare of a joke to catch his victim unaware. Mom and Dad were absolutely thrilled that I'd brought Wyatt into their home, and were deeply conscious of the aura of affection between Wyatt and me.

That night in my bed, we lay naked, whispering back and forth about my sisters and my parents, laughing and kissing. I knew I wanted this to last. I knew without any doubt that I would go to Portland to be with him. The concept of being with*out* him in this life, now that I'd taken great joy in getting to know Wyatt physically and emotionally, made the past seem quite empty in contrast. When he lifted me up, and sat me on top of him, I knew I wanted to always be in his arms.

But I also knew that he would be leaving on Monday afternoon for a flight he'd booked from San José to Tacoma. Riding him slowly during our lovemaking, a small part of my mind was mourning his departure. When I cried out, my pleasure was also my pain.

Sometime around dawn, I was awakened by the sound of whimpering. The crying was soft at first, plaintive and scary, and gained some volume before subsiding. I was frightened, as though visited by a spirit. I turned to Wyatt to shake him awake, but his eyes were already open, because he'd heard the sound too.

"What is that?" I asked softly, as the crying started up once more. "Is it a ghost?"

"I think it's your Rat again, Madeline."

We threw back the covers, and found our clothing, and stumbled through a dark house because we were too much in a hurry to turn on any lights at three a.m. Once I opened the front door, there was enough illumination from the streetlights to see the dog huddled on the porch.

Wyatt picked up Rat tenderly, and carried him to the kitchen table. I'd put down a blanket, and turned on the hanging lamp, and here Wyatt placed Rat gently so we could examine him. Rat was wearing his collar, and there was a section of rope clipped to the ring that had been severed entirely. The straight cut was too perfect to have been worked through by canine teeth. I unclipped the rope from the ring, and set it on the counter near the sink.

"He needs a vet," Wyatt concluded, after assessing Rat's condition. Rat's left hind leg appeared to be broken, poor Rat whimpering in obvious pain. "I think he was hit by a car, though it's amazing he made it here at all." He regarded me for a moment. "Rat loves you, that's why."

We laid Rat on the bench seat of my work truck, and drove him to a veterinary hospital with an on-call vet. They brought Rat to an examination room, and then told us it would cost around two thousand dollars to fix him.

"Do it," I stated without hesitation, signing the paper to acknowledge my financial responsibility, and handing over my credit card. I gave no thought to the cost, only to the suffering of Rat. If he could be saved, that was all that mattered, and I didn't give a shit about two grand, or ten grand, or whatever the hell it took to mend his wounds.

While we sat in the waiting room, Wyatt reminded me that somebody else legally owned Rat.

"I know. I almost forgot."

He touched my shoulder gently, knowing I wasn't in a good place right then.

"Don't you think you should call Jake?"

"I should," I said miserably.

I took out my cell, and called Jake's home number. He answered on the second ring, cursing at me when I told him who it was.

"Shit, Maddie, what the hell? It's only four-thirty!"

"You bastard," I said softly, "shut up and listen to me. I've got Rat. He showed up on my porch again."

"Rat?" He seemed surprised. "No, I tied him up."

I ignored his useless reasoning, and bit my lip because my first inclination was to accuse Jake of neglecting Rat. I calculated that if he had tied Rat up, and two days of four-legged travel were required for Rat to arrive on my porch, this suggested that Jake never checked his dog's food, water, or wellbeing. I concluded that Jake was at the least grossly negligent. With my emotions and hostility in check, I deliberately kept the conversation short.

"Rat was hit by a car," I informed. "His left rear leg is all fucked up." I told Jake where he could find Rat, and then, I hung up before he could say another word.

Wyatt was looking at me curiously.

"If you're wondering, I'm not interested in him," I promised, referring to Jake. "Since meeting you, I've asked myself many times why I ever thought I was interested."

"It's not that. I'm thinking you're very beautiful, and I have a deep respect for you, Madeline."

I wiped some tears away, and then smiled at him.

"He's coming here, so I'd like to go home. I'll tell the receptionist they can call me when Rat's operation is over."

I got up, and rang the bell, and a woman came to the window. I told her that the dog's owner, Jake Keene, would be there soon, and that my friend and I were going home. Would they please call me, and let me know how it went?

"You're not the owner?" I think she was worried about liability, so I set her straight.

"I'm the dog's aunt," I assured, "so use that in case anyone complains."

This time, Wyatt drove us back to the house. Once he got a little lost, but found his way again, all without the aid of GPS or an archaic map like the one Grandpa Feliz had left for me in the glove box of the Mercedes. Thinking of that map reminded me of the folded coffee cup from Road Apples, and I silently thanked the blessings of a higher power that had sought to put us together at such a humble place in time.

Maybe this was the transformational moment when I started to actually believe in fate, and doubt free will, perhaps a fallacy meant to soothe the human psyche. Was it possible that fate was the center of all truth, and the idea of free will kept us struggling vainly against the restraints of destiny?

We undressed, and slipped into bed. He stroked the hair from my face, and told me how he felt about me. Not once did he use the word "love," but I could feel his care in every word, and touch.

"I want to go to Portland," I revealed to him. "I want to be with you. I don't want to be without you. The thought of being without you seems…bleak."

"I should be the one putting on the brakes," he admitted. "I'm older and wiser, and a man, and we men always seem to run away from you women. Except that I find myself running toward you, Madeline."

He smiled that sweet grin from ear to ear.

We slept for a couple of hours, until almost eight a.m., and I hustled up breakfast. While we were drinking our coffee and sharing the newspaper sections like a couple of old farts, the doorbell rang.

I sighed, rising up from the table. "I can guess who that is."

As I supposed, the visitor was Jake, who I let in without a word. He followed me to the kitchen, and then halted in the doorway when he saw Wyatt, as though smacked across the face with a two-by-four.

"What the hell? Who the fuck is this, Maddie?"

"Sit down, and have some coffee," I instructed, and Jake, amazingly, complied. I handed him a cup of coffee in one of those dragon cups again, and he eyed Wyatt while he sipped the coffee, completely oblivious of the cup's implied theme.

Wyatt was smiling with benevolence in his gaze, while Jake's glare was daggers.

Finally, Jake worked up the nerve to ask, in a cautious voice, "Who the hell are you, if you don't mind me asking?"

Wyatt held out his right hand. "I'm Wyatt Earp McLain."

Jake at least had the courtesy to shake Wyatt's hand, but he was taken aback by Wyatt's name.

"Aw, what the fuck? Who the hell calls their kid Wyatt Earp, anyway?"

Wyatt shrugged. "My father did."

"That's bullshit," Jake insisted, which was as clear as calling Wyatt a liar.

Wyatt dug out his wallet, and handed Jake one of his business cards. The card was elegant, with the stylized head of a bear in Quinault traditional art.

Jake stared at that wonderful card, shaking his head slightly. "You're banging him, aren't you," he said to me, a statement rather than a question. He seemed miserable at the possibility that I might have moved on.

"That's really none of your business. Anyway, I wouldn't call it 'banging.' That's just not exactly descriptive of the process."

"Well, Madeline, if I may interject, sometimes it *is* 'banging,'" Wyatt offered, "but mostly I'd call it 'lovemaking.'" He grinned at me from across the table.

Jake seemed more repulsed than angry, and I was relieved. If by chance Jake displayed jealous intentions, I was more prone to believing Wyatt would have the upper hand in any ensuing physical altercation, though the thought of a fight over me was completely distasteful.

"Look." Jake took out his checkbook. "They told me you paid to fix up Rat. What was it, twenty-two hundred?"

"Twenty-two seventy-four point thirty-one," I clarified, to the penny.

"I'm going to reimburse you, Maddie," he proposed, while already writing out the check. "I've got to have a kennel built." He stared at me meaningfully, though I wasn't sure what he was getting at, because I'm so dense.

"May I suggest something?" Wyatt asked.

"What!" Jake was short with Wyatt, but it was understandable. Unforgivable, yes, but expected.

"No matter what contraption you build to imprison Rat, he'll always find his way back here, the first chance he has."

Jake had apparently considered that, which is why he said what he said next, turning his back toward Wyatt to deliberately exclude him.

"So, Maddie, how about I hire you to build a kennel, and then you come live with me?" He seemed dejected after he said it, as though he already knew my answer.

"I decline your offer," I said softly. "I don't want to build you a kennel, or live with you, or really even see you, Jake. The only reason I've seen you lately is because of Rat."

And then, it dawned on me.

99

I reached out and picked up the section of rope on the clip I'd removed from Rat's collar ring, and set in down in the middle of the table beneath the hanging lamp.

"You cut the rope," I said firmly.

"What? No!" Jake seemed rattled that I'd figured it out.

"You bastard, you cut the rope, and let him go, so he'd come here to find me."

At that moment, I wanted to strangle him. I resisted, because the fact of killing Jake would compromise my desired future with Wyatt, and that kept my hands at my sides.

Wyatt clucked his tongue. "My, my, what criminal impulses we have when we pretend to love someone."

"I only did it to make it look like Rat chewed through the rope," Jake said, in his defense, but I swept the rope end into my hand, so that he couldn't reclaim it. I wanted the rope end as leverage, proof that Jake didn't deserve to ever care for an animal again.

"You are a bastard!" I repeated with force. "And you're stupid, too. Rat would never be able to make such a clean cut with his teeth."

"I wanted to get to you, Maddie." Jake was now pleading, which disgusted me. "You wouldn't call me otherwise."

"I wonder what law enforcement would think?" Wyatt shrugged. "Or the ASPCA?"

"You know, fuck you, and the fucking horse you rode in on!" said Jake snidely, accentuating the syllables by poking the air with one finger.

"My people rode in canoes," Wyatt calmly corrected. "The fucking horse is only good for land travel, and ain't too effective in water. Great for hunting buffalo, but lousy if you're chasing whales."

"Christ," Jake muttered, rolling his eyes.

"I'm picking Rat up from the hospital when they're done," I advised Jake. "You're not fit to keep him. You're not fit for love, not for Rat, and certainly not for me."

He sat there for a few seconds, nodding and staring at the tabletop as though he felt like a complete idiot, and then he left, the check curled on the table beneath the light.

Wyatt gazed up at me, because I was still standing there, holding the rope end with its perfect cut.

"I'm proud of you, Madeline," he spoke. "I'm also really, *really* happy that fool doesn't call you Madeline."

"Madeline's for you," I promised, tears on my cheeks.

He opened his arms, and pulled me in. My heart felt good to sit there on his lap, cradled in his embrace.

That afternoon, I drove Wyatt to the San José Airport, and dropped him curbside at Departures. Parting was very difficult, but I knew I'd see him again soon.

He kissed me with those magnetic lips.

"You're magnificent, Madeline," he said admiringly. "You're a woman with grit."

"I just try my best."

Wyatt picked up his travel bag. He was smart—he put everything into a soft-sided gym bag, small enough to qualify as a carry-on. He had joked that not having checked baggage on a one-way flight really irked the TSA, and so he kept his tribal card handy.

I had to leave, because security was giving me the death stare from the sidewalk, but he leaned down into the opened passenger window anyway.

"Do you want to know something? I love you, Madeline." And then he was gone.

I swear, those words meant the world to me, as I watched him walk into the terminal, his beautiful hair whipping in the wind.

Later, after I'd picked up Rat from the vet, I waited for Wyatt's promised telephone call. He contacted me around seven o'clock, our predetermined time, and I knew he'd already been at the loft for a couple of hours. I didn't ask if he meant what he said. He spoke the obvious with those magic words. I just wasn't going to bring it up.

But the statement was the first thing he mentioned. He said, "You put a hex on me, Madeline. Some of the old people used to talk about witches when I was a kid on the rez, but I never believed, because I never met a witch, until I met you."

"Is that a good thing?" I asked, greatly concerned, as witches in the Filipino culture are considered evil beings. Some time later I discovered the same applied to the Quinault, though Wyatt seemed to embrace the latent magic I apparently possessed.

"For me, it is a beautiful thing," he vowed. "I'm under your spell."

We lingered in conversation. He told me he would send me the particulars on the house, and I promised to meet with a realtor to discuss my options. We knew our endeavor would take some effort, but discussing our plans allowed us to foresee the time when we would be together permanently.

When I went to sleep, with Rat dozing on my bed, wedged in with a couple of pillows, I was on cloud nine.

Chapter Ten

My next construction job, post Wyatt-weekend, was in the Niles district of Fremont, a tightly knit neighborhood with a small town feel. I'd secured a contract three months ago to perform a kitchen remodel in a mid-1950s home. Aside from installing custom-fitted cherry cabinetry, we'd be changing out chipped white phenolic countertops for granite, and a stainless steel sink for one of those fireclay farmhouse basins.

I again hired Juan Jiminéz, and a different relative, not Humberto, usually a dependable standby. Juan had recommended a young man by the name of Cucho, Juan's grandnephew.

I didn't like Cucho, but I couldn't put a finger on the why. He was a good worker, never complained, and always did as he was asked, so he earned every dollar and then some.

But he owned this sexual insolence that I didn't appreciate, a sort of a twisted need to subjugate women. I'd hear it in his words when I shuttled him and Juan to the job site each morning for five days straight. They'd see some babe during the commute, and Cucho would say, "*Visita a esa perra. El sexo debe ser bueno.*"

Translated to, "Look at that bitch. Her sex must be good."

Evidently, Juan hadn't gotten around to mentioning to Cucho that I knew conversational Spanish, along with a bit of street slang. Poor Juan was as befuddled as any granduncle would be when they suddenly realize that their young relative is probably headed to state prison for a life sentence, after a brief but violent career in sex crimes.

When I paid off Cucho, I was very careful to give him cash, not a check. This went against my business principles, because I'd never be able to write off labor if I didn't pay my hires with a check, as I did with Juan. But somehow, I felt uneasy about giving Cucho easy access to my home address, imprinted on the top of my business checks.

My ultimate mistake, which I suppose must have festered in Cucho for a long time, was to make a statement after I passed him the envelope.

I said to him in precise Spanish, *"Gracias por tu comentario. Usted es un hijo de puta. Las buenas mujeres no tendrán sexo con usted."*

"Thank you for your commentary. You are a bastard. Good women will not have sex with you."

Juan found it humorous, and laughed audibly, but Cucho glowered, and I knew I would never hire his scary ass ever again.

❖ ❖ ❖ ❖

Marked shortly after the completion of the Niles kitchen job, is when I started to feel ill. The sickness began with a deep weariness, which pretty much floored me when I came through the door that final evening from Fremont. I chalked it up to my weeklong dealing with Cucho, and the man's passive-aggressive hostility.

Whatever the cause, I must have slept for ten hours that night. I was fortunate that Rat was easy-going, and agreeable to lying around while he recuperated from the reset femur, and internal injuries. Both of us off our feet was a sight to see, and I told this to Wyatt in a letter I wrote:

You should see our pathetic selves just lying around the place. I haven't felt this tired in my life. I guess it's just from missing you.

This malaise went on for a week. Though I worked two more jobs with Juan—a granite countertop in a residential kitchen, and a fiberglass shower stall installation—I was never able to shake the ill feeling.

When it hit me hard, the nausea encompassed most of my waking hours, though primarily in the morning. I'd wake up feeling the way I did as a child on my father's fishing boat once he'd piloted out to the ocean swells. I even threw up two consecutive mornings before eating my breakfast, which really concerned me. I was puzzled that eating the meal shortly after vomiting did wonders in settling my stomach.

To add to the problem, I'd missed my period somewhere down the line. Not that I kept track of my cycle, which is an issue with most of us women and menses, sexually active or not. We should know how to answer the doctor when asked, "What is the first date of your last period?" Having slept with two men within a week of each other constituted a gigantic lapse in judgment. I *should* have kept track.

The nausea, and my vaguely missed period made me suspicious about the origin of this presumed illness, though I refused to put two and two together. The symptoms pointed to an obvious cause, but my denial must have been heavy to so casually ignore the source.

I was mystified to feel like crap, and have no accompanying fever. Even Wyatt was greatly concerned that I'd contracted some ominous bug.

"Maybe you got it at the beach," he mused, over the phone. "Sometimes raw sewage floats by, and everyone's swimming with those nasty critters, *E. coli* and *Shigella*."

I thought about the sea, which reminded me again of being on my father's fishing boat, and lying seasick on the deck with fish slime and blood, and I just about wanted to puke.

I finally made an appointment with my OB/Gyn after a couple weeks of feeling sick, and then this vomiting up before breakfast two days in a row. Why I arranged for a session with Dr. Greenberg, and not my regular GP, should have told me that I was trying not to look at the evidence, though I knew the truth in my heart.

At the doctor's office, the nurse requested the "first date of your last period." I asked her to repeat the question, as though I'd somehow come up with an answer, when all I was really doing was buying time. She seemed annoyed, but wrote in the file, "????." One question mark would have sufficed, so I knew the nurse was disgusted in me for her being so inspired to scratch in four.

When Dr. Greenberg read the file, I could tell that she tried really hard not to laugh at the "????" and cleared her throat mightily to maintain a professional demeanor.

"Can you even estimate the date for me, Maddie?" she coaxed, but all I could do was shake my head.

She examined me, did some prodding at my innards, performed one of those degrading pelvic exams, threw in a Pap smear, and then asked me to take a pee test for pregnancy.

"Really," I scoffed. "I'm hardly pregnant."

"Maddie, you don't know when you had your period last, and you told my associate that you've had sex with two different men recently."

"I used condoms!" I defended. "They've *always* worked for me. I don't even get started until the condom's on."

"Condoms have a failure rate of one to two percent. One to two percent is enough odds to result in a pregnancy."

"But I used condoms!" I insisted, unable to back away from that concept. I was beginning to feel rising dread.

"I'm testing you anyway, so please, humor me." She pulled out a simple drugstore wand from a drawer, and told me how to use it in the bathroom.

I sequestered myself in the clinic restroom, and peed on the wand as directed. Even before the allotted time had passed, up came a perfect +.

"Maddie, I could order another test in the lab to confirm it unequivocally, but it would be a waste of my time, and your money. You, my dear, are pregnant."

I leaned into my hand, terrified. What was I going to do?

The pregnancy itself didn't frighten me. I knew I was plenty capable of supporting myself with a child. This had vaguely crossed my mind, that if I never found a man, I did know that I'd want children someday, and might make arrangements to get pregnant, perhaps through sperm donation, though that seemed more of a clinical solution my lesbian sister Margot was prone to turn to.

As for my general contracting business, if the situation arose that I couldn't physically handle a construction job, I had the option to hire workers, and stand in as foreman. I could have been doing this all along under my state license and bond, but I enjoyed working the jobs. The sense of achievement I received when the work had been done timely and perfectly was priceless.

Money and my career weren't an issue at all. I was scared, because I didn't know who the father could be.

When you got down to the facts, my circumstances weren't as bad as Maury Povich's cattle call of hare-brained sex fiends. However, because a pregnancy could be attributed to one or the other of two known men, I almost qualified for reality-television hell.

If Wyatt fathered this pregnancy, I'd be in the clear, at least emotionally.

But if Jake were the culprit, that would mean I'd have that dirt bag in my life for a minimum of eighteen years, give or take the eventual graduations, wedding and grandchildren, if life allowed. The thought of having to deal with Jake Keene for literally decades repulsed me. My lack of control in my libido had put me into a serious quandary.

Still, I was puzzled about the condom issue, as I'd never experienced a breakage, or any other apparent failure of my chosen method of birth control.

When I left Dr. Greenberg's office, I carried a slip of paper that referred me to a pregnancy counselor in the medical plan. I had already decided that I didn't want to have a conversation with an outsider, so the referral would soon find its way into my kitchen trashcan. For now, it was stuck in my clenched fist.

"You may need someone to talk to," the doctor advised, recognizing true signs of emotional agony. "They can help you deal with not knowing, and with having a paternity test done once the baby is born. There are even tests that can be performed in the second trimester." She eyed me carefully. "Maddie, do you want to at all discuss terminating this pregnancy?"

I was appalled, because aborting my child was the last thing on my mind. I knew I owned my uterus, but I wanted this baby, whether Jake's or Wyatt's. The problem, in my mind, was breaking the truth to Wyatt.

So, I declined her offer, and said I was going to go through with keeping it. And then, I went home and telephoned Wyatt.

"You'll never guess why I felt so sick…"

When I gave the news to him, it felt grim of me, like telling somebody over the phone that a loved one has died.

But Wyatt proved incredibly happy, even when I reminded him that not one week before sleeping with him in Tacoma, I'd had sex with Jake. Extremely confident the child was his, Wyatt brushed doubt aside. I had my qualms, and only because I hadn't kept track of dates.

"What if it's Jake's, and not yours?" I asked pointblank. "What then?"

"I would love your child as my child, no matter who the father is," he promised. "Paternity isn't an issue for me."

"At least think about it. *Really* think about it."

"I am thinking about it, and do you know what I think? I think you should just write my name on the birth certificate. Don't bother yourself with that other person."

"I can't, not if it isn't yours. It wouldn't be fair to the child."

But he wouldn't budge. "I wouldn't care if Prince Charles sired this child. I'll still accept him or her as my own." That was the end of discussion, as far as he was concerned.

Even in my strange mood, I elected not to inform Wyatt that I wouldn't sleep with Prince Charles, even if I were paid millions of pounds sterling to do so. I was annoyed that he had picked somebody for an example that wasn't even remotely physically appealing to me.

"I should at least tell Jake," I suggested, and here, Wyatt put his foot down.

"It's none of that idiot's business, Madeline," he growled.

This was a side that Wyatt hadn't a chance to reveal earlier in our association, and a character quality Kate had warned me about when I visited her in Susanville. He didn't express anger exactly, just the force of a man who's decisive, and knew what he wanted. What he *didn't* want was Jake screwing up the deal by having the latitude to meddle in our lives.

I didn't contact Jake, though not due to Wyatt's wishes. I sincerely didn't want any interaction with Jake, so I used Wyatt's opinion as private leverage. Part of me accepted that Wyatt was content to be this baby's father, whether or not he'd actually contributed the genetic material for conception.

For me, however, the facts mattered greatly. I couldn't feel one hundred percent at peace in sharing this pregnancy with Wyatt if I didn't know for certain that he was the father. With the truth between us laid out as clear as day, I still felt as though I were hoodwinking him.

As though to clarify and reinforce his positive feelings about my pregnancy, he flew down from Tacoma on a Friday evening, and surprised me at the bungalow with a jar of whole dill pickles and a quart of half-melted vanilla ice cream. The cabbie must have been flabbergasted when Wyatt asked the man to wait outside of the grocery store so he could purchase these props.

"I hear pregnant women crave this crap, though I still can't figure out why," Wyatt joked, setting me up with a bowl of semi-liquefied ice cream, stuck through with a single pickle. The pickle stood up in the mess as a phallic innuendo. "Do you think Rat would like some?" he asked, of the dog, readily recovered, and wagging his tail at Wyatt's mention of his name.

"Try him," I suggested, though I knew I didn't want any. Just looking at the concoction made me want to throw up.

He placed the bowl on the floor, and Rat sniffed at it once, and then politely left the room.

"Whew, I don't blame Rat," said Wyatt. "I took a bite, and it's a revolting combination."

When I only groaned, Wyatt took pity on my emotional anguish, and physical discomfort. Instead of further jest, he picked me up off the couch, and carried me to the bedroom, where we lay together in our usual talking—or pre- and post-coital—position, face to face.

"Madeline," he said softly, stroking my cheek, "it's not all that terrible. Please don't be upset. I'm not upset at all, in fact, I'm excited that you're going to have a baby."

"I'm so happy you're here, but I hate it that I'm afraid to prove Jake as the father, or even having that as a possibility."

"I don't care." He repeated his opinion from the phone conversation.

"But I do, it matters to me!" I couldn't help the heartache, and I began to sob.

He embraced me while I wept. "You pregnant women. What a power," he teased, as though an emotional tirade of some sort was inherent to my gender.

I admit that I felt very comforted to be held in his arms. After a few minutes, I stopped crying, reminding myself that I shouldn't waste the short time we had to share our thoughts and affection, engaged in foolish tears.

"Let me explain something to you," he started in, once he sensed that I was rational.

"All right, I'm listening. I promise."

"I spent my adulthood adrift, not always in the same town, but I did eventually make a secure life for myself. It wasn't the reservation. It was a new way of living, and of thinking, but I made it work. Sometimes it was even scary for me, but for the most part, I was happy. I'd meet women every now and then, though there was nobody I could hold close, no one who was dear." He paused for effect. "Nobody I loved."

I nodded. What he described was a lot like my life, a plethora of career opportunities, but very few chances for true love, never mind finding a man who was dedicated and faithful.

"And then I happened to meet you," said Wyatt, "in the rain, in the dark, busting chops with your fists, while your dog here practically mauled a man to death. Well, at the time, you thought he was Jake's dog, but I think Rat was yours in his heart all along, Madeline."

That comment made me smile.

"And I wanted you, Madeline, when I saw you with your fists raised against danger, I wanted you. I told myself, 'Here's a woman who knows her own life.' I waited patiently inside that coffee house, hoping you'd talk to me, because I had a lot to say to you. I just didn't know how to start saying it. Once you decided to talk to me, I coerced you into eating with me, and being with me. I wanted you to come home with me. You don't know it, but I had a hard-on almost the whole time we were sitting in that restaurant booth, which is pretty damn good for a man over fifty. Things got really complicated when I realized that we shared these few common facts, and then I knew for sure that I would never be able to get enough of you. And then I wanted you even more."

I touched his face tenderly. "You're so beautiful," I marveled. "You're such a wonderful person."

"No, I'm a hopelessly wretched pervert," he disputed. "I saw you, and at first, all I wanted to do was fuck you. Isn't that creepy? I'm standing in the rain, and all I could think of was getting you into bed. Yes, Madeline, I wanted you *in* my bed, *in* my arms, even if it meant it'd be just for that one night. Except, that you went and changed the game, you kissed my scars, so then I wanted you even more. You put your lips on those hideous scars, and I fell in love with you."

"Wyatt, your scars aren't hideous. I love your scars. I love everything about you."

"We'll see if you still do after I say what I have to say. Because I did something very bad that night, Madeline, I tricked you, I deceived you."

"I didn't do anything I didn't want to do, Wyatt."

"No, it's not that part of it. I know you freely went up the stairs with me. You've done everything willingly, everything you know about."

"What do you mean?"

"I did something to you, and you have no idea, something very serious, and now it affects the outcome of your entire life. What I did to you has filled your calendar for the next eighteen years."

"What are you talking about?"

"That night in the loft, after we first had sex, and then we slept. I woke up, I turned to you, but you were sleeping. You were so delicious, that I entered you anyway, Madeline. You were still asleep, but I put my cock inside of you, just a little bit."

"Oh. I see."

"I'm sorry, I am, it's like a betrayal, I know. I just wanted to feel how you felt, skin to skin."

"But, Wyatt—"

110

"That's all it took, Madeline, I'm sure there was semen. But you felt so good."

"Did you…did you come again?"

"No." He shook his head. He appeared so ashamed, and I couldn't help feeling bad for him. "Just a little bit, I put myself inside of you, while you were sleeping. And then I pulled it out." He buried his face in one hand. "That's why I can speak so confidently about being the father. But I told you the truth, even if I hadn't done this terrible thing to you, this thing that sealed it, I'd still want to be the father anyway, Madeline."

I gently removed his hand from his eyes.

"Is that all you have to tell me?"

He seemed agonized. "Isn't that enough? I royally screwed up. Well, not about making a baby, but because you were asleep."

"There's nothing wrong with it, Wyatt. You didn't do anything wrong."

"There's *everything* wrong with it, Madeline. I betrayed you by doing that, because you were sleeping, and there wasn't any consent. I knew it was wrong when I did it. And then I wrote to you, like a crazy stalker."

"It's okay, really." His admission meant that Jake wasn't the father. My relief was enormous, as was my joy.

"I did that to you while you were asleep," he went on, "and then I sent you that letter. I couldn't leave you alone."

"But I reciprocated. You gave me an out, Wyatt, and I wrote to you anyway. If you're trying to assign guilt, doesn't that prove to you that I'm just as guilty?"

"One would think so, right? But I started it."

"You didn't do anything wrong, Wyatt."

"I came here out of the blue to see you. I wanted to be with you *so* much, Madeline!"

I had to put a halt to his miserable guilt, and useless rambling that was going in circles. I didn't need his confession, as I quite honestly felt exactly the same way that he did.

"Are you a stalker, Wyatt? Because I'm pretty sure your sister thinks highly of you."

"I admit—I've never been this strangely obsessed with any woman. You're all I think about."

"And I think about you all the time too."

"It's got to be wrong to be doing all this thinking about each other."

"I believe that two people who are in love are supposed to think about each other all the time."

"It just makes me into some crafty stalker type, Madeline."

"Then I'm one, too." I placed my hands on his shoulders. "Look, Wyatt, have you ever been convicted of a crime? Or investigated for acting like a pervert?" That final question nearly made me laugh, except for Wyatt's solemn expression.

"No, I've never even gotten a parking ticket."

I looked into his eyes, past his torment, and still saw the man who came out of Road Apples that night in the rain to try to help me.

"We have a problem, don't we, Wyatt?"

"Yes, it's a problem, all right."

"We want so much to be together. First it was *my* issue about not knowing who the father is, and now it's *your* guilt for a minor slip of the dick."

"But you were sleeping. It makes it all wrong."

"Wyatt, listen to me. I was in your bed, and I was naked. I can't blame you for doing what you did. You're a man. You're already prone to making choices like that by default. And anyway, as my father liked to say to his daughters as we were growing up, 'Don't have sex unless you expect to get pregnant.'"

"Your father actually said that to you?"

"Of course. Any good father would."

He seemed to be feeling better, now that he'd admitted his deliberate act.

"I do have to say, you're delightful, Madeline. If I hadn't known it was so wrong, I would've kept going. But I think the moment I put it in, the damage was done."

"I'd like to have a baby before I get too old," I assured. "Twenty-five is a good age, don't you think?"

"Well, fifty-two is really pushing the envelope. I'll be over seventy by the time this child finally is of an age to give us some privacy."

"It's nature, Wyatt. Sometimes you just can't fight nature."

And then, I thought about Juan's relative, Cucho, and shivered involuntarily. Cucho was a child of nature, and a definitive threat to womankind. Conversely, sweet Wyatt was devastated because he'd stuck his naked penis inside of me while I was sleeping. I was only too glad that he did.

112

"I always wanted what my parents have, their 'togetherness,'" I told him, "but it's difficult to find love like that. I feel lucky that I found it with you, when I wasn't even looking."

"That's what I meant about kismet." This time, I didn't laugh at the word.

"I still think you're beautiful," I teased, and he snorted.

"At least this means a temporary reprieve from the condom brigade. No more investing in Brazilian latex plantations."

In the dim of the bedroom, his eyes were full of mischief, and I was inspired.

"Make love to me," I whispered, and he drew me in.

I wanted him, I needed him, and I loved him. These dire feelings were wrapped up in the knowledge that he'd fathered this child inside of me, a burgeoning seed, growing in my basement darkness for the next thirty-four weeks.

I couldn't wait to tell Dr. Greenberg that the condoms *hadn't* failed.

Chapter Eleven

In my mind, I can still see Wyatt standing curbside when I dropped him at the San José Airport, smiling at me. I know he despised flying, and mostly because of the security checkpoint, and the uneducated TSA employees who, in their ignorance, sometimes viewed Wyatt as a hulking, sleeper-terrorist, until he showed them proof of his QIN tribal membership.

I was feeling much better now, and I know it had everything to do with the fact that I had theoretical evidence that this child belonged to Wyatt. Had it been Jake's, I would have been just as in love with the thought of bearing offspring, but somehow, knowing Wyatt fathered this miracle, made it all the more real to me.

A couple of days following Wyatt's flight back to Tacoma, I went to visit a realtor so I could make a decision about my house.

Sherry Flynn was a friend of the Wenstads, the family who sold me the Bassett Street bungalow after Grandpa Gus died inside the master bedroom. Sherry had assisted with the paperwork, even though she never earned a dime from her efforts. I knew she either must love her work, adore the Wenstads, or she was putting her ducks in a row for future business.

When we sat down and talked about what to do with my property, I knew it was likely all of the above. She seemed to enjoy the process, and her advice was priceless. After asking me specific financial questions about the property, and then tapping away on a calculator, she told me I didn't have to sell. I could simply rent the house, and haul in more than enough to cover the monthly mortgage, property tax and insurance, and still pay her monthly fee for property management. She calculated that after all the property-related bills were paid each month, I would actually earn a profit of three hundred fifty-seven dollars to throw into a separate account for income taxes.

"I know you love the house, Maddie," she affirmed, remembering how I'd felt about the place even when it looked like hell. "I think you should keep it. You owe less than one-hundred-fifty thousand, and rental rates are stable in Santa Clara County."

"I could sell it, and make a profit," I said, to put it out there. The thought of ridding myself of the house seemed more painful than renting it to potential house-wreckers.

"You could, but your margin might be a bit thin in this economy. You're better off keeping it, and having it pay its own way. If you must sell, you should at least wait until property values improve. You may even decide someday to return to the South Bay, and if you keep it, you'll have a place to live. Where did you say you're planning on moving to?"

"Portland, Oregon." I felt thrilled when I said it, especially after seeing photos of the house Wyatt wanted us to live in together. The Victorian stood in the Hawthorne neighborhood, and had been built in 1892, with wonderful oak floors and twelve-foot ceilings on the main floor. There was even a shop out back that had been added in the 1970s, where Wyatt could install a new studio.

"Ooh, that's a wonderful city!" she exclaimed. "You'll love it there. I have a brother who lives in Tigard, and he just touts Oregon all the time."

I decided not to ask why Sherry hadn't gone to live there herself, as she was practically an ad for emigration. Instead, I asked her to look up the property on the MLS database for the Portland area, and let me know her thoughts.

She entered the number, and then frowned.

"I'm sorry, Maddie, maybe I entered the number incorrectly. Can you give me the MLS once more?"

I quoted it again, and she tapped it in, but couldn't find the property in the active listings.

"Here, just let me," she said, and I could tell by the sound of her voice that news wasn't good. "Is this the one?" she asked, turning the screen around so I could view the listing.

"Yes, that's it." I felt excitement, until I realized that it was posted as pending. "Does that mean what I think it means?"

"It means that someone's already signed an offer to buy the property, Maddie. It's no longer available for sale."

115

"Oh." I sat back in the chair, deeply disappointed. "Oh, well." I tried to sound nonchalant, but Sherry knew how much I'd wanted the house just by the slouch of my shoulders.

"I'm so sorry, Maddie." She nodded for a moment, and then handed me a packet of paperwork. "Look, sometimes deals can fall through. The buyer can't get financing, or the seller won't agree to certain stipulations. Why don't you take this with you anyway, just in case the buyer's offer falls through, or you find another property."

"What's this?"

"It's the brochure and contract for property management. We can find a renter for your house when you're ready. We even run all the background and credit checks."

I rose to my feet, my body feeling heavy, not just from the pregnancy, which seemed to suggest a lead weight in my midsection, but from the knowledge that Wyatt and I had lost this lovely old house, with its perfect set-up for his art studio. I had actually looked forward to working on her. She didn't need many changes, just some paint, double-paned windows, and refinished floors. Wyatt and I had even picked a place to install a wood stove, based upon her photographs on the real estate listing.

Suddenly, I realized that by referring to the house as "her" and "she," even in my silent musing, I had taken a reach to anthropomorphize a wooden building, just as Kevin had. I had fallen in love, a contractor's curse.

I drove home, wondering just how I was going to tell Wyatt.

Once inside the house, with Rat ecstatic to see me, I had to convince myself that the wish of the house in Portland was only a dream. Pouring out Rat's dinner in the laundry room, I sat at the kitchen table to take a moment for meditation, and that's when my cell phone rang in my shirt pocket.

The number was Wyatt's. *Here goes nothing.*

"Hello, Wyatt."

"Madeline, are you sitting down?"

"Hah. Funny you'd ask, because I certainly am."

He paused, and I know he heard the tone of my voice.

"Is everything all right?" he asked." You sound sad." I heard him chuckle. "Do you need me to come down there right now, and get naked with you?"

That made me smile. "Yes, but no. Don't fly down. It's not all that bad." I told him about the Portland house being in escrow.

"Yes," he agreed, "I knew about that."

"When did you find out?"

"This morning." He cleared his throat. "Madeline, I called you to let you know that I've been doing stuff behind your back again—like the penis thing. Except that you can't get any more pregnant than you are, now, can you?"

I had a bizarre urge to laugh, but wisely abstained. "What did you do?"

"I, uh, bought the house."

I sucked in air, held it and then let it all out.

"Are you there, Madeline?" I know he'd heard the breathing exercise.

"Yes, I'm here. What do you mean, you bought the house?"

"Well, look, somebody else wanted it too. The owner's realtor got an offer, and the seller was going to sign it. I didn't want to lose the house. I know we could always find another, but this one is special, and I thought you'd be as disappointed as I'd feel if I lost it. So, I transferred a bunch of money into escrow this morning, and signed the paperwork."

"Where did you get a loan so quickly? Doesn't that take some time?"

I recalled the hoops I'd had to jump through to get a mortgage approval for the Bassett Street house, a two-week hell of submitting tax forms and authorizing credit reports.

"I didn't get a loan, Madeline, I have, well, all right, brace yourself. I have lots of money in the bank." He then explained how he came by it. "Do you remember when I told you that there was a nurse in California who took babies from Native women?"

"I'll never forget that story."

"About ten years ago, it came to light that not only was there a nurse involved, but also a doctor, and someone in the office of Social Services in San Joaquin County. They didn't just limit their kidnapping to Kate. They also took many others. I think the total count was twenty-three. Some of the people were from tribes outside of California, like Kate, but most of them were from California tribes whose members used the County hospital to give birth, instead of a rural doctor or midwife."

"How does that figure into money?"

117

"My Aunt Doreen's married to an attorney, Ben Barrow, a Quileute from La Push. He's worked for countless Native causes in Washington State. When he found out about Kate, and how she was taken, he filed a lawsuit not only on her behalf, but mine, as well as the Quinault Indian Nation of Washington State. He named as defendants the State of California, the County of San Joaquin, the nurse, the doctor and the Social Services Agency, and the social worker. He wanted to include the foster parents who'd accepted Kate, but they were killed in the late seventies. Apparently Kate's foster father was a Sheriff's deputy who worked for San Joaquin County."

"Talk about being in cahoots," I marveled.

"I know. It went pretty deep. And the defendants' attorneys flung a lot of ridiculous shit at the fan, but in the end, they couldn't hide from the facts. Think of it as an American citizen stealing children who are citizens of another country, because that's what it amounted to. The QIN is federally recognized. It's a sovereign body, and the American citizens who stole Kate were kidnappers. That's the worst kind of terrorism, if you ask me, that hasn't been done for decades, when children used to be stolen from Indian families, and forcibly relocated to government schools for assimilation. That's why we can't speak our Quinault language in its fluent form."

"What happened with the trial?"

"There never was a trial, because the defendants' attorneys knew their clients would have ultimately lost. Instead, counsel put heads together, and came up with a figure. There was a settlement made to me and to Kate, and even a substantial amount paid to the tribe, because they'd been cheated out of a sovereign daughter."

"Is that what put you through school?"

"Oh, no, that was well after I got my master's. I qualified for scholarships and grants. I'm a damn genius, Madeline, with unbelievable test scores and limitless talent. But I did use some of the settlement money for the down payment on the loft, and some to start my business, and to get Aunt Doreen started with hers. The rest I left in the bank, because I really didn't need it. Not until I met you."

"I don't have any need for money," I assured. "I make a good living."

"I have a need for money, if it means I can have this life with you, if it means buying a house that's on the halfway point between Santa Clara and Tacoma. Did I surprise you?"

"You surprise me all the time, Wyatt, every day. It's good surprise, though, so don't worry."

"Do you know what this means, Madeline? It means the deal is done, and we can go there anytime. The world is now our oyster."

We talked some more, mostly about missing each other. He asked when I had time off, and I gave him a date a week away. We planned on meeting in Portland to check out the house together. When our conversation was over, the future felt very full, with the echo of his voice in my head.

Chapter Twelve

I was working on a bathroom remodel in Gilroy, when I realized I would soon have to hire more than one helper at any given job site, especially if the task involved heavy lifting.

On this job were just Juan Jiminéz and I. He finally thought to mention that his cousin, Humberto, had temporarily moved to Santa Fe to help take care of an ailing mother. Humberto had been born in New Mexico, and was a U.S. citizen, despite his preference for Spanish, which so often causes a knee jerk reaction in Yankees in regard to immigration. I've felt that same hostility, being half Filipino, one-eighth Sioux Indian, and though part-Anglo and American born, being referred to angrily as a "wetback." I knew that Juan was also an American, having been born in Nogales, Arizona. The fact that he spoke Spanish more often than English only reflected the depth of his immersion into the Mexican-American community of Santa Clara.

When I drove to the parking lot of the home improvement store to pick up Juan, he was standing in a group of men, and included his grandnephew, Cucho.

That bastard was perched on a concrete parking stop, leering at me. The moment he saw that I'd hired up his granduncle, he ran toward the truck, as though I would be willing to forget what a prick he was about women. Cucho was prepared to wheedle a chance at being included, but Rat had other ideas, and got all up into Cucho's face with his teeth bared and glistening with threat of damage.

Once Juan got into the truck, with Rat's gentle blessing, we drove south toward Gilroy, and I finally asked the question: *"¿Por qué es él su pariente?"* Why is he your relative?

"No sé, Señora Benités." I do not know.

I couldn't fathom it either. Rat obviously loved Juan, whom he'd only just met, but he hated Cucho without so much as a sniff in the air of

120

the man's scent. In retrospect, I think it's entirely possible that Rat picked up on something emanating from me, a hint of fear or hostility.

Juan and I were doing fine with the demolition, but when we had to transport the new tub enclosure into the revamped space that I realized my ability to lift heavy objects wasn't long for the world. There was no way I would compromise this pregnancy, and so I started planning in my head for help at the next few contract jobs that might involve lifting items heavier than thirty pounds.

Juan noticed my discomfort, and the manner in which I gingerly protected my abdomen, even though I wouldn't show for a few months, and he nodded knowingly.

"*Señora, usted está embarazado.*" You're pregnant.

"*¿Qué?*" In my most obnoxious voice, I feigned an inability to comprehend his words, but Juan only laughed, and waved his hand, because he knew I understood, just as much as he knew I was indeed pregnant.

I was fortunate Juan believed I was married. He referred to me as *Señora*, and I could only guess how much respect he would lose in me, had he known I'd conceived out of wedlock. That's a peculiarity of being a woman who hires men, especially men who are of a religious inclination, such as Juan, a devout Catholic. As a man, I could have shared a round of beer, or joked with swear words, but as a woman, my professional integrity was of prime importance, as was my personal moral compass. Being female meant that I had to adhere to a stricter image, and toe the line.

When this job was finished, and I drove him to his house, a small cottage near the home supply store, I asked him if he knew any other relatives aside from Cucho whom he would recommend I hire the next time around, perhaps a more trustworthy man, a man who didn't hate women.

He eyed me carefully, knowing full well his grandnephew was bad news.

"*Mi sobrino no es bueno con las mujeres,*" he said with a sigh, admitting that Cucho was not favorable in his attitude toward women.

"*Gracias,*" I said, glad that he understood.

A couple of days later, I had a tile job on a kitchen floor in Los Gatos, which I was able to handle without a second helper. Concrete backboard is heavy, but not unmanageable, and doesn't exceed the maximum weight rating for pregnant women. Conversely, wallowing around on kneepads kind of cramped my style knowing that little ball of tissue was growing and expanding. But I got the job done, the tile perfectly aligned, and received high praise from the couple, and their intent to refer me to anyone who needed work done in their home.

This secured me three jobs, the first two tiling showers, and the last installing a vintage stained glass window in an 1890 Italianate home. Although the window wasn't heavy, standing on my sturdy Little Giant ladder made me realize that pregnancy went hand in hand with magnifying a predisposition for acrophobia. Knowing the cause of my wavering while standing only halfway up that ladder, I was able to overcome the sensation with time-tested pragmatism.

❖ ❖ ❖ ❖

The jobs were completed, and I was more than ready for Portland. I was planning to drive rather than fly, and meet Wyatt at PDX in my work truck. We reasoned that if by chance we found anything we wanted for the house, we could conveniently stow it in the back of the truck, and simply haul it home. I even thought ahead, and loaded my endless assortment of tools, drill kit and saws, and both of my ladders.

He telephoned me the evening before I departed. I'd been packing clothes, and Rat's food, when my cell phone rang.

"Well, hello, Madeline," he said in that smiling voice. "What are you doing?"

"I'm packing. Remember? I'm driving up to Portland early tomorrow morning, and then I'm picking you up at the airport."

"Too bad you don't want to fly." I could tell he was concerned about the long drive, so I reminded him about my responsibility to Rat.

"Dogs can fly," he claimed, and then realized he might as well have said that pigs can fly. "In a travel crate," he clarified. "Though I think Rat wouldn't like being separated from you."

"That's okay. I'd rather not give the TSA a chance to roast our little fetus in an imaging machine."

"I'll say. I've been zapped so many times you're lucky you even got pregnant. My poor testicles."

We joked around, and then said our goodbyes. I had a good night's sleep, and was on the road by two a.m., in plenty of time to beat the dawn, so I'd be facing north, rather than into the blazing sun.

The drive was lengthy, but rather than becoming tired I felt a slow rise of excitement as the Interstate drew me closer to Portland. My truck is a three-quarter ton, and has miserable gas mileage, so I stopped for gas more often than I had in the Mercedes. There were pauses for coffee, which Dr. Greenberg had said I could still drink in moderation, and stops to pee and relieve poor Rat's need to post on the canine message board at rest areas. The trip went without glitches, and when I arrived in Portland at around two p.m., with Wyatt's flight due to arrive at two-fifty, I was filled with relief.

From Interstate 5 south of Tualatin, I merged onto 205, and drove all the way north, to the Columbia River. Parking the truck on N.E. Marine Drive, I took Rat for a walk. The river was slow moving and wide, with little sport boats riding up and down the current. The strangers I passed on the walking trail were friendly and upbeat. Some smiled at me and Rat, and others said "hello." I understood Wyatt's appreciation for Portland, and by the time, I returned to the truck, I'd been smitten, too.

Going into PDX, I drove through Arrivals three times, before I saw Wyatt standing at the curb, gym bag over one shoulder, and a large carton at his side. There's nothing equal to the emotional moment of suddenly spotting a loved one you haven't seen for a while. When I pulled to the curb, and opened the door, I belted out, "How much!"

And he replied, "Lady, for you, the sex is free."

I had to cover my mouth and my amusement with one hand. He pulled my hand away, so we could kiss, and then we were off to our adventure.

"What's in the box?" I asked.

"It's a surprise."

"I hope it's not eggs." I noted the carton's crushed corners, probably manhandled in transit, but all he would do was grin secretively.

"Let's just say it's not a literal food item, but in real life, it's known as a form of sustenance."

His riddle was maddening, and I guessed all manner of food, like waffles and broccoli, but he only laughed at me.

"You have to think outside the box, Madeline."

He directed me to the house, a twenty-minute drive from the airport to the Hawthorne neighborhood. As I cruised down the street, and even before I saw the house, I fell in love with the trees that lined the sidewalks. You only see that in movies, trees engendering a neighborhood's small town atmosphere. Like an authentic woman, I started to daydream about walking beneath those shadowing trees with Wyatt and Rat, and an as-yet unsexed and unnamed baby in a stroller.

"There's the house," he announced, pointing up at a Victorian, the exterior painted shades of red, brown, green and tan.

I pulled into a short driveway, which only just accommodated my long bed truck without overhanging the sidewalk. We let Rat out, and the dog ran up the steps as though he'd been to the place countless times. Wyatt produced a shining key, and let us in through the front door.

My first thought was that, although the exterior had already been restored, the inside needed work, and I happily looked forward to it. The downstairs floors were oak hardwood, and would require sanding and refinishing. The electrical had been updated, thankfully, as I'm a reluctant electrician. But the walls would have to be painted, and the baseboard had been brutalized at exodus by the previous owners' removal of clunky furniture.

The next move was asking Wyatt to reveal the contents of the mystery box. When he brought it into the house, and set it near the front door, the box had seemed heavy, even in his strong arms.

"Maybe I should keep you in suspense," he proposed, all the while ripping through the packing tape with the edge of the house key. Opening the box revealed a wealth of Styrofoam peanuts, into which he buried his hands. He withdrew out a beautiful metal sculpture of a salmon wrapped in foam sheeting, the peanuts falling away like snow. He laid the sculpture carefully atop the packing material, and stripped away some of the sheeting.

"Oh," I breathed, touching the sculpture lightly with my fingertips. The metal piece was remarkable, and very realistic, and seemed to shimmer with rainbow colors in the light through the windows. "When did you make this?"

"A couple of weeks ago. I wanted to create something we could hang in the house, something with a special meaning. You know, the house *is* on Salmon Street."

I told him about fishing on my father's offshore boat, and laying seasick amidst the bodies of Chinook salmon, the deck slippery with blood while my mother dressed out the catch.

"When they were running, they'd hit the lures hard," I reminisced. "Dad would try to get us to reel them in ourselves, but we were too busy chumming over the gunnels. That's something I never really got over, being seasick."

"I'll have to take you up a river sometime, or out on Lake Quinault. You won't get sick like you do on the ocean."

"Have you ever been seasick?"

"The sea's in my blood, Madeline, but yes, there are times when it was really bad. It just takes some getting used to."

Wyatt decided we wouldn't be able to sleep in the house, not until we bought a bed. The three bedrooms on the second floor had wall-to-wall carpeting in good condition, and were functional, but the walls needed to be painted, and were full of tack holes.

I carried a tape measure, and Wyatt a notebook and pen, and we collected all sorts of calculations of rooms and windows and closet spaces. I determined how much paint and caulking was required. I then got ahead of myself, and knew I'd need to rent a bobtail truck, and pull something, either the pickup or the Mercedes; and what the heck was I going to do about my motorcycle?

I just stood there, the wheels of my thoughts turning fruitlessly. Wyatt noted my racing mind, and put his arm around me.

"Let's fix this room first," he suggested.

We stood inside the largest of the bedrooms on the second floor. The south-facing room contained two double-hung windows, and had its own closet, spacious enough to qualify as a walk-in for me, though Wyatt had to duck his head.

"Why this room first?" I asked.

"So we can have sex in it, Madeline. I think it's big enough for a king-sized bed."

I nodded, as my double bed in Santa Clara had proved too tight for Wyatt's six-foot four-inch frame. I didn't mind being wedged in so closely at night, but I knew that he liked to stretch out.

There was no master bath, though the second floor bathroom was large, with both a claw foot tub and stall shower in one corner, opposite the commode.

"I found somebody to rent the loft," he mentioned, as I inspected the windows.

I was still taking notes, having acquired the notebook and mechanical pencil from Wyatt. I had already decided to save the old wood-frame sash windows, and use them to build a greenhouse in the backyard.

"That was quick."

"The University has a student union, and they found some people who were willing to pay the price I'm asking." He nodded his chin. "What about you?"

I'd completed the paperwork, and passed it along to Sherry Flynn the day after our meeting. I wanted the bungalow paying its way as soon as possible.

"I know the realtor is looking. She's already had a few interested parties."

Wyatt studied me closely. "You love your house, don't you?"

"Of course I do, but it's just a house. It's not like the realtor's going to lease it out to spray paint taggers, or to some jerks with sledge-hammers." I closed the notebook, ready to work. "Let's go."

"Where are we going?"

"A home supply store. I want to change out these windows today, and prep the room to be painted."

He gave me an interested stare. "Are you nesting?"

I grinned. "A contractor is always nesting, even when you're doing a job in someone else's house."

"This isn't someone else's house. This is going to be your home, Madeline."

"You get my meaning, though, right?"

"Well, sure."

He pulled out a smart phone, and, though ponderously slow about it, he looked up the closest home supply store, including the directions. I remarked that I was impressed with his openness to new gadgets, and he grinned at my sarcasm.

In no time at all, we were off in the truck, and soon arrived in the giant box store's parking lot, with its complement of day laborers standing about. The afternoon was cool and partly cloudy, and we felt safe about leaving Rat on guard in the cab with the windows slightly opened.

I'd handed Wyatt the notebook, and he accompanied me while I pushed the flatbed cart. Accustomed to the practical arrangement of most home supply stores, I easily found what we needed, the two double-hung windows that approximated the required size. You can buy them off the shelf as long as the dimensions are equal-to or slightly smaller, and then shim the frame to fit the windows. I chose two-by-four-by-eights, a couple packages of wood shims, some trim, and drywall paste, a box of long wood screws, crown molding, and baseboard. I added mastic for the tack holes, and tubes of caulking for my gun, plus two gallons of latex primer, and painting accessories. We

126

even found a random side aisle dedicated to pet supplies, and chose a cushy new dog bed for Rat and a harness.

We spent ten minutes in front of the dazzling array of paint card samples, trying to decide on a color for our shared bedroom. Wyatt liked blue, and I was partial to earth tones, so he suggested that we should browse through colors that fell outside of our normal tendencies. In the end, we agreed upon a yellow-tinged white for the ceiling, and pale violet for the walls. I was intrigued with the violet because Wyatt said it reminded him of lingerie.

"Can we find *you* some panties in that shade, Madeline?"

I laughed loudly, though unfortunately, the clerk behind the paint counter overheard why Wyatt liked Enchanted Lavender so much.

When everything was totaled at the register, I whipped out my business credit card, and swiped it through the reader. Wyatt was taken aback, until I explained that I intended to use the trip for a tax deduction. He seemed to have a desire to take care of me, which I surely wanted to indulge, unless it meant I could limit my payout to the IRS with allowable deductions. Working on Wyatt's house meant that I might be able to legitimately call it a job.

Loading the truck together, he seemed concerned that the project I intended to undertake wouldn't be finished for days, but I assured him I could complete it before nightfall. And back at the house, I proved it.

He served as a competent assistant. He did everything I asked, including finding the correct tools, and staying far away from the pneumatic nail gun. I surprised him by not only changing out the windows in less than an hour, and installing trim inside and outside (and climbing up my extension ladder), but filling in all the tack holes, measuring and cutting the crown molding and baseboard to fit, then installing, and covering the carpet with plastic in preparation of sanding down the putty once it dried. Just before the last ray of sunlight disappeared behind the graceful neighborhood of old homes, I sanded the puttied walls, cleaned up the dust with my shop vacuum, and rolled primer on the walls and ceiling, while Wyatt used a brush to fill in the corners and molding where the roller couldn't fit.

By that time, we were starving, but we fed Rat first, and then let him out to use the yard. While we waited, Wyatt used his phone to find a nearby Chinese restaurant. Every now and then he'd just look at me, so I asked what was on his mind.

"I've never seen anyone work like that before."

"Like what?" I asked, as we drove to the restaurant, Rat lolling out the window with the tip of his nose, and sniffing the air.

"Like a well-oiled machine."

"Come on, really? Never?"

"Well, okay, fishing. I've seen people fishing as though it were the easiest thing in the world. But I've never seen anyone pry out a window, and then put a different one back in so it fits like a puzzle piece."

"That's what the trim is for, to hide the defects, and all the shims and caulking. It makes it look so pretty and perfect."

I found parking on a side street, and despite the length of the truck I managed to parallel-park the rig. We locked Rat in the cab once more, while Wyatt spoke his admiration of my parking skills.

"I've seen people flub up parking a Volkswagen Beetle, and you just slid that boat right in. Damn, woman, you're great!"

"Anyone can park anything, with enough practice."

"You know, I've worked with people on things," he said vaguely, as we walked, hand in hand. The smell of food in the air was making my stomach grumble. "But it always seems to take forever to change a light bulb in a communal setting."

"I replaced all the windows, plus a sliding glass door, in my parents' house in two days, with one helper." I shrugged. "I guess it looks difficult, if you've never done it, right?"

"Right." There was something in his eyes I'd never seen before. I didn't know if it was admiration or disbelief.

We both ate as though we were famished, so there was nothing to take with us at the end of dinner. Wyatt wasn't too conversational, unlike his normal self, which is usually buoyant, the inveterate jokester. I didn't mention his somber mood, though I wasn't oblivious to the change. I had a feeling that actually seeing me doing my business had triggered something in him he'd have to work out.

We knew we wouldn't be able to sleep at the house, so we found a motel that allowed us to keep Rat in the room. The motel was closer to downtown Portland, and I think we both felt cagey with the sound of traffic, and tall buildings of the skyline, but we were together.

After we showered, we remained naked and lay in bed, facing each other. He still seemed to be deep in thought, and I mentioned this to him.

"You're right, I am preoccupied," he said miserably.

"What is it?"

"Well, after seeing you work so quickly, you're going to be done with the house in no time flat. And then what?"

"What do you mean?"

"Are you planning to stay, or is this just a job to you?"

His fears were understandable yet preposterous, and I started wondering if I'd somehow misinterpreted this renovation project. I knew using my credit card that day for the purchase might have fazed him. I decided reassurance was the correct answer to his dilemma.

"Of course, I'm going to stay. Why wouldn't I? I want to be with you, Wyatt."

"Maybe you need a linchpin, like a marriage proposal, because I'd marry you, Madeline, if you need that to stay here with me. Do you think you'd like to marry me?" He seemed so worried, but I had the impression he had led me straight to the subject he most wanted to address.

I took a deep breath, and looked him in the eye.

"I would love to marry you, Wyatt." This was the utter truth, and had less to do with my pregnancy than simply enjoying his company. The concept of losing him offered a desolate feeling.

"I'm an old guy, Madeline. Would you be happy with this old guy?"

"I won't be happy at all, unless I'm with you, Wyatt."

He cheered up after that, and we started to make out like a couple of horny teenagers. Soon he disappeared under the sheet, and did some fancy moves on me with his tongue. When the moment arrived, orgasm moved through me in a way I can only describe as a freight train.

Wyatt seemed concerned about entering me, but I promised him that nature had designed a woman's body to receive a man all the way through pregnancy to labor (or so my own mother had once mentioned in passing to an aunt, one of those conversations children are not supposed to overhear, or understand).

"We were pretty vigorous before we knew I was pregnant," I pointed out. "Knowledge doesn't suddenly make me breakable."

He obliged, with tenderness that made me feel as though I were connected to him, not violated by the act. He was large—both in stature and equipment—but knew what to do when making love to me, and our differences were absolved by the sweetness of heat and ecstasy.

Afterward, we lay entwined, which seemed more like being wrapped up in Wyatt.

"Nobody has ever asked me about marriage," I said softly.

"I am surprised, though I can kind of see why some men would be intimidated by a woman who can fix a sink clog, and then do the nasty. Those aren't the kind of men I'd want you to marry."

"What kind of man do you want me to marry?"

"Me. You're too good for anyone else. Especially that idiot you were seeing before we met. He's the type of person who's destined to hurt women."

"Well, I'm not hurt by him."

"I wouldn't hurt you for the world, Madeline," he told me in a sleepy voice. "I need you to know that."

"I know."

"I would hurt the world, if it meant saving you," he promised. A moment later, he was asleep.

Maybe I was deluding myself. I'd only known him for a few months. There are many ways for one person to hurt another, and usually emotional trauma remains long after any physical damage has healed. I had simply closed my eyes and jumped in without first testing the waters. Like the ocean at sunrise, I assumed I was safe from harm. I had taken stock in Rat's opinion from the first moment outside of Road Apples, when Wyatt had spoken, and Rat had returned obediently to my side. Any other unanswered questions about Wyatt were solved by faith.

The idea that Wyatt would deliberately protect me from harm was troubling. I have always been self-sufficient. I like to believe I'm street-smart enough to know how to avoid danger. Thinking about Wyatt standing between me, and an unknown menacing force, both comforted and disturbed me, and it took some time before I was able to sleep.

❖ ❖ ❖ ❖

The following morning, after taking our breakfast in a neighborhood diner close to the motel, we started early on the house. We rolled paint in the master bedroom, first the ceiling, baseboards and crown molding with Creamsicle, and then the walls with Enchanted Lavender. When the paint dried, we stripped off plastic and blue tape, and admired walls alight in faint color that complemented a carpet marbled in earth tones.

"I like it," he declared. "Panties look real good on a bedroom wall. Let's go shopping. I want to sleep here tonight."

With the new bedroom windows left open to the breeze to help the paint cure—and Rat content to stay in the fenced yard—we drove around town. We bought furnishings for the bedroom, plus a dining room table, and a set of chairs. These loaded readily into the bed of the truck, as they were packed in slim boxes, and required assembly.

"But I know you'll have that done in no time flat," he concluded. "You're a whirlwind, woman."

I had great fun shopping with Wyatt, and making discoveries about our preferences, which seemed to fall along similar lines. That's why it was easy to choose sheets and towels and a comforter set without any debate.

We were able to persuade the mattress store to deliver the king bed and headboard the same afternoon, and then found a grocery store so we could stock up on a few day's worth of food. Walking down the aisles with Wyatt turned a mundane chore into an event. He never failed to crack jokes about certain food items suggestive of human sexual organs, always with a finesse that required the listener to wonder if he *had* actually said what he'd said. I was beginning to think he'd pulled himself up from his earlier funk.

In the truck, I mentioned how much fun I had with him, and he seemed relieved.

"I worry about that sometimes."

"Why? Can't you see how I feel about you? You're always making me laugh. That's very sexy in a man."

"That's great news. But I don't think the statistics on May/December relationships are promising."

"I don't think about our ages at all. I'm just focused on you."

"Well, you *should* consider the age difference every now and then. *I* do, and frankly, I'm terrified."

"What scares you about it, Wyatt?"

I was confused, as I'd given him no reason to think I wasn't interested in his company, or was planning to back out. The very fact I was in Portland sharing the particulars of furnishing the house and fixing it up made my intentions clear, or so I thought.

"Things can happen, Madeline," he said cryptically. "You know, one moment you're laughing and theme music is playing in the background, and then suddenly, *crash!*"

"I'm an excellent driver," I promised, a meaning extending beyond piloting the truck.

"You never know when a tree's going to fall in the wind."

131

At the house, while we awaited the arrival of the bed, I took out my cordless drill, and proceeded to assemble the bedroom and dining room furniture. Just as he had when I'd replaced the windows, Wyatt proved the perfect helper, and by the time the truck arrived with the mattress, box spring and headboard, we not only had our dining set completed, but the bureau and night stands for the master bedroom as well.

That evening, with a new bed to lay on, and new wood blinds in the bedroom windows to block curious eyes, we made love to christen the room. In passing, I thought about Kevin's mention of champagne sex by Oregonians, and I smiled to myself.

I knew we only had three more days in this house until I had to leave for the Bay Area. There weren't any jobs on my immediate schedule, as I'd started to refer them to other contractors I was familiar with, including my cousin, Jerry. I'd even received a text message from Sherry Flynn confirming that she'd found a renter for the Bassett Street house, and would need my approval of a date when I would expect to vacate the premises, so she could have the contract signed. What I wanted to do was to start packing, and move up to Portland.

When I told Wyatt about Sherry's text, he perked up, and decided to put away the gloom and doom.

"I know, I acted silly," he admitted sheepishly. "What can I say?"

"You can just keep telling me when you feel insecure, and I'll keep giving you reasons not to feel that way."

"What good is that?"

"You get to vent, and I get to reassure you."

"And then we get to have sex," he added cheerfully.

Early the next morning, I donned a bunny suit and respirator, and started in on the wood floors on the main level with a power sander. The floors were old and the finish scratched, but the wood itself was not too damaged, and I was able to get the floors cleaned up and varnished.

While I studiously worked, Wyatt and Rat kept each other company. Wyatt amused himself tinkering around in the shop behind the house, and sketching plans for his future studio configuration. The two of them even made a pizza run in the truck. I knew that if he could maneuver a Crown Victoria, he could handle my truck without any worries.

That night, we tucked in with the windows partially open, Rat curled on his bed. We were impervious to the damp Portland cold what with Wyatt's two hundred pounds of muscular body heating the bed. A

132

breeze moved through the room, and rain drummed the eaves, but being exposed to the night air was far better than inhaling the odor of curing varnish.

I remarked on the humidity in Portland, and Wyatt only laughed softly.

"I grew up in the rain. Portland seems like a desert after Taholah."

"How much rain do they get in Taholah?"

"In Quinault country, they measure rainfall in feet, not inches." He pulled me close, and gently touched my face. "When I was a boy, there were stories about *Misp*, the deity who created a habitable world for all living beings, both animals and plants. *Misp* had the power to change the landscape and the creatures in it, including humans, in order to strike a balance."

"Every culture has mythological beings, and stories of creation."

"Well, I know that, Madeline. It's not like I actually believed in *Misp*. The stories are centered more on reminding me about what it means to be Quinault. I don't believe in *Misp* any more than I believe in the Christian God the evangelists broadcast on nighttime television. But I do like the idea that the world can be changed in order to find balance, even on the tiniest level."

"I like that idea, I feel less insignificant, though I do believe in higher power."

"That higher power is contained in everything that is." He kissed my nose. "When I lost my parents, the world spun out of control, and I began to find my own order in small things, whether it was bringing home a salmon to feed me and my aunt, or making birds out of aluminum cans."

I would have asked him whether he felt that our current venture had balance, but I didn't want misunderstanding. I imagined him sitting bolt upright in the bed, traumatized with the thought that my construction savvy might set the world out of whack, instead of simply being my contribution to this new place we would call our home. So, I merely snuggled up to him, and pulled one of his arms around me in an embrace. The physical touching soon evolved into lovemaking, our whispers drowned by the falling rain.

Most of the time we slept naked, though it was impossible to actually fall asleep with his erection against my back until we made love. Wyatt had some kind of quality or a perfect aphrodisiac, the elixir to turning me on. Sex seemed to be a sleep drug for Wyatt, but it kept me awake, dreaming of the wonderful years to come.

If only Wyatt could put away his fears, that terrible waiting for the other shoe to drop. I told myself this habit of his was deeply embedded in losing his parents at an early age, and then finding out he had a sister who'd been hidden away for years. Though he'd built his life in certainty, everything beloved lay in the shadow of peril, and he was terrified of losing it.

Chapter Thirteen

At breakfast—bagels toasted in our new toaster, served with the perennial drip coffee made in our new coffeemaker—Wyatt told me he'd decided to accompany me on my return drive to the Bay Area.

This was exciting news, because it meant that I could delay our parting. I had already begun to mourn the moment I'd be dropping him at PDX. Knowing he planned to be my travel companion absolutely thrilled me.

I had learned early on that Wyatt was spontaneous, prone to changing his schedule very effectively around gallery openings or other events, though he never jeopardized his professional obligations. On the other hand, I was less able to veer suddenly from a projected course, as my life and my income depended upon a predetermined schedule, and meeting my contracts in a timely manner.

But, of course, Wyatt's impulsivity was part of his charm.

"What about your plane ticket?" I asked, and he told me he'd already changed it out for a flight from San José to Tacoma for a week from today, in case he needed to use it.

"I did the phone thing," he explained. "It's similar to the penis thing, and the house thing, which was so much like the penis thing too."

This was another proof of his will, that aside from impromptu course changes, and a jovial wit, he was also an excellent planner when the situation dictated. I imagined him setting a date on his calendar as to when the labor was expected, and then wanting both of us to traipse off at the last minute. The idea was ridiculous, though fairly on the mark with Wyatt's personality.

"I'm going to miss this house," he said sadly, admiring the bright tone of newly finished oak floors.

"We'll be back," I reminded. "I have to finish replacing the trim downstairs, and then we'll paint the walls. When we return, it'll be for good. You know, we still have to pack up your stuff, and move it down from Tacoma."

"I think I'll hire professionals to do that. I've got all that metal, and it's brutal to move it around. You should see what's involved in getting a large piece moved to a gallery for a show."

"What do you have to do?"

"There's this outfit I usually hire. They're licensed and bonded, and come with a flatbed, and a piggybacked forklift. My studio has double doors, and they can load the really big pieces right out of the back alley."

We packed up my work truck, and included the meager groceries we had procured into a hastily purchased cooler stowed on the floor behind the driver's seat, and covered with the dog bed. This way, Rat could curl in the bed, perched on the cooler, attached to the seat belt by his leash and harness, and yet and stick his nose out the window crack, while I sailed along at seventy miles per hour on cruise control down Interstate 5.

"Do you mind if we stop in Susanville?" he asked, when we were already headed out of Portland.

"I don't see why not. It's kind of on the way. Did you want to go see Kate?"

"Of course. Do you want to see your sister, too, while we're there?"

"Sure, I'll call Miranda. I know she'd like to meet you."

At a rest stop while I walked Rat, I telephoned Miranda and told her voice mail we'd be in Susanville that night. I also called my father, and asked if Wyatt and I could stay at their property outside of town. Once again, Dad displayed his fervent hope that my relationship with Wyatt had promise. I believe the phrase Dad used was, "Hold onto a good thing, Maddie." He gave us his blessing for the use of the mobile home, and told me where the guest key was stashed.

This time, I drove I-5 to McCloud, California, and then took all the two lane back roads through the mountains to Susanville. The scenery is spectacular, and the highway is usually in good condition. The trip was nine-hours, factoring in pauses for gas, food, the bathroom, and Rat.

We killed the time with conversation, never having a loss for words, which convinced me that I was really getting to know him. I was familiar with facts about his childhood on the Quinault reservation, things about Kate and his Aunt Doreen, and the harrowing ordeal of losing his entire family.

He mentioned a few women he'd dated, though there seemed to be no particularly serious relationships, which mystified me. Wyatt was even-tempered, but also passionate, especially when it involved art, music or sex, so the fact that he'd had no affairs that suggested a more serious progression toward marriage vaguely worried me. Something as important as the way in which a man approaches an affair, positive or negative, can be repeated in subsequent relationships, and only emerges with the recount. I suppose if he'd wanted me to know everything about his past, all of the pieces to his life would be revealed on their own accord. And foolishly, I never asked.

By six o'clock, we were rolling onto my parents' property on the Lassen Grade. The place was incredibly quiet after the noise of Portland, what Wyatt called its "bustle." The motel had been surrounded by urban clatter. Though set in a peaceful neighborhood, the Hawthorne house was nevertheless affected by vehicle traffic, the occasional emergency siren, and high-flying aircraft. I promised Wyatt that once all the windows had been replaced with double paned, the outside noise would be substantially dulled, though never fully blocked.

We walked with Rat through the woods on the property, and listened to the birds and the wind. That's all there was, not even a whisper of traffic from the highway, because the house was set so far back in the trees.

"Too bad we didn't get a place up here," he reflected.

"I'm sure we could borrow the house anytime." That had always been my parents' intent, an heirloom vacation spot for immediate family.

"Would you like to go see Kate tonight?" he asked.

I admitted that I was both excited and daunted by the prospect. On one hand it had proved quite simple to seek out a man's sister to get the lowdown on him, but now I was practically part of the family, and everything mattered.

"Can you call her? Invite her and her husband out to dinner. There's a really good family-style restaurant in Chester, and we can take them there."

"I'll try, but you don't know Kate. She likes to entertain, instead of being entertained."

He used my parents' landline, and telephoned his sister. I allowed him to talk in privacy, by putting our dirty clothes into the washing machine, though his conversation was brief. Wyatt soon found me, and leaned through the doorway of the laundry room.

"We're going to the ranch for supper, Madeline. Isn't that exciting? Aren't you stupefied?"

I knew he was teasing me, and he could tell I was pensive, so I explained about the "mattering."

"Kate likes you, Madeline, and I love you, and I'm positive there's no reason to worry."

"It's something she told me when I came to Susanville to talk to her."

"What is it?"

I really tried to remember her exact words, and then they just popped into my head, in Kate's kind, reasonable voice: *I have my doubts.*

To say anything seemed almost cruel, so I only shook my head.

"It's nothing, just a general concern because I'm so much younger than you are."

"I can't imagine Kate being bothered about the difference in our ages."

"I think she was more worried about certain people being set in their ways." Now I felt I'd said too much.

"I wouldn't worry about what Kate thinks. You should see the guy my niece Kristina dated in college. Geez, he's old. Talk about being set, that guy's set in concrete."

He had apparently gotten over his unease about our May/December situation.

Rat returned to the porch, and was asleep in the dappled shade. We took the free time to go inside the cool of the mobile home, and make love on one of the couches in the living room. Naturally, during the focus of the moment, I pushed away negative thoughts or worries.

We showered, and then, with Rat in the cab, headed toward Westwood, and the Spotted Horse Ranch. My apprehension was relieved by the welcoming attitude of the Sumner family. The loving circle that greeted us in the gravel yard included Kate, her husband Paul, and their youngest son Dakota. Dakota was at that gangly, teenaged stage, nervous energy and hijinks, balanced with the poise of a seventeen-year-old who knows everything (or so he thinks).

I'll never forget the expression on Kate's face when Wyatt teased her by calling her "Katie." I even got to shake Paul Sumner's hand, experiencing that sensation of being in the presence of greatness, due to the winery connection. Kate's husband was down to earth, and genuinely interested in what Wyatt and I had been doing in our spare time, so I relaxed almost immediately.

Dakota fell in love with Rat's friendliness, once he moved past the dog's initial physical presentation. The two took off running, and the last I saw of them before we ate, were the boy and his dog friend leaping over boulders and playing around the creek that cut through the center of the ranch.

Inside the house, Paul invited Wyatt down to the wine cellar, and I helped Kate in the kitchen with dinner. She referred to the meal as "supper."

"You don't call it dinner?"

"No, that comes at midday."

"I'd always thought the midday meal was known as lunch."

"Maddie, lunch isn't even in my vocabulary."

I thought about Wyatt having claimed that "love" was a term he never used. Suddenly, I ached for candor with this wonderful woman, who was now almost my sister-in-law.

"Kate, I don't know if Wyatt's said anything to you recently, but I think you ought to know. I'm pregnant."

She paused, holding dry spaghetti over a pot of boiling water. There was an odd expression on her face, and I immediately assumed I'd made a social blunder. She saved the moment by dumping in the pasta, and then grabbing me for a hug.

"I'm so happy for the two of you," she said gently. "I can't wait for a niece or a nephew."

But something was bothering her.

I picked up a cracker from a dish Kate had set on the kitchen nook table, and nibbled.

"I remember what you told me when we first met, Kate. About having your doubts."

"Ah, yes, I remember that, too." She studied me carefully. "You seem happy with my brother. You must have already figured out his quirkiness."

"I know he's spontaneous, though he also has a way of making plans and following through."

"That's Wyatt, the misnomer of the family."

139

She set an egg timer for the pasta, and then, pouring us both glasses of water, she joined me at the table, sliding a glass over to me.

"When did you get pregnant, Maddie? Was it just before we met?"

"Yes." I took a sip of the water, and could feel the cold all the way to the pit of my belly.

"Surely you used protection."

"Surely, I did. I'm very careful, and it wasn't deliberate, Kate. Wyatt snuck through the back door when I was asleep."

"That's Wyatt," she said, repeating the previous thought. "And it's a first."

"What do you mean?"

"Wyatt's generally a responsible person. I would almost characterize him as rigidly cautious, which is why your initial visit to me was so surprising. To take a chance like that with you implied that he felt you were worth the risk."

"What did you mean exactly when you said you had your doubts?"

"I was speaking from experience. Wyatt's rarely had the inclination to settle down. He always seemed too afraid to lose a good thing, and yet he wouldn't take one step past a certain point and commit."

That's when I told her about Wyatt buying the house in Portland, and then asking me to marry him.

"I take it all back, Maddie. Sounds to me like Wyatt's running with the ball."

"I know he's afraid of losing everything that means something to him. He even told me early on that he'd never used the word "love" in a relationship."

"That's true," she agreed. "Maybe that's why he lost his fiancé six years ago."

I paused, totally floored. I hadn't known Wyatt had ever been engaged.

"Oh, boy." Kate interpreted my bewildered expression. "I take it Wyatt hasn't told you about Celeste."

"No, I don't know anything about anyone named Celeste."

I sat at that table, imagining the fetus inside of its water darkness, and felt a grief I've never experienced in my life. I felt as though someone had taken my heart firmly in hand, and wrenched it from my chest.

"It's fine," I went on bravely, to avoid giving in to tears. "It's all so soon, and so new. We have a lot of time to get to know the small details about each other."

"I wouldn't call a broken engagement a 'small detail,' though I *am* surprised he hasn't said anything about Celeste. He's usually a glaringly honest man."

"Maybe I haven't asked the right questions. Or, maybe he just doesn't want to talk about her."

She laid a hand on mine, and I looked into her kind face.

"You should know, Maddie, that I see a huge difference between you and Wyatt, and Celeste and Wyatt. I hadn't the heart to tell him directly, but I was relieved when their engagement was broken, and Celeste didn't marry my brother. She wasn't good for him, there wasn't any light to his spirit that I see with you." She laughed softly. "Celeste never would have driven out of her way just to talk to me about loving Wyatt. Personally, I don't think she really loved him, so I guess there wouldn't have been anything for us to talk about."

"Why didn't they get married?"

"Well, it had nothing to do with *my* feelings about her. Wyatt's got his own mind, and his own way of doing things, which I'm sure you've familiarized yourself with. But it's possible that he never got around to telling her that he loved her, and mostly, I think it's because he finally wised up, and knew that he didn't."

"Wyatt *has* told me that he loves me. He hasn't said it often, but he's said it."

"Which makes it special. What else has he done that's out of character?"

"I'm not exactly sure. He went to church with me once, does that count?"

"He went into a church? A Christian church?"

"It was a Catholic church."

She seemed astounded, but also impressed.

"My, my! I think there's conversion going on, and I'm not talking about the religious kind. I grew up as a Catholic, but for all the times Wyatt's visited, not once has he ever joined my family going to mass. I think you're quite remarkable, Maddie."

"Don't get too excited. I think going to church was more of a clinical experience for him."

"That may be true, but I also believe he went with you, because he wants to get to know who you are."

She stood, and returned to her spaghetti to give it a stir, and pour in a dollop of olive oil to prevent it from boiling over. I knew I had to rid myself of the despair that had filled me at the mention of Wyatt's past life, a life he'd kept a secret from me, and making my hands busy might be a temporary solution.

"Can I help you with something, Kate? Maybe set the supper table?"

She seemed pleased I'd asked, and that I'd used the correct idiom for the evening meal, directing me past the swing door, where I could find all I needed in a built-in hutch.

As I pulled out salad bowls and dinner plates, and found the drawer with the flatware, I thought about the beauty of the hutch, standing in its wall niche for years, and tended by women in loving concern over their families. The house was over a century old, and I had no idea who owned the place before Kate's family, but I could see the house had become a sanctuary of familial warmth and cohesion.

Once the table was set, I examined the artwork hanging on the walls. Kate was an artist, and her oil paintings burned color in the living room and dining area. I thought about the large painting of Kate's hanging over Wyatt's stone hearth, and that brought me back to our first night in his Tacoma loft. I recalled the emotions I'd felt, tangled up with physical passion, how the moment convinced me there was no reason to hold back. Now, knowing about this person named Celeste, I felt at a loss as to how to proceed.

I was standing there, trying to lose myself in the themes of Kate's paintings, when Wyatt and Paul climbed up the stairs from the wine cellar. They each carried two bottles of wine, and were laughing over some joke Wyatt had obviously told, because his amusement was familiar, while Paul appeared to have been taken by surprise through a jest.

When Wyatt met my gaze, he must have seen a trace of the sadness that had passed through me, though I'd done my best to put it aside until I could talk with him in private. Instead of asking me if something were wrong, he put a reassuring arm around me, and smiled his Wyatt smile, and then kissed me on the lips, which settled everything for the moment.

The dinner was served at a table shared by family—Wyatt and his wisecracks, Paul with his viticulture and history lessons, and a bit of friendly banter between Wyatt and Dakota, while Kate sat back, and drank it all in. I felt included, and yet apart, by virtue of Kate's disclosure.

Wyatt eventually announced the impending birth of our child. I was seated next to him, and he turned and met my eyes with his sly grin, all the while receiving heartfelt acclaim from his brother-in-law and sister.

"You know, this baby is going to be Quinault," Kate mentioned, when the commotion settled down. "Have you given any thought about what that might mean?"

"No," I admitted. "I'm still getting my mind around the house in Portland." I remembered what Wyatt had said about being a man of two nations. "I think what you've said means that our son, or daughter, will become a citizen of two nations."

Wyatt nodded, and reached out to hold my hand.

"I remember when Kate stood before the Enrollment Committee," said Wyatt. "That was an exciting time, Madeline, to see my sister become an enrolled tribal member."

"How old were you, Kate?" I asked.

"I think I was around your age, Maddie, twenty-six, maybe. When my children were born, I brought them to the General Council to ask for their enrollment—except for my daughter, Sara. Her father's *Sicangu Lakota*, so Sara's enrolled with the Rosebud Sioux tribe."

"Tell Maddie about Rickie," Paul prompted, and Kate's eyes gleamed suddenly with tears.

"A few years ago, my eldest son, Rickie, located me." She briefly wiped her eyes. "He'd been taken away to Mexico as an infant by his father."

"That was the year I was stabbed in my loft," Wyatt reminded. "A couple of life-changing events for both of us."

"Yes, they were," Kate softly agreed. "When I brought Rickie before the General Council to ask for his enrollment, the experience was particularly moving, because he'd been gone from me for almost thirty years."

"How did Rickie feel about it?" I asked.

"Rather wonderful, I would think. He currently lives in Taholah."

Wyatt laughed. "Yeah, imagine that, my nephew with the Mexican accent, who looks Quinault, and works in the tribal cannery."

This family seemed complicated to me. I was still chewing on the revelation of Celeste, yet avoiding the truth to keep my poise.

When the time came we had to depart, I was more than ready, but also sorry to go, though I had a positive feeling I'd be back again.

We spoke our goodbyes, and Paul handed over two bottles of Clay Creek Reserve Red. Wyatt said something quickly to his sister, words that caused her to laugh outright, and then hug him tightly. I embraced Paul, and kissed Kate, and then Dakota made a fuss over Rat before the dog was loaded into the truck.

There were ten miles to travel back to the mobile home, ten miles of conversation that started as soon as we hit the highway.

Wyatt initiated. "Kate told you about Celeste, didn't she."

"How did you know? Did Kate tell you?"

"Kate didn't tell me she'd said anything to you. I just saw your face, Madeline, when I came up from the cellar. You always wear your heart in your eyes, so I could tell you were hurt. I knew it had to be about Celeste."

"Don't be sore with Kate. She had no idea that I had no idea."

"Why would I be sore with Kate? It's you who should be angry with me. I should've told you about Celeste a long time ago."

"I'm not angry, Wyatt. You aren't obligated to tell me anything about a relationship you had long before my time."

"Well, yes, I am obligated, Madeline. Because you might think one relationship has a lot to do with another." He gazed out at the darkness, and sighed.

"Do you want to know what Kate told me, in case it needs correcting?"

"I'm sure I can guess what she told you. That she didn't appreciate Celeste, that I didn't love Celeste enough to make it into a marriage, and that's why she left me. Kate's right about most of it, but not about how it ended, or why."

"Kate said that when you were with Celeste, there wasn't any light to your spirit that she notices when you're with me."

I could see the flash of his teeth as he smiled.

"Really!" He was silent for a moment, pondering. "She's right," he agreed, of his sister's assessment. "It's very different with you."

"How so?" I saw the left turn, and slowed, so I wouldn't hit the gatepost.

He held onto the grab handle, as I turned the truck into the yard.

"You're exciting, Madeline, power tools and all. With you, I feel alive, and I get to be my genuine self. I can also tell that you're not a woman who withholds. But with Celeste, I felt like I was dying. I felt trapped, and principally because I wasn't happy."

I parked the truck, shut off the engine, and we just sat there, listening to the clicks and pops as the engine cooled. When I spoke, I tried my best to keep my tone neutral.

"How did you meet Celeste?"

"She's an English professor at UW, Tacoma. I had an exhibit at Lanier's Gallery in downtown Seattle, which she just coincidentally happened to attend."

"A brush with fate?"

"It's not the same, not at all like it was when I met you, trust me. That's why I was reluctant to say anything to you about Celeste. I was concerned that in the telling, you'd think it would diminish our experience, our chance meeting."

"You can tell me what happened, Wyatt. You need to know I'll always listen with an open mind."

"I do know that." He sighed. "At the Lanier's show, Celeste asked me where I was from, and I told her, Tacoma. I'm so used to mentioning the rez when anyone asks about my life, but Celeste seemed too upmarket, and anyway, we lived in the same city. I didn't feel a need to mention my background."

"That doesn't sound like you."

"Which part of it? Wanting to get laid by an elite, attractive and educated woman? Because let me tell you, a man needs sex, sometimes regardless of the source. It's true love that seals the deal forever."

"No. I totally get men and sex. But not telling somebody where you came from, because you think they're too high class to accept that you were raised on an Indian reservation? That doesn't sound like you, Wyatt. And to be ashamed of your origins, when they're so humbly relevant, that's also out of character."

"Well, you're right. That's not part of me. I did a lot of things with Celeste that weren't a part of me, not who I am. I didn't act normally. I refused to be myself. But you know, Madeline, it wasn't me being a counterfeit man that did us in, though I'm sure that we would've ended in divorce, had we ever married."

"Was it because you couldn't tell her you loved her?"

"That's fairly simplified, but yes, it played a minor role. And the fact that I didn't like who I was when I was with her was very crucial. But it had to do with something else, and after all the time I spent with her, I found out what she was really after." He tilted his head at me in the half-light of the cab. "Tell me, Madeline, what do you look for in a relationship?"

"I want companionship, hot sex, and true love. I want the man I'm with to be my best friend."

"Are you looking for security?"

I frowned, searching for my own definition of 'security.'

"If you mean a lifetime of wonderful memories with somebody I can't live without, then, yes."

He turned away, and though I could only see his profile in the dim, I swore he was close to tears.

"You've met my parents, Wyatt," I continued. "Do they seem happy to you? Do they look like they're in love?"

"Yes."

"Then let me tell you something you'd never expect. My father had an affair when Mom was carrying me. I'm sure he didn't intend for the other woman to get pregnant, but she did, and she kept the child. She was married to a temperamental man, who happened to be a cop, and she told her husband the child was his. But when the husband died, the woman made sure her son knew about whom he really was. And then this son came looking for my father."

"And your mother knows about this?"

"My mother's known about the affair since she was pregnant with my sister, Margot, but my half-brother was a surprise to all of us, especially to my father."

"And that didn't end their marriage?"

"I don't know what happened when my father told my mother, but I do know that they're still married, and that they're still in love. They're the model of love and forgiveness."

"That's a wonderful story, Madeline. But I promise, I'm in no mood to engage myself with anyone except for you. I'm too old for games. And though I admit I've had women in my life, I've never been much of a player. I've always wanted a good thing, not a string of pussy."

"I believe you. And I just want you to know what kind of person *I* am, Wyatt."

"Oh, I know who you are," he said confidently. "I could see how wonderful you were, right away."

"You didn't tell me what Celeste was really after."

"Didn't I?" He laughed, but there was no mirth. "Come on, let's go inside. I would think Rat's hungry."

We let Rat out to do his toilet thing, and then went into the mobile home, which was warmer than the night air. I fed Rat in the laundry room, and then joined Wyatt, who was seated on a couch in front of the wood stove, staring at the cold box. I asked if I could get him anything, but he shook his head, and motioned for me to sit down next to him.

"It was a crazy affair," he admitted, about his relationship with Celeste. "We went out for a few months, and then I found myself engaged to this woman."

"How did you manage that?"

"What do you think about this? Celeste asked me to marry her. It was surreal. I'm not the type, not like my sister. Kate always wanted children, and a home with a loving husband. I was content with my studio, with gallery openings and the adulation of single women. Not that I'm a slut, Madeline, but I'm no saint, either, though I make it a point to stay away from married women, and complicated situations, and never date more than one woman at a time."

"I believe it's good to have rules, and play by them."

"Rules went out the window with Celeste. I was pretty overwhelmed by her. She was gorgeous and educated, with a doctorate in English from Harvard. She was white, too, which I found kind of intriguing, and also off-putting, because of my inability to get past that mind-block, and tell her who I really was." He rubbed his chin. "I guess I was shallow back then."

"I don't think that being attracted to those qualities in a woman makes you shallow."

"It does, if all you're looking for is pussy, and you're willing to pay for it with your soul."

"Celeste sounds like she's an interesting person," I disputed. "There must have been an intellectual attraction once you moved past the sexual part."

"It all comes down to the fact that neither of us had very much in common with the other. I mean, come on, she loved opera, which I can't listen to if my life depends on it, and she absolutely hated seventies rock. At least you like *Journey*."

"That's true, and lucky. What was Celeste after?"

He shrugged. "The settlement money."

"Why would she be after money, with a university job?"

147

"Being a tenured English professor doesn't necessarily mean you're rolling in the dough. Celeste came from a family where she grew accustomed to certain privileges, and had a taste for the finer things in life. I think she felt she was inhibited by her income and profession, and of course, greed's part of human nature." He raised his brows. "I told you that Aunt Doreen's husband, Ben Barrow, was the attorney who filed suit for me and Kate."

"I remember the story."

"Ben was interviewed by a journalist from *Indian Country Today*, and the names of all the players were mentioned in the article. The amount of the monetary settlement was included. The *Associated Press* even picked up the story, and circulated it to major news outlets."

"What does that have to do with Celeste?"

"I started to feel anxious about the relationship. At first, I thought it was because I was getting cold feet, you know, being scared to settle down. I almost got stupid and talked myself into following through with what I'd promised her. But something wasn't adding up, Madeline."

"What was that?"

"My meeting Celeste at Lanier's."

"You and I first met in the parking lot of a coffee house named after horse shit," I reminded, but he waved me off.

"That's different. That was innocent. You were sincere." He paused, and studied me thoughtfully. "I can't explain it any other way than to call it intuition. When I had the chance, I poked around her apartment, and found a file folder with enough evidence to convince me that Celeste was out for money."

"What did you find?"

"A list of my shows. A printout of the original article from the *Wall Street Journal* about how the lawsuit panned out."

I was starting to feel uneasy with his mention of the money secured from the lawsuit—I had no concept of its sum—and he'd already alluded to the money's ability to buy his happiness.

"Then she already knew about your origins," I pointed out. "She knew you grew up on the reservation."

"Of course. Which makes me the greatest liar of all, after Celeste."

"Maybe she found the article after meeting you in the gallery in Seattle," I reasoned.

"I'd have believed that, except the article was printed off the web, and the header was dated *before* our alleged chance meeting in Seattle.

And then, there was a list of my gallery itinerary, with the Lanier's date highlighted in bright yellow. I began to have trust issues, and that's what ended it."

"What about me, Wyatt?"

"You, Madeline? Wow, I think your problem is that you trust too much."

"No, I mean—why did you trust me, after having a relationship with a woman who proved to be so untrustworthy?"

"Oh, that's simple. When I saw you in the rain, you were like glass. I could see right into you. You and Rat were kicking those guys' butts. If you were the kind of woman that Celeste proved herself to be, there's no way you'd be fighting alongside a dog. I couldn't help but trust you after seeing that. And don't take this the wrong way, but you're not as socially sophisticated as Celeste. I just can't imagine you involved in a diabolical scheme to catch a man." He nodded appreciatively. "As I said, I can see right into you."

"Why did you talk about fate?"

"I said every word to you with meaning, Madeline. I still believe we were put together for a purpose. For all we know, you were supposed to get pregnant, and my sneaking in was part of fate's objective."

"I have a difficult time believing that your choice to slip it in was some universal plan."

"Why? Do you think you and I would be this far into a committed future, if I hadn't gotten you pregnant?"

"Yes, I really do. And anyway, that just proves my point, that it wasn't fate. It was a matter of choice."

"Madeline, whatever you think, I still feel that we were put together at a moment in time for a reason. And I can't shake that belief. Some things are greater than human puniness can imagine. Does that figure into how I feel about you? Maybe. But I can also blame your total lack of deception, your intelligence, and your great body."

"Has there been anyone since Celeste? Besides me."

"After Celeste and before I met you, I had a few passing affairs. Nothing serious, just sex. One woman was seeing another man while she was seeing me, because I could smell it on her, which was why I didn't continue. But I hadn't had any sincere, profound relationships since breaking it off with Celeste. That's about six years of loneliness, Madeline."

"Maybe I would've been just another passing affair."

"If you want to get to the facts, then all right. It's true. I wanted you that night for sex, and I've already admitted it. But…you touched me in so many ways, right from the very beginning. When I first saw you in the rain, I didn't want to let you go, and the rest will be our history. I guess you know by now how stubborn I can be."

He leaned his head on my shoulder, and traced his fingers across my abdomen. I loved his hands and his touch, the connection I felt whenever we were physically close, but this was a gesture that made me feel sad for him. His loving touch promised that nothing had changed between us, and yet, after his admission, everything was different.

"Why didn't you find anyone after Celeste?"

"After the stabbing, I was very conscious of the scars. Sometimes I couldn't even look at myself in the mirror, it was that bad. It took some getting used to before I could accept how much I'd changed on the outside. The very last woman I dated before I met you admitted to me that she couldn't bring herself to have sex with me because she considered them a grave disfigurement."

"You took your sweater and shirt off right away. As soon as we were in your bedroom."

"I had to know, Madeline, and I wanted to be honest with you. If you found my scars repulsive, I needed to know before I committed my heart, so I could let you go. But you touched them with your fingers, and you put your lips on them. I knew if you could kiss my scars, then maybe you could love me too."

"I couldn't help touching your scars. I wanted to touch each of them. The scars tell me who you were, and your regret in the killing tells me who you are. I've never thought of them as a disfigurement."

"I realized that." He stroked my cheek. "Everything I have, I want to share with you, Madeline."

"I only want everything you are."

"But I have money."

"I don't want your settlement money, Wyatt," I told him in a low voice, fierce with my passion for him. "I don't even want to know about it."

"It's a lot of money, Madeline," he continued, insisting on sharing despite my need to remain clueless. "And I can't possibly spend it all myself. It's fucking hundreds of thousands of dollars."

"*Don't* tell me. I *don't* want to know!"

"When they paid us off, and after Ben got his cut for representation, I received over a mil."

I felt sick to my stomach, as though I'd been betrayed by the fact of numbers in a bank account. Wyatt wasn't trying to buy me. He could know with confidence he would never find himself in a position where money meant more to me than his love. I simply wanted to go back to the time before I even knew the money existed.

The tears fell, but I doggedly clung to his hand, kissing his fingers. His mouth was tender with his love for me.

"Wyatt." My agony would pass, and perhaps we would forget this moment of revelation, though he had more to tell me.

"While I was growing up, we were rich in so many ways, but also very poor in a monetary sense," he finally revealed. "It was a beautiful time, because my aunt cared for me deeply, but the world was haunting too. I learned to care for her, and for my life, by following her example.

"Sometimes when we were hungry, I'd go up river, and catch salmon, or kill a deer on the reservation. You go to the shore at low tide, and dig clams, and maybe you have beach food for a day or two. Aunt Doreen, she kept me from eating all that crap the BIA distributed, like cheese loaf and macaroni, cold cereal. She grew a vegetable garden. She bought dried beans by the hundredweight, and taught me how to gather wild food, like seaweed. And she turned a blind eye when I brought home salmon, or venison. I have to thank her for my good teeth, and the fact that I don't have diabetes."

He sat up, and gazed at me. There was no deception in his eyes, no fever to shove money down my throat. We almost seemed back to square one, only now I knew about Celeste. I also knew I wasn't in her league. I was a plain-speaking woman with few demands, other than what came cheap, and remained true.

"I'm not a materialistic man, Madeline. Most of that money's been...just sitting there, and it'd sit there until my dying day. There aren't any ambiguities with you. You just are who you are. And you seem the most logical person to share my money with."

"Why?"

"Because." He smiled sadly. "You don't want any part of it."

The time was late, and we were exhausted from conversation. We pulled out the sofa bed on its creaky frame, and made up the mattress with fresh sheets from the linen closet. We then lay down naked, our usual posture.

I touched his scars, where the knife in a human hand had been plunged through skin and muscle, down to the bones of his left shoulder, deflected from piercing his heart by his rib cage and broad chest, and the swinging talon that ultimately halted the attack. His arms were strong when he lifted me, but they trembled with unseen scars, a fear of loss, and the memory of hunger.

Chapter Fourteen

In the morning, there seemed to be a deeper connection, an understanding that transcended fate or sexual attraction. When I looked at Wyatt, I could see to a greater depth. I'd formerly been guided by faith in his humanity, and he was now less of an enigma to me.

I recall waking up, and being cradled in his arms, and the expression on his face when he spoke to me. The previous night's conversation had managed to clear the air, but I think it also reinforced to Wyatt who I am.

We sat at my parents' dining table with our usual coffee, the air filled with love and kindness. The magic reminded me of the morning after we'd first made love, whispering our thoughts, as though in fear of breaking the spell.

"Thank you, Madeline," he told me, "for being exactly who I know you are."

"Why are you thanking me?"

"A lot of women who would dump a man at roadside for concealing a fact like a broken engagement."

"And those are the type of women I wouldn't want you to be with, or to marry." I repeated his argument from that night in the Portland motel.

After breakfast, I washed the bed linen. Wyatt folded away the sofa bed, and then we took a walk with Rat. I'd found a plastic ball in an old toy box in the extra bedroom, and Wyatt and I took turns throwing it for Rat to chase. The dog would run the ball down, snap it up in his teeth, and return it for another quick flick of the wrist. He never seemed to tire of the game, and Wyatt suggested we take the ball with us when we leave, for future play.

He wanted to meet Miranda, though I doubted we'd have a chance, as she was probably on her work shift with the California Highway Patrol. I called her cell anyway, and she answered while she was patrolling up north by Ravendale. She offered to meet us for a late lunch at a place called Pablo's Bar & Grill south of Janesville. When I hung up, I knew that Miranda wasn't a local, or even remotely schooled in rural culture, as Kate would have called it "dinner."

We locked up the mobile home, and hid the guest key once more, not intending to return once we left Susanville. Rat ran around and left a few more urine markers, and then we loaded into the truck.

"What's your sister like?" he asked with interest, as I merged onto the highway. "Is she hot like you?"

"Hotter," I claimed. "Especially in uniform."

"You know, Madeline, I have to confess something to you. I find it hot that you're pregnant."

"You couldn't even tell if I hadn't told you already."

"It doesn't matter. I *know*. You're like the ultimate woman, in my mind." He whistled. "My poor aunt would really scold me if she knew I desired a pregnant woman."

"Why would your aunt be unhappy with that?"

"I'm sure she'd find a reason, something forbidden that a man shouldn't do with a woman. You know, like during a woman's cycle, there's the thought that it's unclean to have sex when a woman's on her period. I wouldn't have a problem with having sex with you during your cycle, Madeline, but it is an old taboo."

"Do you think your aunt would like me?"

"Absolutely. She'd take one look at your drill set or nail gun, and equate you with the ideal feminist. She's why I respect women so much. Well, I think there's a little fear there, too. Sometimes on the rez, a man would drink alcohol, and then beat the crap out of his wife, and Aunt Doreen would use the tragedy as a teachable moment to explain to me that the abuse was an anomaly, a freak of nature. She called it a curse from the whites. It kind of made me reluctant to drink too."

"But you drank wine the night we met."

"I don't drink very often. Did you know that bottle of wine came from the top of a case Paul gave to me when I was in Susanville last year for the wedding of my niece, Sara? I hadn't even opened the box, until the night we met. Talk about fate."

We arrived at Pablo's, and could see a California Highway Patrol cruiser parked in the lot, between a pickup truck with an Allison diesel engine, and a beat up red Cadillac Seville. Wyatt made a comment about how all the vehicles in Lassen County were either diesel pickup trucks, or pieces of junk ready to fall apart. He spoke with a straight face, and the undertone of a joke, though we both agreed there was some truth to the remark.

I parked around the side of the building where the shade was cool enough to leave Rat safely in the truck. We left the windows cracked for a cross-breeze, and proceeded into the restaurant.

Miranda was seated at the bar, one leg hooked over a stool, and the other propped straight beneath her, as though only half-sitting on the stool while on duty was a loophole exempting her from unethical behavior. She was having a conversation with the bartender beneath the mounted head of a rather large Roosevelt elk that peered down severely at the walnut bar from its imposing height. I thought about the evening drinking crowd lined up beneath the head, and given a disdainful once-over by the elk's glass eyes.

She noticed us, and waved us over.

I hugged her, and introduced Wyatt, and Miranda shook his hand.

"Whoa," he commented at my sister's strong grip. "You've got a hand like a bear trap, Trooper."

"Is this your father?" the bartender asked Miranda, who only shook her head, without offering explanation. I had thought that Miranda would accuse me of having daddy issues in front of a total stranger, but she kept her poise, and merely nodded to the waitress, Bethany, by the nametag, who waited patiently to lead us to a booth.

Once we were seated, and handed menus, Miranda put hers down, as though she already knew her choice, likely catalogued from a habit of consuming meals regularly at Pablo's. Miranda then commented on the bartender's mention of Wyatt's age.

"That must happen to the two of you a lot."

"No." I shook my head. "This is a first."

She appraised Wyatt with the suspicious glare of a law enforcement officer.

"Maddie barely looks twenty, but I think you might be able to get away with being thirty-five."

"Thank you." He made an exaggerated motion of relief. "That takes 'fatherly' out of the equation. My intentions toward Madeline are more of a carnal nature."

"I gathered." Miranda rolled her eyes. "She told me *all* about you."

"Really?" He seemed surprised. "I was under the impression that the two of you hardly ever saw each other."

"Yeah, Wyatt, is it? Have you ever heard of a modern invention known as the telephone?"

Miranda had donned the mask of being difficult, but in fact, already exhibited a general partiality toward Wyatt, or she wouldn't have been so caustic.

Wyatt had a way about him in the joke department, and was always prepared to ramp up the wordplay.

"Is that some kind of communication device?" he asked.

"Gee whiz." Miranda picked up the menu once more, if only to hide her face.

"After I saw Kate, I spent the night with Rat in a motel in Reno," I explained to Wyatt. "Miranda called me around two in the morning, and I may have said a thing or two about what happened in Tacoma."

"A 'thing or two'?" Miranda smirked. "She painted you as God's gift to Maddie."

Our waitress, Bethany, having come to the table to take drink orders, overheard Miranda's comment, and gave Wyatt a sideways glance of curiosity. We restrained ourselves, and ordered sodas, and then stayed quiet until Bethany was out of earshot.

"They make a mean burger," Miranda spoke up, though that was the bulk of the menu, except for the Cobb salad, which Miranda advised me not to order. "Watch out for salmonella," she warned.

"I think I'll have the chili," Wyatt concluded, setting aside his menu. "I kind of have a soft spot for pinto beans."

"You should see what the chef puts in the chili. But if you must have the chili, Maddie's going to have to open up all the windows on your way back to Santa Clara." Miranda then made a farting noise.

Bethany returned, and took our orders, still deliberating Wyatt from the corner of her eye. I was amused to see her standing near the door to the kitchen, jawing with the other waitress in hushed voices about the tall, broad-shouldered man seated with two diminutive women.

Wyatt eventually excused himself to use the bathroom, and that's when Miranda leaned in for the scoop.

"Tell me," she said, batting her eyes. "What's it like?"

I knew exactly what type of information Miranda was angling for, but I could see Bethany approaching with our orders. I was reluctant to have this conversation in front of the waitress, so I pretended to be mystified by Miranda's query.

"What's *what* like?"

"You know." Miranda nudged me under the table with her boot. "Is his dick as big as his physique suggests?"

Not that I'm a prude, the proof being my affair with Jake Keene, and that first night with Wyatt. But I was loath to discuss a lover's physical attributes, especially in a man I intended to have more than just a good time with. As Bethany placed our meals in front of us, one eye on the passageway to the bathrooms, I simply wiggled my pinky finger.

"No way!" Miranda burst out, and the startled waitress fled.

Wyatt had no idea when he arrived from the restroom that my sister now thought he was a sadly disproportionate man, and I must appreciate him for more than just his small penis, or else I wouldn't be dragging him along on a road trip.

"What's going on?" Wyatt asked, seeing my grin and Miranda's expression of horror. "What's so funny?" He couldn't resist a good joke, which he'd incorporate into his mental archive, and save for the ideal moment.

"Nothing to be concerned about," Miranda assured, as she shook her finger at me. "You're hilarious, Maddie, really amusing." I knew she'd seen through my smokescreen, though it required a few minutes.

The food was pretty good, and Pablo's made a brisk business, despite being out in the middle of nowhere. Truckers and ranchers came and went, and the two waitresses seldom had a free moment to give Wyatt the eye, and whisper about him.

At some point, I announced to Miranda I was pregnant.

Her burger was poised in midair for a bite. She stared at me dumbfounded, and then she put down the burger, wiped her hands with a napkin, and asked carefully, "Does Dad know yet?"

"Nobody knows, except for you and Kate Sumner's family."

Miranda didn't speak further, and simply looked back and forth at the two of us.

"Say something, Miranda," I prodded.

"I don't know what to say," she admitted. "You're the last sister I'd ever have thought would get pregnant, let alone find a man like this one."

"I think she's paying you a compliment, Madeline," Wyatt said with a shrug.

"Please say you're happy for me," I begged. I felt like a little girl again, trying to get my kick-ass elder sister to respect me.

157

"I *am* happy for you Maddie," she said sincerely. "I'm happy for both of you. I'm just a little dismayed, I thought I'd have kids before any of you, because I'm the one who got married first."

After Miranda's personal disappointment, I felt terrible for insisting. I had always thought that her career in law enforcement meant more to her than starting a family.

She patted my hand. "I'm happy for you, Maddie, for both of you," she repeated.

At least she was sincere about her happiness in our news, though she did make a point to remind me that now I'd have to tell Dad.

"Yeah, good luck with that," she said with a smirk.

When we were through with the meal, Wyatt grabbed the tab, and headed off for the cash register, while Miranda adjusted her uniform. We followed him outside into blinding sunlight, and said goodbye to my sister, before she climbed back into the cruiser.

She had put on her sunglasses, and was giving Wyatt a solemn expression. Certainly sternness was more believable when you couldn't see her eyes.

"Wyatt," she warned, "you'd better be gentle to Maddie with that huge thang."

She turned a tire smoking U out of the parking lot before merging northbound onto the Interstate.

To Rat's great joy, we got into the truck, and I turned southward toward Reno.

Wyatt, however, regarded me steadily from his side of the bench seat.

"What did you say to your sister?" he asked, but I only shook my head.

"What *would* I say?"

"You can tell me that when I went to the bathroom, you were discussing my shoe size, not describing my penis."

"She asked me if you were as large as your build suggests," I said, paraphrasing Miranda.

"And you *told* her?" He seemed terribly embarrassed. "I mean, you actually told your sister that I've got a large penis?"

"I didn't have to say anything, she had you figured out already."

"Madeline, no matter how humbly grateful a man is about what tool nature has provided him with, that doesn't mean he wants women talking about him behind his back, even if the subject matter is framed as such to be blazingly complimentary. Women can be thoughtless when a man is well endowed. They treat him like a sex object, instead of as a person."

"I didn't say anything," I repeated. "All Miranda has to do is look at me, and she knows I'm happy. She doesn't have to be told why."

He seemed to be considering my statement, while gazing out the window at the line of rugged hills.

"Is that the only part of me that makes you happy?" he finally asked in earnest.

I was thinking that, yes, size *does* matter, but I knew that wasn't why I was happy. I was also aware that just because Wyatt knew what to do with his "thang," great sex alone would never be enough to keep me happy. I was thankful our relationship had deepened since that rainy night in his Tacoma loft. Even then, I'd been pleasantly surprised—and extremely relieved—that our lovemaking hadn't been impeded by the contrast in our physical sizes. Wyatt was a practiced lover from the start, and knew how to satisfy me.

"It's only a part of the whole of why I'm happy when I'm with you," I promised. "I also happen to like you. You're intelligent and funny. You're considerate. You care about other people, and you're honest, even if it's sometimes difficult to process the information."

"Well, but I wasn't so forthright about Celeste, was I?" He sighed. "Tell me, Madeline, do you like having sex with me?"

I knew I had to be patient. I understood he was getting himself worked up by the insecurities that had evolved over the years starting from childhood loss. The insular world of growing up on the rez, being acclimated to living "outside," and the cavalcade of attractive women that must have marched through his life without forming more permanent attachment—these experiences could cause anyone anxiety.

"Yes, I enjoy having sex with you very much," I said softly. "But it's not just your penis, it's everything about you that makes sex with you so sexy."

"I'm relieved, and I'm happy, too, Madeline. It's important to me that you get pleasure when we have sex, that you enjoy making love with me. I have encountered women who didn't enjoy sex. I don't know if it was me, or the dick between my legs, but I've always been aware that a curse like mine requires sensitivity."

"I've loved and enjoyed every moment naked with you, Wyatt. I look forward to many more naked moments."

He seemed pleased, and reached over to squeeze my shoulder.

"I like you too, Madeline. You're small, but you pack a punch." He pointed at a sign that indicated Reno was twenty-five miles distant. "What do you think about spending the night in Reno?"

"I'd love to, but what about Rat?"

"You said you went to Reno after you saw Kate. When your sister called you at two in the morning? You had Rat with you then."

"I found a motel that let me keep him in the room. If you don't mind that it's kind of a shabby dive, though it is clean."

"I like a sleazy motel. It gives off just the right sense of lewdness, don't you think?"

I laughed, and then told him about the man who'd had the hooker in his room, and how they were smoking outside while I walked Rat, waiting for the dog to finish peeing. The picture created seemed to amuse him, though he expressed curiosity as to how I'd recognized the woman was a prostitute, so I laid out my analysis.

"She was standing outside their motel room smoking, dressed in just a skimpy bra, G-string and high heels."

We arrived in Reno, and found the motel, booking a room two doors down from the room I'd stayed in on my way home from my Astoria trip. In our privacy, Wyatt turned on the air conditioner, while I fed Rat in the tiny bathroom and laid out his doggy bed. Everything about the room was miniscule—the double bed, nineteen-inch television a bulky CRT, not a flat screen. The walls were painted off-white, with green shag carpeting reminiscent of the 1970s. A side chair upholstered in avocado Naugahyde completed the garish theme.

He asked if I was hungry, and I said I wasn't, so we lay down on the bed together, and just looked at one another. I touched his face, a gesture that inexplicably brought tears to his eyes.

"Madeline," he whispered. "I love you. I know I haven't said it except for a few times. I just want you to know how much I love you."

"Is there really a way to measure such a thing?" I joked, but this time he was adamantly serious, and grabbed one of my hands, placing my fingers over his heart. His chest was broad, the muscles firm from working as a metal sculptor, and I could feel his heart beating beneath my fingertips.

"Madeline…" He continued speaking my name softly while he undressed me. Soon I was naked on the bed, and he ran his hands along my curves. His fingers and palms were rough with calluses, but he knew how to touch me, just as he knew how to make love to me, slowly and thoughtfully. The intensity of our emotions enhanced the physical nature of our act, and when we were through, we were both drenched in sweat.

We lay in the darkness, breathing deeply, with just enough light to see by, and touched each other in wonderment.

"I was so lonely, until I found you," I admitted.

"Even with Jake?"

"Especially with Jake. I think that's why I was so willing to settle for him."

"I was lonely, too, Madeline. But I think I knew you were coming to Tacoma."

"How could you know?"

"I had just come back from Taholah, and then I had a sudden urge to go to the coffee house. I walked in the rain, but it was a nice walk, because I like the rain, and it wasn't falling too hard at first. I felt as though I had to get there quickly, just before it started pouring, and then I didn't even order coffee. I just sat at a table all alone, and looked out at the parking lot."

"You must have seen me arrive."

"I saw your car come in and park, and then I saw the struggle. I got up, and I ran outside."

"Did you hear us, Rat and me?"

"No, I couldn't. It was raining too hard, and the café had music playing over the PA." He smoothed the hair from my eyes. "But I saw you fighting back, Madeline. All I could do was stand there, watching. I'm so sorry."

"I remember, you told Rat to let go of the man he was biting."

"I know. That's a stupid thing to try to tell a dog, but at least he listened to me." He kissed my mouth with soft lips. "I fell in love with you so many times that night."

"I fell in love with you, Wyatt, when you said 'kismet.' I laughed, but that's when it happened to me."

"What the hell are we going to do, Madeline?"

"We're going to live together in Portland. And we're going to have a baby."

He nodded, as though mulling over my words, and then he pulled me close and looked straight into my eyes.

"Madeline, would you marry me? Tonight?"

He wasn't smiling, so I knew not to expect a punch line. I suppose that the few seconds I paused were enough to make him jump out of bed, and turn on the light.

"Come on," he urged, gathering our clothes, and laying them on the unmade bed.

"Where are we going?"

"I want to prove to you that I don't have cold feet, or any doubts."

I began to untangle my various articles of clothing from his, and dress, though I knew I needed a shower after that sweaty, profound sex.

"Yes, but what are you doing? Where are we going?"

"I want to marry you, Madeline. I want to prove to you that I don't have any second thoughts about being with you forever."

His spontaneity was mind-blowing, especially in contrast to a ceremony I'd always thought I'd receive as a sacrament in the Catholic Church. But, in our post sex glow, I was tempted to get caught up in the crazy fervor of wanting to be married to Wyatt. I could forsake the expectations of a regimented world, and take a chance with love. That's what the decision boiled down to—either my life with Wyatt, or the alternative, and I didn't want to be without him. To dig in my heels uttering phrases meant to bring us back to reality made no sense in light of my pregnancy, or this Portland endeavor. Though I certainly didn't need the finances or validation of a man, I wanted Wyatt, and I knew that marrying him would complete the circle.

Before the courthouse closed, we bought a marriage license. Sailing along through stars and fog, we chose a wedding chapel off Virginia Street, where the Justice of the Peace was only too happy to marry us for a fee. Standing at altar with the reek of sex trapped beneath our clothing, and Rat at our feet on leash, we spoke our vows. I couldn't discern if the magistrate truly liked us, or if it was only part of his job function, but his broad grin certainly added to the mood.

The gaudy lights of Reno flashed like a carnival. A billboard of half-naked female dancers clad in scanty, beaded outfits reared up above the chapel, fortuitously named The Chapel of Eternal Love. I swore I had a screw loose in my head to allow me to act so impulsively, and yet, I rode the crest of the wave of foolhardiness as a willing participant.

Back in the motel room, Wyatt and I stood together in the dinky shower, and washed off the previous sex act, and then, afterward, we committed another in the heat of our emotional and physical arousal. Ours was a wild ride, and I accepted the future with an open heart and

162

without fear, embracing Wyatt's attractive impulsivity, and his raging passion. If sealing our fate with a madcap Reno wedding was our destiny, then so be it.

Chapter Fifteen

The drive home was memorable, executed as a newly married woman with my husband at my side, and our child *in utero*.

When we arrived in Santa Clara, the time was almost one o'clock. I let Rat out in the yard, and then opened up the windows to rid the house of stagnant air. Wyatt rambled from room to room, and studied my life on display as though in a museum—family photographs in mismatched frames, and souvenirs I'd collected over time, such as my ceramic box of train-flattened pennies.

"I've done that," he said, about the coins, once he'd removed the lid to the discovery. "I found myself in a lot of trouble from Aunt Doreen, because of what money meant."

"I know. Dad forbade us from ever mentioning our tradition to my Grandpa Feliz, as he would have been furious that we wasted something as precious as money. I doubt there's more than fifty cents in that box, but it *is* money, after all."

"Still," he mused, setting the lid back on the coins, "it's precious, because of memories you made with your father and your sisters. At least you'll never spend it, right?"

"Yeah, because defacing pennies is illegal."

"Really?" He left the coin box, and put his arms around me. "*Really*, Mrs. McLain?" he repeated, kissing my neck, while I giggled like a schoolgirl.

"Why, Mr. McLain, are you thinking what I'm thinking?"

"What *are* you thinking I'm thinking, Mrs. McLain?"

"Are you thinking about doing me, Mr. McLain?"

"I'm *always* thinking about doing you, Mrs. McLain."

That statement led to us fooling around on the couch. Wyatt looked so good bare-chested, a delicious treat. We made our way to the bedroom, dropping articles of clothing as we went. We passionately consummated our first sex act in the house as husband and wife. This wasn't Oregon, but the intent was exactly the same.

When we were done with round one, I pointed out the clay proof of the halibut he'd given me in Tacoma, propped on the bedroom fireplace mantel. I know he'd seen it the very first time he visited, though drawing attention to it prompted more kissing, and another round of newlywed sex. Only afterward did I realize the implication of opened windows to the ears of my immediate neighbors, as Wyatt and I could be outspoken during our lovemaking.

Finally, exhausted from acting out, we showered and dressed, and then lazed around the living room, discussing inconsequential subjects, such as favorite foods. We both acknowledged a shared a taste for wild salmon.

I sighed, and studied the room around me.

"I've got to get a plan together to pack this shit up, and move it to Portland."

Wyatt asked for the notebook we had used to record the measurements of the Hawthorne house, proving he was wonderfully organized and straight thinking when required. I retrieved the spiral-bound pad from my luggage, and he helped me make a list of the items I wanted to keep, like all my old refinished furniture, and the stuff I was willing to part with, such as the exercise bike in the laundry room that I'd not used once.

"Why even have it?" he asked.

"It used to belong to my mom," I explained. "She'd ride it when she was pregnant." And then it dawned on me. I could actually use the exercise bike now. I mentioned this to Wyatt, who only pretended to wince painfully.

"Listen, Madeline, a true Indian woman walks," he argued sensibly. "She walks for miles and miles and miles."

"For miles and miles and miles?" I echoed.

"Right, and then she stops for a moment to drop the baby on a blanket, using the same blanket to wrap the baby in, and then she gets up and walks again for miles and miles and miles."

His casual mention of such a process horrified me. "That sounds like forced relocation, Wyatt, like the Trail of Tears."

"Yes, Madeline, it does, doesn't it?" He closed the notebook, and hitched his hair behind his ears. "Is there anyone in particular you would like to tell about your husband and child?"

165

"Well, there's my parents," I listed aloud. Wyatt opened the notebook again, and wrote on a fresh page. "My grandparents, my sisters. Everyone else can hear it through the Filipino grapevine."

"Ah, a bunch of gossiping folks, huh? Sounds like the rez." He put down the notebook. "What do you say we host a dinner of some sort, and have everyone over?"

Thinking about having to cook for more than just me, and the addition of Wyatt's stomach, put me off. I love my Wedgwood stove, but I don't enjoy cooking, a foible of mine Wyatt understood early on. Fortunately, he loves to cook, and I don't mind washing dishes, so we strike a perfect balance of opposites. I thought about the Quinault tale of *Misp*, and knew we'd been blessed.

"I was thinking we could just visit people," I said, "and then break the news."

"That's a good idea, but be forewarned that news like ours can often get away from itself. It's like wildfire, Madeline."

"Boy, do I know it."

"Oops, I almost forgot about something important."

He disappeared into the bedroom, and then returned with his gym bag, which he canvassed for a tiny parcel in a blue velvet sack. The item proved to be a box with a gold wedding band imprinted with tiny flowers and vining leafy plants.

"This is for you, Mrs. McLain." He slid the band onto the ring finger of my left hand. "It totally slipped my mind last night, because I was so heavily intoxicated with sex and love."

I marveled at the ring, so very beautiful. I knew he'd had to special-order, and estimate my ring size. Keeping in mind that I used power tools, he knew a diamond would get in the way.

"When did you buy this?" I turned the ring so I could grow accustomed to the sensation on my finger.

"A couple of weeks ago, around the time I made the metal salmon for the Portland house. I was hoping when I got around to asking you to marry me, you'd say yes, or else I'd be stuck with it." He paused, perhaps reading the amusement in my gaze. "All right, so it's the penis thing all over again. I put a little piece of paper around your finger when you were asleep way back that time you were crying about not knowing who the father of our baby was."

"That's so honorable of you." The gesture and the preplanning that went into buying the ring, even the sneaky part, were tremendously thoughtful, and I started to cry.

"Easy, girl," he soothed, as though I were a mare, instead of human. "It's not all that bad. Would you have preferred a diamond? I know how you girlie-girls love your bling."

"Don't you dare," I admonished. "I love this ring, it's—"

"Like the perfect wave?" he asked, brows arched. He'd quoted my letter, where I'd written, *there is the sea, and the tide, and I hit the perfect wave.*

"I acted like a fool last night," I told him in a rush. "I was terrified. It was so overwhelming, but I was so excited too."

"You didn't act like a fool, Madeline. If anyone's been a fool, it's me, with my stupid insecurities. You have a way of making everything fall into place. At least you married me. Now I'm an honest man."

Something occurred to me. "We have to buy a ring for you. No way my husband is going to walk around looking like an advertisement for the single life."

"Oh, yeah, I forgot about that."

He dug another box out of his gym bag, containing a man's ring, a simple gold band with braided edges.

"This once belonged to my father," he said softly. "It was one of the only things I ever got to keep all these years, and the only part of him that survived the crash. It used to be scratched up, but when I bought your ring, I asked the jeweler to shine it up, and make it look like as new as we are."

He showed me an inscription inside the band, *Randall Scott & Elizabeth Eagle.*

"Are those the names of your parents?" I asked.

"Yes." He studied me for a moment. "Would you consider using part or all of their names for the baby's name?"

"I was thinking of something more along the lines of 'Doc' Holliday, even if it's a girl."

"Be serious, woman. Don't act like me, all jokey and stuff."

"Of course I would. I'd be happy to."

I agreed, as I hadn't given the naming bit much thought. I had never been the kind of girl, who as a child forecast my life—from the man of my dreams up to the house with the white picket fence. There were no dolls or stuffed animals reflecting the preplanned names of my future children. I had hopes of happiness, much like my parents' lives, and I know such high expectations often have a quirky way of being fulfilled when one isn't looking.

"You never played like the other girls?" Wyatt asked, reading me clearly.

"I was too busy building the house. I didn't have time for social games."

"I remember as a boy that even on the rez, the girls liked to play at marriage. It must be a girl thing in every culture. I was always agreeable to going along with it, until I got old enough to want to see under their dresses, and then Aunt Doreen wised up and kept me home. You know, girls and their tits. Imagine me! I might have gotten someone pregnant."

He shrugged, the inexorable drive to procreate his variant of "house."

I looked at my watch, and realized it was getting close to dinnertime. I suggested that we could invite my parents over that evening, maybe for a drink, when my father was finished teaching his music students for the day. Wyatt thought it was a great idea, so I telephoned my mother, and set a time of eight-thirty.

I called my other sisters, first Margot, because we are so close, and then Miranda, who knew about my pregnancy, but hadn't been privy to the hasty Reno wedding. Margot was excited, and started planning for a post-Reno wedding party at the house she and Julie shared in Saratoga. I asked them to hold off telling anyone, until Wyatt and I had a chance to break the news to Mom and Dad that evening.

"Your sister lives in Saratoga?" Wyatt marveled. "The town with the trillion-dollar houses? How did she manage that, did she marry a sugar mama? Or, is *she* the sugar mama?"

"Margot and Julie bought a very tiny, very old house, and then hired Benités Construction to fix it up."

"Ah, I get it."

The last person I called was Mallory, my eldest sister. She didn't answer her phone, otherwise occupied, probably teaching a step aerobics class at the gym. I was tempted to leave a message about as front-heavy as I would soon become:

Hi, Mallory, I just wanted to call and let you know that Wyatt and I got married last night in Reno. We're expecting a baby, and thought we'd hasten our nuptials. Call me back!

But I didn't speak these words. I simply asked her to call me when she had a chance. Telling Mallory so flippantly that I was pregnant would be cruel, as she suffered from a medical condition that precluded her from ever having children. Despite Mallory's angst, I love my eldest sister, and would never deliberately hurt her.

When I hung up, I thought about our half-brother, Jesse Ibarra, the one Dad had fathered a quarter-century ago, the man Mallory nearly married in an attempt to throw acid in our father's face. Jesse is a police officer in Los Banos, which had made me leery of him at first. But Jesse *is*, after all, my half-brother, so I called him. His cell went to voice mail, and I left a message similar to Mallory's.

"What about your grandparents?" Wyatt asked.

"We should go see them."

"Don't you need to call first?"

"You're kidding, right? They're always at the house."

I explained that my grandparents were seldom away from home, as their property, small as it was, constituted nearly the densest suburban orchard in Sunnyvale, plus a lush and complex flower garden, requiring daily watering on regular rotation that often took an hour or longer to complete.

Leaving Rat to his own amusement in the back yard, we loaded into the Mercedes, and drove to my grandparents' house. Just as I'd thought, there was Grandpa Feliz, seated on a lawn chair in the shade of the garage overhang, reading the newspaper. He smiled and waved when I pulled into the driveway, but he didn't get up from his chair. I knew this was due to culture, that there was an expectation that I would go to my grandfather, and greet him in his own home.

I kissed Grandpa Feliz on the cheek, and then introduced Wyatt to him. Wyatt towered, a bastion of shade to save Grandpa's eyes from the merciless sunlight. This time, Grandpa rose to his feet.

"Wyatt," Grandpa repeated the name.

"Yes, sir, I'm Wyatt Earp McLain." He shook my grandfather's hand firmly.

"You go inside. Grandma's there."

He directed us through the garage and into the house, where we found Grandma Enida seated on the sofa, watching television. She wore a camel hair coat to keep warm, as Grandpa never turned the thermostat up higher than 50 degrees, even when Grandma was recuperating from major surgery. In the midst of summer, the air was reasonably warm in the house. The last time I'd visited, she was in the hospital, being tube-fed painkillers. On this day, she was bright-eyed, sitting up, a TV tray in front of her, and eating half a Hawaiian papaya with a teaspoon.

"Grandma," I spoke, leaning over to kiss her warm cheek. "How are you?"

"Madeline, you are here." She seemed very pleased to see me. "Who is this?"

I introduced Wyatt, who shook Grandma Enida's hand. Grandma, a charmer, was gracious, and invited us both to sit down and talk, using the remote control to mute the television with a trembling hand.

"You got married," she observed, as the two wedding bands were as clear as day, especially to my grandmother, who has sharp eyes. "When is the baby coming?"

"I...uh...in twenty-six weeks, Grandma," I told her.

"Shee!" Grandma cussed out her approval. "Maybe I stay alive to see the baby. You think? Your Grandpa, she's always sitting outside, you know, I got the colon surgery, and your Grandpa spends too much time out there, she's never sitting with me anymore and watching the television."

This was a tragic statement, my grandmother protesting my grandfather's current state of mourning, as though her colon cancer spelled the end of their over sixty-years of marriage.

We talked some more. Grandma Enida was interested in Wyatt's childhood, which she compared to Narvacan, in Ilocos Sur, Philippines, during and after World War Two.

"Except you got no guns." Grandma referred to the Japanese occupation, and the death toll of war.

"Well, we had Joseph DeLaCruz." Wyatt proceeded to describe the late Quinault leader, instrumental in preventing commercial loggers from accessing tribal land by organizing a blockade of the Chow Chow Bridge in Washington State in 1971. Wyatt spoke from memory, having been a protestor on that very bridge at the age of thirteen.

"He set us free from the U.S. government," he explained, "so we could have self-determination."

"Ah," said Grandma knowingly, "your DeLaCruz is like our Rizal. She is your national hero."

Grandma Enida recognized my happiness. She respected Wyatt, and I knew she would be my advocate to Grandpa Feliz, who was hard of hearing, and would require a lengthy explanation to decode my sudden pregnancy, and our spur-of-the-moment Reno wedding. I imagined Grandma setting it all out in the simplicity of Ilocano, and I loved her quiet wisdom.

She told us to go and eat, another expectation in the house of my elders. At the dining table were whole boiled prawns, cold steamed rice, and an Ilocano stew made with pork, tomatoes and *tabungao,* a Philippine calabash. Despite her shaky hands, Grandma fussed over us with plates and canned drinks, flattering Wyatt on his appetite, as the *tabungao* steadily disappeared.

"I've got to ask your grandmother how to cook this, Madeline," he complimented.

Before we left, I asked Grandma about her prognosis.

"The doctor said I would have chemotherapy." She waved her hands in a gesture of giving it all up to God. "Well, I lived a good life, I'm eighty years old, and I asked your Grandpa to come to America, so she did, and your daddy could grow up, and you, too, Madeline, in America. If we don't come to America, you don't meet Wyatt, *Nakong.*"

The tears stung my eyes at her calling me her "dear little one."

I kissed her, and told her I loved her, and Wyatt shook her hand once more. We did the same with Grandpa—only he saw the flash of my ring, and, grabbing my hand, laughed out loud.

"You're a good girl, Madeline," he praised, and shook Wyatt's hand again firmly.

"They remind me of Quinault elders," said Wyatt, on the drive home. "I'll bet if you took your grandparents to a powwow, everyone would think they're Indian. Well, until they opened their mouths, then they'd know they're Filipino." He eyed me. "That's hot, you know?"

"What's hot, my grandparents?" I touched his cheek with the back of my hand. "Are you feeling all right?"

"No, not your grandparents, but that you're part Filipino. You always see white guys with Filipino women. The white half of me sees the point, you're luscious."

"What about the Indian half of you?"

"I'm my mother's son, so that half likes the white woman in you."

"I *am* part Sioux Indian."

"No, I'd only believe that if you call yourself 'part Lakota.' None of this 'Sioux' nonsense."

"My mom's birth mother, Grandma June, calls herself 'half Sioux.'"

171

"Grandma June needs re-education, too." I realized he was joking. I never quite knew which was a joke, and which the grave, but when required to be serious, Wyatt had the capacity to rise to the occasion.

He certainly rose to something. When we arrived back at the house, there was a familiar car parked on the street, a BMW 740i. A woman sat behind the wheel, staring at the front door.

"Jesus Christ," I cussed, parking the Mercedes in the driveway.

"Why? What's going on? Did you just have a religious vision?"

"No, that car, the BMW? That's Jake's mother."

"Relax, Madeline, let's have a little fun with the lady, shall we?"

I flashed a smile at him. Wyatt used my key to enter the house, and I walked over to Charlotte Burgess's imposing car, just as she unrolled the window.

"Hello, Charlotte." I tried my best to keep my voice subdued. "What can I do for you today? Are your toilets still working?"

I had installed low-flush toilets at her winery headquarters many months ago, and figured it would be an acceptable conversation prompt to mention to this woman, who'd only visited me once. That was when Jake left for Seattle for the book signing tour, and had broken off his engagement to Sophie Whipple in the public eye of the San José Airport. Charlotte then drove up from Tanner Valley Vineyards to denounce my involvement with her son. Though she had adopted Jake at an early age following the deaths of his biological parents, she still acted as though it were her umbilical cord that had fed the fetus. By her consistent behavior, I was starting to think that she believed the cord was *still* attached.

"Well!" She seemed offended, and highly inconvenienced, but I knew this time, as at our previous encounter, her attitude was mere posturing, and I had the upper hand.

"Would you care for some coffee, Charlotte?"

"Yes, of course, Madeline."

She climbed out of the BMW. I had forgotten how tall she was, nearly the height of Wyatt. To me, at that very moment, she seemed painfully withered from whatever cause she had decided to take up on Jake's behalf.

She followed me into the house, which smelled of brewing coffee. This signified that Wyatt had already started, and I was grateful for his intuition. I suggested to Charlotte that she could sit on the couch, and then I disappeared into the kitchen.

172

Wyatt was setting up a tray with coffee mugs, sugar, half-and-half, and a plate of packaged cookies. I noted that one of the mugs happened to have the dragon motif, and he smiled mischievously.

"Did I pick the right one?"

I hugged him tightly. "How did you know to make coffee?"

"It's the same with my Aunt Doreen, and with Kate, when company arrives. I assumed it's an Indian thing, but I notice you and your mother do it too."

When the coffee was finished brewing, I poured the cups, and Wyatt carried the tray out to the living room, setting it on the low table before Charlotte's tightly pressed knees.

Charlotte's eyes were just about popping out at the sight of Wyatt, who'd taken the extra care to dress up in my apron. The formerly white apron was covered in bloodstains, a result of that time I'd assisted my father in butchering a half-dozen chickens for *sapsaporicket,* an Ilocano blood stew prepared for the engagement party of my sister, Margot, to her partner, Julie. I never minded the bloodstains, which languished in spite of repeated washings.

The apron was a perfect touch, much too small for Wyatt, and strained against his muscular girth. Add in his long silky-dark hair, bronze skin, tiny gold-hoop earrings, and beautiful exotic eyes, and Wyatt was a perfect recipe for provoking Charlotte.

"*Who* is *this!*" she demanded.

"Oh, how could I forget? Charlotte, please meet my husband, Wyatt Earp McLain."

Wyatt curtsied, lifting the hem of the apron with his fingertips. "Pleased to meet you, Ma'am," he spoke, using his best fake British accent.

"Your *husband!*" Her face was flushed, a net of mottled red spreading across both cheeks.

"Yes, now Wyatt, dear," I said kindly, as though he were an idiot. "What is it that you do again? Are you a roofer, or a dock worker?"

"Darling, you know I simply do both, because I'm ambidextrous. It seemed the best use of that naughty master's degree." He kept up an accent, though his speech now suggested Irish brogue.

"Madeline, I must ask you to halt this charade at once!" Charlotte barked.

Wyatt only tittered, and sat in one of my armchairs, helping himself to coffee and a couple of sugar cookies.

I finally relented, feeling a little sorry for her.

"What can I do for you, Charlotte?"

"I'm here about Jacob, of course." She lifted the dragon mug to her lipstick-red mouth.

Wyatt snorted softly at the cup's implication. I warned him to simmer down with a roll of my eyes.

"I think Jake was your issue the last time you visited," I said. "But, you see, Charlotte, Jake's not *my* problem."

"Jacob has simply locked himself in that hovel of his, and refuses to come out."

She was referring to the Santa Cruz Mountain retreat in Ben Lomond where Jake resided. In Charlotte's snobbish opinion, the former 1920s hunting estate qualified as squalor despite its renovated charm.

"You could call someone from Mental Health," Wyatt offered, in his true voice. "That's what they do in Washington State when people start acting all weird and antisocial."

"Kindly keep your opinions to yourself," Charlotte snapped, without looking directly at Wyatt.

"Hey, I'm fifty-two, I get to have an opinion," he returned in his sweetest voice.

I was having a difficult time *not* looking at him, and my amusement in the apron was mounting.

Charlotte finally turned a tortured glare his direction. "Are you *really* those things?"

"What things?"

"Dock worker. Roofer."

"No, Ma'am."

"What *are* you, then?"

"You heard Madeline, I'm her extremely satisfied husband."

"That's *not* what I asked." Charlotte was becoming peevish, which only meant Wyatt had full control of the conversation.

I leaned forward. "Didn't you say to me once, Charlotte, that 'some roofer or dock worker' will someday see my value?"

"In good stead," she finished stiffly, and then sniffed.

"I don't have anything to do with Jake's latest behavior," I said with conviction. "He's a man, and he's got to decide for himself what he wants to do."

"He claims that he wants to be with you." Charlotte's statement was evidently highly unpleasant for her to make.

"Then you need to ask him why he can't handle a monogamous relationship, Charlotte. That's really his first step for a future with any woman he meets."

She regarded Wyatt with interest, now that she knew he wasn't a longshoreman or general contractor, vocations that Charlotte considered very far beneath even her contempt. If she knew the secret of Wyatt's hands, what my naked body had grown to love, every honorable callus, she might have turned her haughty nose up in disgust.

"Really, what is it that you do?" Her desperate curiosity required as much satisfaction as Wyatt had professed to receiving from me.

"I'm an artist. A metal sculptor, to be exact."

"A metal sculptor?" Charlotte blinked, likely confusing Wyatt and his work with modernist Albert Paley, or the hulking creations of Jack E. Anderson.

"That's right." He was openly amused at her internal conflict. "Or, if you'd prefer, since you think so highly of dear Madeline, I'm a blacksmith, though not to be confused with a farrier, who shoes horses."

"I must know." And here, she licked her lips. "Are you famous?"

"Well, I'm rather well-known in the Pacific Northwest, especially on the Seattle arts scene." He squinted at her, as though is disappointment. "I've met people just like you, at gallery openings. You know, with a full champagne flute in one hand, and a checkbook in the other."

Charlotte was vainly trying to hide her sharp interest behind her stuffiness. She leaned forward, shoulders straining against the blazer of her tailored suit.

"Where in the world did Madeline find you?" Charlotte's query suggested my lowly stature could never land a brilliant artist in a billion years.

"Madeline found me in a café, in the rain," Wyatt said softly, his eyes on me, and love in his voice. "At the appointed hour, when the dog struck two."

Charlotte scoffed, pissed at being handed cryptic code. To complicate matters, her scent must have drifted out of the house, and into the back yard, as Rat came to the laundry room door, barking up a storm.

"So, *you* have that animal!" she cried, pointing a finger at me.

"That's only because Jake set Rat free." I described how Rat had come to me twice on his own accord, but the third time, had been

175

literally cut loose by Jake, and then suffered a terrible injury, probably from being struck by an automobile. "He admitted his guilt," I added, about Jake's collusion. "That's why I have Rat, because Jake's incapable of loving anyone except himself."

As though to shore me up, Rat continued to bark and snarl at the back door.

"I've seen enough!" Charlotte rose shakily to her feet. "You and yours are evil, Madeline, and I want no part of it."

"So. Huh. Then what were you here for today, Charlotte?"

"She *was* going to ask you to go see Jake," Wyatt observed, a student of human nature. "Even if it meant that you'd marry her boy. Isn't that hilarious?"

I turned to her, my eyes and heart fierce. "Is *that* true? Is that why you're here?"

"Desperate times call for desperate measures," Charlotte conceded.

I walked to the door, and opened it wide. "Goodbye, Charlotte," I said meaningfully, and she stomped back to her car. I heard the door slam, and then Charlotte launched into the roadway with a scratch of expensive tread.

As soon as my front door was closed, I let Rat in. He whined and growled while sniffing at the spot where Charlotte's ass had rested on the couch. Satisfied that the woman was indeed gone, Rat curled up beside the front door, and promptly fell asleep.

"Whew!" Wyatt exhaled, wiping at his forehead in a melodramatic gesture of weariness. "That was impressive, Madeline." He sat with one leg hitched over an arm of the chair, the apron bunched up beneath his armpits.

I fell onto my knees before him, laughing and kissing his face. He pulled me into his lap, if only to stop me from smothering him with my lips.

"Tell me, aren't you glad you caught Jake kissing another woman?" he asked.

"Blest be to God!" I declared passionately.

"It would only have been a matter of time, and you would've caught him eventually, if not in Seattle, then inside of your own bed. And you would have seen more than just kissing." He tenderly stroked my cheek.

"Thank you, Wyatt."

"I only did what a good husband should always do for his beautiful wife."

"You're such a great husband. But I think you had a better time with Charlotte than I did."

"That's true. What do you think about inviting her back again someday?"

"She probably wouldn't come. I don't think she enjoyed being made into a joke."

My stomach reminded me of dinner. Rather than driving to a restaurant, I cooked eggs on the stove, while Wyatt, having removed the apron, hovered behind me as an assistant. I think he was more interested in my body, as he couldn't keep his hands to himself. Nevertheless, I soon made a nice light meal of scrambled eggs with tomatoes, and wheat toast.

We went to bed for a couple of hours, naked as usual. Our interlude started out as a bonding thing, but ended up with sex. I'm telling you, a man as physically hot as Wyatt with the double indemnity of humor is impossible to resist.

By eight, we were up to shower, because my parents were expected around eight-thirty. When they arrived, Dad embraced Wyatt immediately. Mom hugged Wyatt too, but first she kissed me on the cheek.

"Your grandmother called us," Mom said, and I smacked my forehead dramatically, having totally forgotten to ask Grandma Enida not to inform my parents until I'd had the chance to tell them myself. Of course, Grandma couldn't imagine that she would be handed the news before my own father, but I couldn't fault Grandma's enthusiasm.

I served Mom and Dad each a glass of Clay Creek Reserve from the stash Paul had passed to Wyatt at the Spotted Horse Ranch.

"This is great wine," and Dad hoisted the glass toward the light. "So, what are your plans from here out?"

"We bought a house in Portland," Wyatt informed.

I turned to him at the mention of "we," because I'd always thought it was Wyatt's house in Hawthorne, and that I had simply climbed onboard to fix it and live within its walls. Though my parents blended their finances, I had never allowed money and community property a single thought, just like my lacking, girlish dreams.

177

My parents were happy for us, but they were also sad at my leaving. I reminded them that Portland was only a lengthy day trip north on I-5, or a short flight from San José Airport.

We told them the story of how we met. "At the appointed hour," Wyatt had said to Charlotte, "when the dog struck two." The tale seemed too farfetched to believe, but because we both owned the same facts, we were totally credible.

"I'm proud of you, Maddie," my father said, when we were done with our narrative. "The two of you are one in a million, just a twist of fate."

Wyatt passed Dad the other bottle of Clay Creek Reserve as a gift. I was amused to realize that my father's new son-in-law was his junior by a mere eighteen months.

Mom helped me carry the glasses to the kitchen—three in all, because I wouldn't consume alcohol during pregnancy—and then I asked her how she had managed to make her marriage last.

"You get close every day," she advised.

"What do you mean by close?"

"You talk, you forgive...you make love, Maddie." This exchange could have been awkward, but here I was, a wife and soon-to-be-mother, and I needed the wisdom of my own mother.

"That's easy."

"Of course it is. You decide, do I want to live without this person? Or will I just dry up and blow away like dust if he's gone? If you love him, you do everything you can, not to dry up and blow away in the wind." She hugged me tightly. "I love you so much, Maddie."

After my parents were gone, Wyatt and I discussed what would need to be done in the next few days. We'd post all the free stuff to the Internet, or truck it to Salvation Army or Goodwill, and then pack up the rest. We would need to make arrangements for the rental of a bobtail truck, a flatbed trailer and a car dolly for a one-way trip to Portland, to carry all my personal property, plus the work truck, the Mercedes and my big cruiser motorcycle. Wyatt was planning to help me drive up to Portland, and he called the airline to cancel his flight.

Our plans were settled, and we were tired, so by the time we went to bed—naked, of course—we were asleep almost right away.

Chapter Sixteen

Our undertaking seemed massive, yet we managed to clear out the house in readiness for the renters, who were due to take possession on the first of the month, less than two weeks away.

Packing up was accomplished through purchasing cardboard boxes and packing material, and then hiring Juan and Humberto to help us load the many boxes, and furniture into a bobtail truck.

"Who do you know who has time to help?" Wyatt asked, the morning following our meeting with my parents.

I mentioned Juan. "He's a regular of mine, and I trust him."

"Can you call Juan?"

"Well…that's not exactly how I get in touch with Juan." I explained the procedure of hiring day laborers.

"He's not an illegal immigrant, is he?"

Wyatt wasn't politically correct in his descriptive, though I couldn't blame the man, whose own people were known as Native American.

"Not at all. I would *never* hire somebody I couldn't report to the IRS."

We loaded into the work truck with Rat, and drove to the home improvement store in Santa Clara. We were lucky to find Juan standing with a bunch of his *compadres,* waiting to be hired. Usually I was mindful to try to hire Juan early in the morning, as he was a tradesman with an excellent reputation, and seldom passed a day without one job or another.

"*Señora Benités!*" He grinned, happy to see me. He caught sight of Wyatt, and grinned. "*¿Es este su marido, Vito?*"

Juan wondered if Wyatt were my spouse, allegedly named Vito, a character I had created long ago to dispel any doubt men might have in working for a single woman. Back then, I'd told Juan that the fictional Vito was *muchos grandé*, or "many large." I was relieved that at least Wyatt fit the original bill.

179

"*Sí, él es Vito*," I motioned toward Wyatt. "Right, Vito?"

"Yes," said Wyatt carefully, able to grasp my exchange with Juan. "I mean—*sí!*"

I told Juan what we needed, just a day or two of assistance in loading up a moving truck, and he nodded his assent to be hired.

"*Humberto ha vuelto*," Juan informed. He then waved to a man who stood in the middle of the group of day laborers.

I determined that Humberto, having nursed his sick mother back to health, was back in town to pick up day jobs.

"*Informe a Humberto I contratará a usted y él.*" I told him to let Humberto know I'd be glad to hire the two of them.

Juan ran back to his cousin, and passed along my hiring proposition. Humberto followed Juan, along with a man I had never wanted to see again, the unsavory Cucho.

Rat saw Cucho immediately, and without so much as catching scent, started to bark and kick up a fuss. Cucho remembered the dog, remembered my polite opinion of his obvious disdain toward women, and stopped about twenty feet from the truck, scowling.

"That guy's bad news," Wyatt said, about Cucho. He didn't dare point, as that gesture wasn't only a Native *faux pas*, but also an indiscretion in any culture, calling rude attention to whomever you were discussing.

"Absolutely," I agreed. I briefly related the story of hiring Cucho once, and never again, due to the man's hostile language regarding women. Even Cucho's own granduncle had deemed the young man a danger to females of every age.

Juan and Humberto climbed into the truck, much to Rat's delight. The dog sat between the men, with tail wagging furiously. We departed without incident—except for the chilling vision of Cucho in the rear-view mirror, arms crossed, following the truck with angry eyes.

The day's work was productive, in that we packed most of the boxes, and loaded most of the furniture on the truck, holding back the items we intended to give away, and the mattress to my bed, which we needed to sleep on, and pack last. Wyatt noted the double bed would be perfect for the extra bedroom whenever guests came to Portland to visit us.

Wyatt put himself in charge of the packing and loading, directing Humberto and Juan in what little crude Spanish he knew. He could say things like *derecho* and *la izquiera,* or *hasta* and *abajo.* There was enough Spanish in Wyatt's memory to offer these simple directions, though the joke was on Wyatt, because Juan and Humberto were perfect English speakers. None of us bothered to inform Wyatt, as he was making an honest effort to accommodate.

I was responsible for the giveaways, the stuff posted to the Internet, like the battered aluminum pots and pans, and my Walmart dish sets. At one point, I brought six boxes of used items to a non-profit donation center. I also made a pizza run, and fed us late in the afternoon. I then drove the two men back to Juan's place, while Wyatt cleaned the house with a vacuum and dust mop.

I told Juan I'd be back at his house early in the morning to pick him and Humberto up, and we shook hands on the deal.

"*Señora, voy a extrañar mucho cuando te hayas ido,*" Juan spoke, holding back his emotions, because he was a man.

I will miss you when you go.

That night, Wyatt and I were completely done in. The day consisted of positive forward motion, but also had proved extremely hectic. We ate the rest of the pizza—cold, since the microwave was packed in the truck. After a shower, I settled Rat to bed in the laundry room for safekeeping, not wanting him to access the back yard, where he might encounter a skunk or a raccoon. I wanted no glitches in my desire for continuing this wondrous life we'd set sail upon. Rat obeyed, and curled up on his special padded dog bed.

Wyatt and I retired to bed, simply a sheet-covered mattress on a stark wood floor, in our usual naked glory.

"Madeline," he whispered, often a precursor to lovemaking, but we were both so tired, that I fell asleep with his soft voice breathing my name.

❖ ❖ ❖ ❖

I awoke, choking, my body stretched to the limit. In the background, I could hear Rat raving like a rabid wolf, throwing his body against the door, but I was quickly losing consciousness. My vision swirled with black circles, and I could just make out the face of the man who loomed over me, knees spreading my thighs. Pants down around his ankles, he was about to drill me with his penis.

In cold terror, I realized the man was Cucho.

Cucho was ranting angrily in Spanish, while Rat continued to hurl himself against the door, shaking the walls. Cucho was trying to get into position to force his penis into me, but I thrust my fingers into his face.

Raking his cheeks, I caught one of his eyes with my nails, and he jumped back, cursing at me, calling me "*Perra!*"—a bitch.

Free of Cucho's hands, I could see the bedroom window had been broken. The blinds were tilted crazily, and shattered fragments of glass remained in the frame. But there was no immediate sign of Wyatt.

"Wyatt," I rasped, my throat aching, and I clambered for the edge of the mattress. I found Wyatt on the floor, a knife stuck into his belly.

"Wyatt!" I screamed, the wails of Rat's bloodlust and Cucho's rage filling my ears.

A small line of blood slowly trailed behind Wyatt, who, ashen, grasped the knife butt with one hand to protect his abdomen from further entry, while he tried to crawl across the wood floor using the other arm. While he dragged his body, the shards of glass littering the floor tinkled like chimes.

Cucho jumped on me again from behind, and I hit him in the face with the back of my skull. He tried to pull my arms behind me, but I kept kicking him, punching him, using my nails and my teeth and every ounce of my strength to keep him from harming the baby. I struggled to reach for a piece of broken glass, but the second my fingers touched upon a splinter as large as my hand, Cucho hauled me backward by one leg.

Wyatt made it to the door, just as Cucho grabbed one of my arms, and yanked me around, the other hand on my throat, trying to throttle me again. I clocked him in the privates with a foot. But he wouldn't let go, no matter how hard I gouged, no matter how many times I kicked him in the groin, or slammed his knees with my feet—and I was steadily losing consciousness.

Behind Cucho, Wyatt had managed to stand upright by leaning against the wall, and bracing himself with the free hand. He let go of the knife handle protruding from his abdomen, and pulled open the door, the knob slick with blood from his palm.

Rat charged through the gap, and leaping on Cucho, began to tear into the man with his teeth and nails. Cucho let go of me, and tried to grab the dog, but Rat's Shar-Pei dam had imparted a loosely fitting skin, and Rat was able to turn and continue biting Cucho's arms and hands, and then, his throat, drawing blood that turned the floor into a slippery danger zone.

Cucho screamed in abject terror, hastily yanking up his pants, and fleeing through the bedroom door, Rat on his heels. There was a session of fierce snarling, and a struggle with the front door, which Cucho slammed behind him to prevent Rat from chasing him down Bassett Street like a weasel.

I could hear sirens advancing. In the midst of all the commotion, Wyatt had dragged himself to his cell phone, and called for emergency paramedics. Now he lay, naked and bleeding, his beautiful, agile body curled around the knife handle.

I knelt beside him, begging him to live. He seemed to be trying to remove the knife, but I pulled his hands away. I knew that taking out the blade would be worse than leaving it in.

I whipped the blanket off the mattress, and wrapped it around Wyatt. He was in shock, which kills faster than most wounds. I found my robe, quickly dressed, and then hauled Rat into the bathroom, shutting the door. I did this for Rat's safety, as I feared a cop with a gun, seeing all the blood, would be more likely to assume the worst about Rat, and shoot the poor brave dog. All Rat did was lay on the bath carpet, and cry like a baby.

"Good boy," I croaked, my voice hoarse from being throttled.

The paramedics arrived with the fanfare of two full sized fire trucks, followed by five police cruisers, and an ambulance. Wyatt was awake, but his skin was turning gray, and his eyes had started to wander.

"Wyatt," I begged, touching his face with my lips. "Please, stay here with me."

He couldn't speak, as though saving strength, but he kissed me a few times, before the paramedics intervened, and began trying to stabilize him for the gurney ride to the hospital.

The cops wanted to impound Rat. They explained that since the dog had bitten a man, he would need to be quarantined, and swabbed of blood evidence. I argued that Rat had saved us from further harm, and pleaded with them not to euthanize Rat.

"Write that in your report!" I kept insisting. "His name is Rat, and he stopped the attack, he saved our lives!"

The cops promised me that Rat would not be killed, and would be well taken care of, in all likelihood returned to me within a few days. When I brought Rat from the bathroom and snapped the leash to his harness, he was clearly upset, but he went readily with a compassionate police officer. Rat's body language indicated he believed he was in trouble, and I suppose allowing the police to remove the dog from the house may have reinforced Rat's anxiety. The last I saw of him on that night, he was walking with his head down and tail between his legs.

They whisked Wyatt to Valley Medical Center, the county hospital. I went too, riding in the back of the ambulance, naked beneath my robe. I held his hand, and he tried to look into my eyes for as long as possible, the oxygen mask blocking our kisses, before he finally passed out from the pain, and loss of blood.

In the hospital, Wyatt was put into emergency surgery to address the knife sticking out of his muscled belly. The triage nurse saw the other knife scars on Wyatt's shoulder, and horrified, inquired about their origin, while I dismissed them impatiently as old wounds.

A female police officer from the sex crimes unit brought me into an examination room, and interviewed me, while a nurse scrutinized my physical state. The entire interview and exam were caught on video. The cop asked if I knew my attacker, and I named him without hesitation, even going so far as to giving them Juan's address, so they could hunt that bastard grandnephew of his down.

The nurse scraped under my nails, where Cucho's skin and blood had collected during my defensive actions. Though I mentioned that I hadn't been penetrated, she found semen on the inside of my thighs, and collected samples. I knew it wasn't Wyatt's, as we hadn't had sex that night, too exhausted from packing and loading to be intimate. The only answer was that it belonged to Cucho, and that the violence of his attempted rape had excited him so greatly, that he hadn't needed to complete the act to get his rocks off. I was so physically repulsed, that I nearly vomited right there on the examination table.

I told the nurse that I was pregnant, and she checked the fetus, using ultrasound. A woman usually experiences this beautiful moment in her doctor's care, but the first time I heard my baby's heartbeat, I was being examined following a sexual assault.

When the nurse had finished with the exam, and collected the pertinent evidence, I was allowed to shower in one of the rooms. The nurse provided me with two gowns and a pair of socks, until I could call Margot or Mallory, and ask someone to bring me some clean clothes. Everyone was kind and professional, and really helped me get through the difficult period, post-assault. The police officer even let me use her personal cell phone, and I called Margot, who drove out right away with Julie, bringing me some of Julie's clothes, because all Margot wore were dresses.

❖ ❖ ❖ ❖

Wyatt was in surgery for a few hours, and then in recovery. They said to me, "Your husband is in recovery, Mrs. McLain," and then brought me to him. It felt strange to be called "Mrs. McLain" by anyone other than Wyatt.

He was unconscious for nearly an hour, before he awoke from the anesthesia. They had Wyatt trussed up like Grandma Enida, on drugs and fluids, because, as the doctor explained, they'd had to repair his intestines and the abdominal wall, so it might be a couple of days before they would allow him to eat solid food, in case they had to go in again.

"Why would you have to go in again?" I asked.

"Possible infection," the doctor explained. "Hope for the best, but we'll wait and see."

Once he awakened, Wyatt was relieved to see proof I was physically unharmed. He was moved from recovery, and into a semi-private room on another floor. As his wife, I was allowed me stay with him as long as I wished.

"Madeline," his said, in a strained voice. He'd spoken my name to put me to sleep the previous night, before awakening to our nightmare.

"I'm fine. Our baby's fine," I promised, and he smiled weakly, obviously reassured by my words.

"I love you, Madeline," he murmured, and then he drifted off in drugged sleep.

He had periods of sleep and wakefulness, and I was always there when he awoke. Margot brought me some of my own clothes, and my cell. I telephoned Kate in Susanville, and told her what had happened. I was struck that neither Wyatt nor I had thought to call Kate and tell her we'd been married in Reno, but then, she said she already knew.

"Wyatt told me he was going to marry you in Reno on the way home. He asked me to keep it a secret, because he was going to surprise you."

This revelation really hit me hard, proving that Wyatt was an excellent planner, from purchasing the beautiful wedding ring he'd secretly sized, then brilliantly arranging a conversation in the Portland motel room, so he could propose to me, all the way up to our marriage at the Reno wedding chapel.

"So it wasn't impulse?" I asked.

"Of *course* it was impulse, but at least he planned the impulse. In fact, he was down in the wine cellar with Paul when he planned it. Paul told me that Wyatt used the landline to call the chapel, because he couldn't get cell reception on the ranch."

"Oh, Kate. And here all along, I'd thought he was being reckless. I felt like I was being foolhardy, too, except that I knew I didn't want to live without him." A sob rose up in my throat, and reflexively choked me. "I just can't live without him, Kate," I admitted, tears burning my eyes.

"It won't come to that, Maddie," she assured me bravely. "Everything will be all right."

Before we ended the call she promised to let Aunt Doreen and Ben Barrow know what had happened to Wyatt.

❖ ❖ ❖ ❖

A Santa Clara police detective arrived in Wyatt's room, and asked to speak with us. The detective informed that Cucho had been arrested, turned in by his own granduncle, Juan Jiminéz.

Wyatt had recovered enough to sit up weakly in the bed with assistance. He accepted the information from the detective with calm indifference. When the cop had gone, Wyatt explained why he'd been able to let go of his anger.

"I know why we were put together, Madeline, and I know why Rat kept coming back to you. So we would be united when this terrible thing happened. So Rat and I would be there to prevent you from being raped and murdered."

I haltingly told Wyatt that although I hadn't been penetrated, the nurse had discovered semen on the inside of my thighs, so in a manner of speaking, I'd been sexually assaulted.

"I love you, Madeline," he insisted, covering my announcement with words of love. He was adamant about his love for me. Nothing could dissuade him from believing in a purpose for us being together, both to get through that awful night, and to strive for our future.

I mentioned what Kate had revealed, about Wyatt's silent plan to snag me, which had culminated in our Reno wedding. In the face of this astounding disclosure, Wyatt never even blinked.

"Kate told me you were a force to be reckoned with," I added, recalling that conversation with his sister in Susanville, when Wyatt was just an unforgettable one-night stand.

"Yes, that's true," he agreed softly. His weary face reflected the depth of his feelings for me. "I wanted you, Madeline. It was a choice to either be with you, or lose a chance at real happiness. I read your eyes, and I assumed that you felt the same way."

"It happened that night when I first saw your scars. I knew you were a kind man, a loving man." I lay my fingertips against his cheek. "When did you put your plan into motion?"

"From the moment I stood there, watching you drive away. And then I went inside, and I wrote to you. I took a chance, I put everything I had into that letter."

"What would you have done if I hadn't written back?"

Wyatt faltered, as though the thought hadn't occurred to him, but then he surprised me.

"If you never wrote back to me, I guess I'd still be waiting." He smiled wanly. "That was the longest six days of my life. All I had was hope."

"And a plan."

He reached out, and grasped one of my hands, and I could feel him trembling from the effort.

"That first night, I knew I wanted to be with you, Madeline, and later, on the beach, I was overjoyed when you told me you loved me. But I never wanted to own you. I never saw you as a conquest or as a possession." His eyes were heavy, lids half-closed as he fought the pain medication. "I kept coming back because I was so sure you felt the same way about me."

"I do. I feel exactly the same way."

"Madeline," he spoke my name, trying desperately to focus.

"I love you, Wyatt," I promised, kissing him, and reassured, he surrendered to sleep, hand in mine.

❖ ❖ ❖ ❖

Kate and Paul arrived from Susanville by diesel pickup truck. Aunt Doreen came by air with her husband, Ben Barrow, and Ben's adult son, Burly Dog Barrow, also an attorney. Burly Dog stood in Wyatt's room looking like a cranky hit man, and scaring all the nurses, until he opened his mouth and poured on the charm.

"So, you're Madeline," Aunt Doreen nodded her approval. "Wyatt's been writing me all about you. I've been wanting to say *Sio'kwil*, to you, Madeline."

"*Sio'kwil?*"

"A Quinault expression of gratitude."

187

Aunt Doreen was about my height, with a face that reflected ageless elegance, and deep love for me, though we'd never met. I asked her why she seemed to love me already without ever having met me, and she smiled.

"Because, you love Wyatt, and he loves you." That truth was all that mattered to her.

My side of the family visited—my parents, grandparents, aunts, uncles and cousins, and Margot and Julie. Miranda came from Susanville with her husband, Gilbert, and whispered in my ear that she had just discovered she was pregnant. Mallory arrived with Jesse Ibarra, and blushingly announced their engagement was on once again. I knew it was for love, not for some childish retribution against Dad. This time, I knew they had a chance.

❖ ❖ ❖ ❖

The doctor estimated Wyatt could go home in a couple of days. They'd decided to put him on soft solids, and once Wyatt had a bowel movement, they'd sign him out. He was on his feet now with the assistance of a walker, up and down the hallways accompanied by a nurse or family member, and IV rig, always in need of support to sit up, because there was still tenderness in his abdomen. Wyatt used a bar hanging on a chain over his bed to pull himself into an upright position. When he grasped the bar, his wedding band flashed in the light, and I would blush with the knowledge that he was my husband.

Most of the time, I was at the hospital living and breathing beside Wyatt, loving him without the sex, because that would have hindered improvement. He kept suggesting various positions and techniques that might circumvent injury to his abdomen. He tried to crack jokes, weakly, but it often hurt too much for him to laugh with any gusto.

❖ ❖ ❖ ❖

Animal Control released Rat to me on the fifth day. I received a call on my cell while I was watching Wyatt sleep, and agreed to pick Rat up at the Animal Control Authority in Santa Clara. I awoke Wyatt to tell him. His skin seemed a little warm to the touch, but he was coherent, and overjoyed that Rat would be allowed to come home.

Ninety minutes in slow traffic was required to drive to the shelter, and sign Rat out of the animal prison. He was happy to see me, yet penitent. He seemed to understand that attacking a human was wrong, but like the incident in Tacoma, he had only resorted to offense to save me.

188

This time, however, he seemed almost depressed, and when I brought him home, he lay prone in the laundry room, despondent, staring at his food dish with little interest. I held him gently, speaking his name, telling him what a good friend he was. He wagged his tail once or twice in response.

I telephoned my father, and asked if he could check in on Rat that night. I left an extra key inside one of the redwood planter boxes on the front porch. Knowing the dog's state, Dad promised he would come within the hour, and spend some time with poor sad Rat.

When I arrived back at Valley Med and approached Wyatt's room down the short corridor, I knew right away that something was amiss. I could hear him arguing with several people, a behavior that was simply not his style. If Wyatt were in disagreement with another, he would use the leverage of a joke or verbal interplay to mitigate the tension. He was a man of peace, not an aggressor, so the elevated volume of his voice was an immediate cause for concern.

I entered the room in time to see two female nurses and a lab technician at Wyatt's bedside. Wyatt's face was flushed and a bit bloated, and he seemed totally out of sorts.

"Oh, good," one of the nurses said, recognizing me. "His wife is here." She turned to Wyatt. "Mr. McLain, your wife is here!" She spoke loudly, as though Wyatt had gone deaf.

I went to him, and held his hands, but he seemed not to recognize me. He was really burning up now, and sweat drenched his skin and gown.

"What's wrong?" I asked, fighting panic.

"He's developed a fever," said the other nurse. "We need to draw blood, but he won't allow us. We think he has an infection, and we need to identify it, so the doctor can determine a course of treatment."

"Wyatt," I said, foolishly thinking to reason with him. "Can this person," and I pointed to the lab tech, "can he take a little blood from you?"

"No!" Wyatt roared, which caused my hair to stand on end. "They want to kill me! They think Indian Health won't pay, they need me to die!" He was angry with the medical staff, and furious at me for conspiring.

"Mr. McLain," said a nurse, holding up a couple of tablets in a small plastic cup. "We need to address your fever. Will you take this Tylenol?"

"No!" He knocked the cup of pills from her hand, and they flew across the room. "It's cyanide, you want me dead!"

"Please," I begged the other nurse, "how high is the fever?"

"One-hundred and five." She shook her head. I knew that one more degree up the scale, and he'd *really* be dead, not simply be a figment of his delirious imagination. I was terrified.

"How else can we get him to take Tylenol?" I asked.

"By suppository," the first nurse said, but she looked a little frightened. Wyatt was two hundred pounds of muscle and bone, and willing to put up a fight in his delusional state, even with the debilitation of the abdominal wound.

He yanked up his gown, revealing not only the wound, but also his genitals. I'm sure this wasn't on purpose—the genital part—and he poked at the wound. The edges had been closed with stainless steel staples, and seemed to be red, tender, and slightly swollen.

"Do you see?" he asked me, his fingers really pressing hard. I saw puss ooze to the surface. "They want me to die, they've cut me up, and made it happen."

At that, he lay back on the bed, drained of the desire to fight, as though a fuse had popped, and left him defenseless.

"Wyatt?" I asked, trying to connect with his gaze.

"Madeline," he moaned, his eyes roving, unable to locate me. "Where are you?" Realizing I was absent, he began to cry.

"Quickly," I told the nurses, "let's get that suppository in."

I helped them roll Wyatt onto one side, and they slipped the acetaminophen into his anus without any resistance at all from the patient. The lab tech performed the blood draw, and then it was just a matter of waiting.

And waiting. The countdown clicked back to zero, an absolute to square one. His fever came down a notch, but barely. When I'd arrived, it was 105.2. After the Tylenol, it dropped to 104.1, and stubbornly remained.

"Mrs. McLain," said a man, who introduced himself as Dr. Strauss. "Your husband has septicemia."

"What the hell is that?"

I was sitting at Wyatt's bedside, holding one of his hands, though it lay limp in my own, without response.

190

"A precursor to sepsis, a blood infection. We believe that the original knife wound may have allowed bacteria to be released into his body."

He said much, much more, but I don't remember. All I thought of was how I needed him to be there when our baby was born. I needed him to share this life we'd planned, and I refused to accept anything less.

They treated him with intravenous antibiotics and steroids, in order to both kill the infection, and heal the damage. They packed him in bags of ice to cool his body, but the fever was a living thing, independent of medical intervention. Up and down the fever went, rising again as high as 105.3, but without the rage that had manifested before. All Wyatt did was lay there, eyes closed, as though he had given up. His body was hooked up to a respirator, and he urinated into a catheterized bag. Thankfully, the EEG recorded brain activity, as vibrant as the man I'd known before this agony descended upon us, before this living hell.

The terrible situation dragged on for almost three days. His relatives returned from Susanville and Washington State, not knowing if their vigil was for Wyatt's healthy recovery, or a funeral.

❖ ❖ ❖ ❖

Jake Keene showed up, and stuck his face around the curtain. He was the last person I wanted to see, and I'm sure my expression spoke this sentiment. I could also sense that he was contrite, and felt a need to express this to me.

"How is he?" he asked, shamefaced.

I shrugged. "Wyatt's kind of out of it right now."

Wyatt's hand was limp, and in the background the respirator rhythmically forced the breath of life into my husband's body.

Jake slowly walked up to the foot of the bed, and stood uncomfortably. His movements were painfully deliberate, and demeanor oddly respectful, for this man who formerly hadn't the time of day for true love.

"I read what happened in the paper, and it's been all over the television news, too, and I'm sorry." He shuffled his feet. "I'm really glad Rat was there."

"So am I," I agreed. "That's the second time Rat saved me. The first time, he fought off a couple of carjackers in Tacoma."

"I didn't know there was a first time, Maddie."

"Of course not, because after I saw you in Seattle, that was really it for me, Jake. I didn't have anything more to say to you."

191

"I realize that now, and I don't blame you. I want you to know how really sorry I am. Sorry about this awful thing that happened, sorry about being an asshole, sorry I was so insensitive."

"I already told you, you're forgiven."

"My mother said she'd been out to see you."

When I merely nodded, he took a breath and continued.

"She said I should have married you before I flew to Seattle."

I smiled woodenly, and then thought about what I would have missed had I married Jake, had I followed my itinerary from Astoria to Seattle perfectly, and never caught him straying. Of course, with me, he'd been straying from his engagement to Sophie Whipple, but I knew that between the two of us there existed a slim measure of honesty.

"And what did you tell Charlotte?"

"I told her that was the only thing she's said to me in a long time that made any sense."

"You know, it's strange, about you and Wyatt, you both lost your parents at a very young age."

He seemed surprised. "I never knew he'd lost his parents."

"You had no reason to know. But that's the only commonality. You're both very different people. Wyatt's an honest man, even if the words are sometimes difficult to hear. But you, Jake, you're a liar. And I'm so glad I caught you in the lobby of The Edgewater, because then I never would have met Wyatt."

He just stood there, nodding—how could he dispute the truth?

"I'm going to have a baby," I blurted. "It's Wyatt's," I added, to dispel any fantasies Jake might have had in reconnecting. I didn't want Jake to somehow misinterpret that he was responsible for my pregnancy.

"Well, Maddie, congratulations," he said with kind sincerity. "I wish the two of you all the happiness in the world. I know you probably don't believe me, but I want you to have happiness, Maddie, even if that means being with Wyatt, and not with me." He sighed. "Because, let's face it, you wouldn't have been happy with me."

"That's true," I politely agreed.

When he departed, I was afraid he was going to try to kiss me, or touch my hand, but for once, he respected my emotional distance, and only spoke his farewell. And that was the last I saw of Jacob Keene.

❖ ❖ ❖ ❖

At one point, when I was alone in the room with Wyatt, I prayed. Not promise praying, which is what making deals with a god entails. I chanted the simple word, over and over again, "Please." I needed a miracle. I loved Wyatt, but after all, I was nearly twenty-six, and he almost fifty-three, and I knew that I would, in all likelihood, outlive him. In my human selfishness, I wanted more time with him, a desperation that often begets a hasty, one-sided pact with a deity—but all I could do was repeat that single word, "Please."

I spoke to *Misp*, asking for a reprieve, unconsciously acknowledging my union with Wyatt as one existence: *Our life doesn't require change. It's already balanced.* If *Misp* were there to listen, then perhaps I'd be heard through my great love for Wyatt, a son of the Quinault Indian Nation.

I even thought about Cucho. I had tried with all my heart *not* to think about that bastard, because I was so enraged. I wanted him dead. I wanted to kill him with my own hands, if I were allowed to try. I had deluded myself into believing killing Cucho was possible, temporarily forgetting that I'd been choked twice. I only remembered fighting him off, before Rat arrived and preempted my chance to complete the execution.

I wondered how a man could become somebody like Cucho. Why would a man hate women with such passion, rather than directing the same energy into loving, the way Wyatt did? There was something baffling about that missing piece, a skewed element, an empty space that thrived on hatred, rather than love. I felt sorry for Cucho, and my compassion brought me humility.

Somewhere in these thoughts, in calling upon *Misp* for amnesty, and the single word of prayer, "Please," I forgave Cucho for what he'd done to Wyatt and to me, and to our beautiful life. I knew, without any doubt, that night in Tacoma in the falling rain had been a gift, and I was happy for the little time I'd had with Wyatt. If I were destined to go forward without him, I'd accept the consequence. I would never be happy again, not truly, except for what it would mean to our child, though I knew I'd find the strength somewhere, if I had to.

❖ ❖ ❖ ❖

At the end of the third day, I received my miracle. Wyatt's kidneys held strong, his fever dropped, and he awakened from whatever place he'd been away journeying.

"Madeline."

He could barely speak my name, as his throat was so dry after they removed the breathing tube. But his voice was sweet music to my ears.

193

"Where have I been?" he asked.

"You're in the hospital," I explained. "You were stabbed, and started to recover, but then you developed a really nasty blood infection. I've been here with you the whole time." And I couldn't kiss him enough.

"But..." He seemed confused. "No, I wasn't really here, Madeline. I was somewhere else."

He described a place where he had been able to see his parents, and some of the elders who'd died. He had spoken with people from his own generation, people he'd grown up with on the rez, who passed away in youth from alcohol poisoning, or car accidents, or the scourge of cancer.

"And then I saw a fence," he described, "dividing me from everyone else."

"Is that why you came back?"

"I came back, because I couldn't find you, Madeline. I couldn't find you, and everyone was telling me you weren't in that place. It was a really beautiful place, peaceful, and I couldn't feel physical pain, but I didn't want to stay there without you. That's what hurt so much I didn't want to have a forever without you."

This spiritual experience, from a man who'd only gone to church once in his life, and that had been on clinical assignment.

Our families were told he had improved, and they all gathered around, so many in fact, that the hospital would have threatened to eject most of them, had Wyatt not just been on the threshold of death. Of course, nobody wants to interfere with Indians, and Native custom, especially when Burly Dog Barrow is standing guard at the door.

❖ ❖ ❖ ❖

When I brought Wyatt home, we were together for the long haul.

I had left my credit card information at the truck rental company, so I racked up quite a fee for the many days we used the bobtail for storage. I discovered my father and mother had come to the house, and had not only taken Rat home with them to care for, but they, along with Kate and Paul, had cleaned up the blood, and disposed of the stained mattress, and replaced the broken window glass in the bedroom. Though we'd missed moving out by the first of the month, the realtor, Sherry Flynn, had acquired an extension from the renters, who decided the fifteenth was fine for the move in, due to extenuating circumstances.

We made it to Portland, and we created our home together. Wyatt is alive, and we treat every day of our precious time together as an incredible blessing. In the hospital, I had accepted the consequence of losing him. Having him whole would never be taken for granted.

We arranged for our baby's birth at home, just as my mother had given birth to me, just as Wyatt's mother had given birth to him, with the aid of a midwife. When the midwife laid our daughter, Elizabeth Eagle McLain, in her father's arms, I recalled a café, in the rain, at the appointed hour, when the dog struck two.

I still have that creased and folded cup from Road Apples. I know exactly where it is, leaning on the mantel behind the wood stove in our home. If I have my way, it'll be there forever, collecting dust and memories.

About the Author

A California native, Karen Kennedy Samoranos has a deep and abiding love for the Golden State, reflected in the settings of her books. She believes in love at first sight, undying passion, and the rare balance of two souls in sync. As an author, all of these elements are a constant theme of her work. By day, she and her husband are committed to a music education business that forwards the cause of live jazz stage performance for children, ages 4 through 18. Family is the ultimate fulfillment—the author has four adult children, and six grandchildren.

www.ingramcontent.com/pod-product-compliance
Lightning Source LLC
Chambersburg PA
CBHW071237250626
47163CB00001B/222